THE DARKEST GAME

ALEX SIGMORE

Storm
PUBLISHING

ALSO BY ALEX SIGMORE

Emily Slate FBI Mystery Thriller

His Perfect Crime

The Collection Girls

Smoke and Ashes

Her Final Words

Can't Miss Her

The Lost Daughter

The Secret Seven

A Liar's Grave

The Girl In The Wall

His Final Act

The Vanishing Eyes

Edge of the Woods

Ties That Bind

The Missing Bones

Blood in the Sand

The Passage

Fire in the Sky

Oh What Fun

Ivy Bishop Mystery Thriller

Her Dark Secret

The Girl Without A Clue

The Buried Faces
Her Hidden Lies

Forgotten

PROLOGUE

"Hand me one of those, will ya?"

John looked over to his right, to the frail woman in the knit tank top and cut-off jean shorts. Her brown hair was a mess about her face, and she had the distinct odor of someone in need of a good bath. Not that he could say he was much better. They'd been in the car for the past two days straight with barely a break to sleep. While they weren't exactly in a hurry, there was no sense in wasting time either. But it had been a long drive, and he wasn't making the biggest trip of his life alone. Thankfully, she'd barely even put up a fight.

But *Jesus*, couldn't she at least take care of herself a little?

"You... really think you should be drinking?" she asked.

He scowled at her, giving her the look that had become his norm over the past few days. Immediately, she cast her eyes to the side, looking away from him, and recoiled, almost like a stray that had been kicked too many times.

"You are absolutely useless," he said, reaching over and pulling a cold one out of the cooler at her feet. He popped it with one finger and took a long pull from the can, keeping one eye on the road as he drove. They were on back roads, staying off the Interstates and highways. He preferred the surface roads. The world was more scenic out here. Not all billboards and fast-food shops.

As he drank, his mind drifted back to better times, back before the world decided to go and wreck itself with technology. Everywhere he looked people couldn't seem to get enough of the stuff: phones, computers, headphones, televisions, internet, and all faster, faster, faster. *Better get more of it as quickly as possible 'cause it will never be enough.* People engorged themselves on the stuff, suckling that teat like it would dry up any second.

But it never would. There would never be an end to the glut. One day they wouldn't be able to tell where people ended and the technology began. And he was sorry to admit that day was probably coming sooner rather than later. He only hoped it was *after* his time.

It was all just another kind of control. A way to keep track of what everyone was doing—just so they could sell you something every second of the day. One day they were going to figure out how to beam commercials into your fucking dreams.

He finished off the can, tossing it out the open window as the wind rushed by.

"That's... littering," the woman beside him said.

"They'll get it," he replied. "They always do." Some church or Boy Scout troop or, hell, some prison regiment out on their mandated constitutional would come along in a month or two and pick it up, all in the name of *saving the environment.*

But one empty beer can wouldn't make a bit of difference. A million cans wouldn't even make a dent. This world was primed for destruction, either by the hands of people or when the planet finally decided to burn them all to hell and start over again. One way or another, their days were numbered.

So why not have a little fun while you could?

Heading east, John took in the sunset in his rearview mirror.

Out here it was mostly farmland, giving them a perfect view of the sun as it set over the horizon. They'd been driving for nearly twelve hours straight, and with little to eat or drink other than what he'd packed in the cooler before they left, he found himself growing anxious. But fate had made his decision for him. How could he ignore its call?

"We're almost there," he said. "You don't have to fret much longer."

"You still haven't told me where we're going."

He didn't reply. Instead, his mind was alight with the possibility that it might work this time. He might actually get what he'd been working for all these years.

Part of him couldn't believe he was going back. Last time he'd miscalculated, gotten too impatient and had almost lost everything. This time, he needed to be slow, methodical. He had to take his time and plan his moves. Otherwise, he might find himself on the run again, with his tail tucked between his legs. And another opportunity like this might not come along again.

He glanced at his companion. Staring out that infernal window like it was her job. Bringing her had been a risk. But had it been a mistake?

"Maybe we should part ways here," he threatened, emboldened by his own power. "Out in the middle of nowhere. No homes, no warmth." It was still the middle of February after all, and outside the temperature was just above freezing. She didn't even have a jacket, instead relying on the truck's heat ever since leaving Arizona.

He hadn't argued at the time. But looking at her pale skin had grown tiresome. And she hadn't proved to be the talkative companion he'd hoped for.

"I don't want to leave," she finally muttered.

"We don't always get what we want," he replied.

About ten minutes later they crossed the line into Oak

Creek, population twenty-five thousand. It was one of a dozen little towns that dotted the landscape around here, all built around the turn of the last century back when industry ran this country. And he couldn't help feeling his heart pick up the pace as he drove closer into the downtown area. He checked his watch. Five fifteen. According to the information online, the store would still be open. Which meant *she'd* be there instead of at her home. He'd considered stopping at a motel first, getting his head straight. But doing that could also be risky. No, he needed to be decisive. If this was going to happen, he needed to make these moves now, before random chance took him off the board again.

The town's downtown area was nothing more than a meager collection of buildings built around a square, all under three stories tall. Most of the buildings were empty on the upper floors, some of them had even been boarded up. A few stores remained, though he didn't imagine the square attracted the same number of people it once had. There were signs a revitalization had been attempted—mostly around what appeared to be a decaying gazebo in the center of the square, but the lack of activity told him that people didn't spend their time here. This wasn't a bustling metropolis.

Which, in a way, was apropos.

On one side of the square a sign stood on the sidewalk advertising rooms for rent (*Cheap! Clean! Color TV!*) It was like he'd stepped back in time a few decades. The town hadn't changed at all—nor would he expect it to. Oak Creek was the epitome of a town that had stalled out, which made what he needed to do much easier. In fact, it was the only way he was going to pull this off. He drove around the square until he found the building he'd been looking for. It sat right between two other businesses, the front window full of canvases.

"Oh," his companion said, looking out the window as they pulled into one of the spots along the square. "An art store."

"So you have eyes after all," he said, killing the engine. He could just barely see inside the store. But there she was, sitting behind the counter, her nose in a book.

"Who is that?" the woman beside him asked, watching him closely.

"No one you need to worry about," he replied. He took a deep breath, then turned to her. "I can't say I'll miss you."

Worry etched her face. "W-what?"

"I thought bringing you along would be good for me. That you would keep me company. But you've been nothing but a pain in my ass this entire trip."

"I don't understand," she said. But she scooted back to the far side of the truck. Good. She *should* be scared.

"Understanding is not required," he said. "We're done here. You can go."

Her brow was drawn in concern, then fear. He slipped her a smarmy smile before grabbing the keys and getting out of the truck, heading for the art store's front door. When he turned to look back at the vehicle's cab, she was gone.

"Good riddance," he said under his breath. He paused, his hand inches from the door. He'd waited so long for this moment —why was he hesitating? He'd been given a beautiful gift, a second chance. And there was no going back.

He was ready. He could do this. It would all be worth it in the end.

Opening the door, he steeled himself as he walked toward the front counter where the woman reading hadn't yet noticed him. *Good, she won't see me coming.* With a snake's quickness, he approached the counter, rounded it and grabbed the woman by her oversized sweater, putting his hand on her mouth and pushing her up against the wall.

"Good evening," he said, his muscles taut as he held her up, her eyes wide with fear and recognition. "I'm interested in some art."

ONE

The thundering rhythm of the bass synchronized with the thumping of her heart.

Detective Charlotte Dawes hadn't been in a situation like this in a good ten years. Sure, she'd seen her fair share of tense standoffs, whether they be robberies, domestic abuse situations or kidnappings. But she never thought she'd find herself strolling across the dance floor of a trendy Chicago nightclub, dressed in full regalia, preparing to make one of the biggest collars of her career.

She and her partner, Dale Givens, had been working this case for six months. Gathering evidence, tracking down leads, flipping informants. All for this one chance to nab one of the biggest drug movers in the city.

Charlotte didn't get nervous. That was something for rookies and officers who couldn't handle the pressure of the job. Her biggest strength was that she was rock-solid, always had been. But given the amount of resources and time that had been spent on this case, and the fact that it all boiled down to this one interaction, she couldn't help but feel the pressure.

And yet, her visage betrayed nothing of her underlying

anxiety. She was as stone-faced as they came, a skill she'd picked up in her youth. *The only way to stay one step ahead of everyone is to never let them see who you truly are.* She deftly stepped around a couple gyrating to the beat as her father's words echoed in her head, a remnant of some long-forgotten pep talk after she'd taken a few too many hits in the ring. He had always been there to lend a supportive voice, or practice tough love when she'd needed it.

And she'd been practicing it all her life. She'd been in high-stakes situations before—being on the force for over twenty years would do that to a person—and yet this one felt *bigger*. More important. She'd had a series of bad cases lately, and this was her chance to turn it all around. To prove she still had what it took to make it in this game. This was how she showed them all that there was no expiration date on a good cop.

Victor Karkoff had a reputation for being shrewd—and ruthless. He wasn't known to waste his time or suffer fools. The man hadn't built one of the biggest and most elusive drug-running operations west of New York by being stupid.

All she had to do was keep her cool, play the part and do the deal. The club was already surrounded, and her boss was in a nearby van watching the whole thing play out from the signal being broadcast from the tiny piece of jewelry clipped on her blazer. Thirty minutes and it would all be over.

But as Charlotte pushed through the bodies of the nightclub, making her way to the VIP section in the back, her attention was drawn to the faces in the crowd. They all seemed so *young*. Had it really been that long since she'd been one of them? And were these kids even old enough to be here?

That was one of the cruelties of life, thinking you were still young when your body told a different story. There had been a time when Charlotte would have fit in here without another glance, but as she passed the groups of bouncing dancers, she couldn't ignore the stares coming from some of them... probably wondering what someone their parents' age was doing in a place like this.

Never let them see...

It had been advice applicable to every aspect of her life. And Charlotte focused on it as she pressed through the crowd, finally emerging at the other end. It didn't matter to her what a bunch of kids thought. She was here to make a deal with a dangerous criminal and get him off the streets. And if all went to plan, no one in the building would even know what had happened.

As she reached the edge of the crowd, her eyes flitted to a man just to her right. He was tall, leaning against the railing and doing his best not to look out of place. But to Charlotte, Givens stood out like a sore thumb. He had a stiffness about him that screamed discomfort, like he wanted to be anywhere else but here. Which was why when she passed by, she didn't even bother acknowledging him. Because no doubt there were other eyes on her and she didn't want to risk breaking cover. She just hoped that she didn't look as out of place here as he did.

Charlotte climbed the short flight of stairs, keeping her posture relaxed, even as she reached the two men standing with their hands clasped in front of them. Her thoughts immediately went to the weapon hidden in her waistband, tucked firmly out of view. The two men appraised her, their eyes steely and hard. Apparently, it was up to her to make the first move.

"Tell him Charlie is here," she said. Both men were built like linebackers and could no doubt physically remove anyone in this building if necessary.

The two men exchanged a glance before one of them moved to the side. "In the back."

Her heart nearly sank into her stomach as the reality of heading into the back of the club without backup hit her, but she was determined to see this through. Would she be in trouble if something went wrong in there? Maybe. But they had worked too long and too hard to make this deal happen, and Charlotte was damned if she wasn't going to finish the job.

The man opened the solid black door for her, allowing Charlotte to pass through. The room on the other side was immune to the heavy bass from the club, apparently insulated with some kind of soundproofing. Decorated in heavy velvet curtains along the walls, with plush cherry red couches in the corners, the room screamed privacy. Two slender women sat on one of the couches, fully relaxed into it. They barely even acknowledged Charlotte as she entered and she did her best not to pay them any attention either. But her heart went out to them. More than likely they had been lured here under false pretenses, and had few, if any, chances to get out. Women like this were the reason Charlotte was here—to stop Victor and those under him from preying on the desperate. With any luck, these two would be sobering up under the supervision of a counselor soon enough.

Seated at the desk was a man in a suit as dark as Charlotte's, though it was a lot more stylish. He wore an extravagant pair of glasses and was hunched over a computer facing away from Charlotte as she approached. Another man, similar to the linebackers out front, stood behind him, a bulge in his blazer barely concealing the weapon hidden under his arm.

The man in the glasses typed away on his laptop for a moment, its screen reflected in the lenses he wore, before he finally looked up. Victor Karkoff had a hard face, one that had undergone more than one cosmetic surgery to fix scars from some of his more intense encounters. It was evident in the way he appraised her, where certain parts of his face didn't move as they should, modified by the miracles of vanity.

"Charlie, huh?" he asked.

"That's what they call me," Charlotte replied.

"You're older than I expected," he said, closing the laptop.

"Sorry to disappoint."

He made a *tsk*ing sound and stood. "Just an observation. No need to get upset."

She hadn't. But he was testing her, seeing how she would respond to pressure. "I assume you're Victor."

"Just you by yourself?" he asked, rounding the table. She didn't miss the subtle nod to the man standing behind him. He followed Victor around the table so both men were standing in front of Charlotte.

"Problem with that?" she asked.

"No," the man said, emoting a swagger she didn't like. He was enjoying this too much. Toying with her. "When Argos vouched for you, I just had a different picture in my mind. Someone a little younger. And generally, people don't come alone, at least not on the first meeting. They like to bring an entourage, show off a little. Either that or they're wearing ten-thousand-dollar watches, or sporting jewels in their teeth. *Something* that telegraphs just how important and rich they are. You're none of that."

"I don't waste my time on bullshit," she replied.

"Fair enough," he replied. The other man had circled around her, effectively blocking any chance of an exit. "But that doesn't mean I trust you."

Charlotte narrowed her gaze. "That's your criteria? Someone who wears gaudy clothes or expensive-looking accessories?" Taking her eyes off him was not an option. She could feel the man behind her closing in. She'd read the dossiers, watched all the surveillance film. But there was something about meeting the man in person that unnerved her. It was like he was staring *through* her, seeing her for exactly who she was. Charlotte could handle a lot of things, but not that.

"Not criteria," he said, lowering his voice. "Just little things that tells me someone is on the up and up. But when I look at you, all I see is a woman out of her depth."

She forced a smirk, keeping her focus on the job at hand.

"That's because I don't need it. People do business with me because they know I don't fuck around. Now, you can either tell your man to back off or I can break his hands and show you just how serious I am."

The thing about threats is you really need to mean them. And Charlotte, who at one time in her life was on the short list for a kickboxing championship, had no problem reaching back into her past and pulling out the intensity needed to make her threat real. It was her shield against his intense gaze. Her way through.

She shot a glance over her shoulder to the man standing right behind her. He must have seen it in her eyes because he took a step back.

"Interesting," Victor said, intrigue seeping into his voice.

"I didn't come here to be jerked around," she replied, turning her attention back to him. "Now, are we going to get down to business or not?"

A subtle look from Victor and the man behind Charlotte moved back into her view, heading to the far side of the room. "May I offer you a seat while we wait?" Victor said, indicating the couch containing the two women. If either of them had been aware of the energy in the room, they didn't show it. Their eyes were so glassy Charlotte was pretty sure neither of them was even still on this planet.

"I don't plan on staying."

"I'd offer you a sample, but I think we both know that'd be a waste of time," he said, sitting down beside the two women. "You don't strike me as someone who partakes."

Victor then locked his gaze on Charlotte, that stare back in his eyes, and somehow even more potent than before. She thought she'd done a fair job of disarming his suspicions, but with the way he was staring at her, she wasn't so sure. Did he know? The hand in her left jacket pocket trembled slightly.

No, not now.

Finally, his cohort returned with a medium-sized black briefcase. He opened it for her, showing row after row of tightly wrapped white powder. Charlotte thought back to Givens outside. He was waiting for her to exit with the briefcase before they called in the cavalry.

Victor removed one of the packages from the briefcase. He seemed to be feeling the heft of it, before tossing it in Charlotte's direction.

She wasn't ready for it, and as she attempted to grab the package, her hand seized and she grimaced, the package falling to the ground.

Unnerved, Charlotte scrambled to pick it back up. Her hand hadn't spasmed like that in months, why of all times now? Thankfully, the package hadn't ruptured as it had fallen. But one look back to Victor told her that if he'd been suspicious before, he was on a hair trigger now. He sat perched on the very edge of the couch, watching her very closely.

"Yeah. Looks to be all there, as agreed," Charlotte said too quickly, replacing the package back with the others. Though she couldn't help her hand from continuing to tremble as she did. A tremble that could be easily misinterpreted.

"Of course it is," Victor replied, though it came out as almost a growl. He motioned with his head. "Problem with your hand?"

"Old injury," Charlotte replied. "It's not important." But she could already see the flash in Victor's eyes. That one little slip had been it he'd needed. In an instant he was on his feet, a gun in his hand almost as if it had been produced out of thin air.

And Charlotte was staring right down the barrel.

TWO

"Six months!"

Charlotte rubbed her temple as she sat in the recovery room of Northwestern Memorial, while her boss, Lieutenant Jeremy Whiteside, paced back and forth in front of her, spittle flying from his mouth as he spoke. It had been nearly eight hours since her escapade at the club, and as the sun came up on a cold Chicago morning, Charlotte found herself enduring her boss's latest tirade. It might not have been so bad had the hospital staff not kept her up all night for fear of a concussion, though thankfully they'd cleared her mere moments before Whiteside showed up.

"Six months of police work... of tracking down informants... of meticulous planning... of coordinating with other departments, all of it blown up in one night because you decided to play cowboy!"

Charlotte sighed. "I didn't play 'cowboy.' I already told you; he made me and I didn't have a choice." Charlotte had barely made it out of Victor Karkoff's club in one piece. Had it not been for her partner and the glut of officers they'd had on standby who managed to infiltrate the club and arrest Karkoff, her body would most likely be in some cold freezer right now. Needless to say, the operation had *not* gone to plan.

"You always have a choice," her boss replied. "When you convinced me to let you take this case, you *assured* me you could handle it. *I* said you should work the van, run things from there, but no, for some godforsaken reason, you insisted on meeting Victor Karkoff eye to eye. I knew it was the wrong call then, but did I listen to my gut? No, I listened to you, because you're a good officer and you've had a run of bad luck lately. I allowed myself to get sentimental, so I swallowed that load of bullshit you fed me, and now here we are."

She began to protest, feeling an urge to defend herself. "It wasn't—"

He cut her off. "Were those not your *exact words* to me?"

"They were," she admitted.

"So what the fuck happened?"

"He was—" She tried to come up with a word for it, but her words hung in the air. The fact was, he *had* seen right through her and she wasn't sure if there was anything she could have done to prevent it. Despite her best efforts, she'd cracked under the pressure and allowed some piece of trash drug dealer to get under her skin. Charlotte had to face facts. She had been in this job a long time. Maybe it was finally starting to wear on her. "I mean, it's not like I've never been undercover before."

"That was five years ago, and before you started dealing with your... condition," Whiteside shouted, throwing an errant glance at her hand. "You know it will be a miracle if he even survives. Taking him by force was not part of the plan. And if he recovers, his lawyers are going to drag us up and down Michigan, asses first."

"C'mon, Jer, the guy had a back room full of Colombian nose powder," she protested. "He's not getting off." Her mouth tugged at one end. "Assuming he makes it."

"Maybe, maybe not," her boss replied. "But the fact is, this was only part one in a multi-part operation. And now thanks to you, parts two, three and four are down the drain. No, not just down the drain. They're through the sewer, out to sea and at the bottom of the fucking ocean!"

She stood to face him, though it caused an ache in her rib cage. "So I should have just let him shoot me, is that it?"

"You never should have been there in the first place," he said before taking a deep breath. "That was my fault."

"What are you saying?" she asked. "Are you canning me?"

Whiteside worked his jaw, averting his gaze. "The doctors clear you yet?"

"Yeah," she replied. "Why?"

"Go home. Get some sleep. I want you in my office first thing tomorrow."

"What about the case? I still have to file the paperwork, not to mention we need to interview—"

"Givens will take care of that. You go home."

"Don't do this, Jer," Charlotte said, hating the pleading she heard in her own voice. "I've worked too hard and too long on this case to just give it up now."

"Detective Dawes, that's an order," her boss replied. "End of discussion."

She sighed, giving him one last glance, but her boss wasn't about to budge. She'd had her fair share of screwups over her career, but she'd never seen Whiteside like this. There might as well be steam billowing out of his ears. And no amount of arguing would change her mind. If he decided to bench her, there wasn't much she could do about it.

Charlotte gathered up what few effects the hospital staff had set aside and headed out the door. She almost ran into the nurse on the way out.

"Whoa there, Detective, where are you going?" the nurse asked.

"Self-discharge," she said. "I'm going home."

"I'll need to let Doctor Barnabas know. And you'll need to fill out the proper forms before—"

"Mail them to me," Charlotte said, heading past the woman. She didn't stop for her protests, instead headed for the elevator which she took down to the street level. As she exited, planning on calling an Uber, she spotted Givens out of the corner of her eye. He was leaning up against the building much in the same way he'd been leaning on the railing in the club, except now a cigarette hung from his mouth.

Upon seeing her he dropped the cigarette and put it out under his foot before approaching. "How bad?"

"He wants me to go home and *rest*."

"Ah," her partner replied. "Need a lift?"

"I can just grab something; you don't need to drive all the way over there."

"No, but I'd feel better if I did."

"Oh, well, if *you'd* feel better, then by all means," she said, motioning for him to lead the way. She'd been partnered with Givens for the past six years and in that time they had become as close as anyone could without being blood related. The fact was, Charlotte didn't have many people left in her life and Givens was the one constant, despite the fact he was a below-average undercover officer. Then again, after last night's performance, she didn't have any room to talk.

"Think he'll bring the hammer down?" he asked once they were down in the parking level and in his car.

"Your guess is as good as mine," she replied. "But I wouldn't be surprised. I may have pushed things too far this time."

"It was bad luck, that's all," he said, pulling out of the parking garage and onto the main roads. Because it was the weekend, thankfully there wasn't much traffic in downtown. They were able to make most of the lights without even waiting.

Bad luck didn't even begin to cover it. Charlotte hadn't closed a case in nearly two years, despite being a veteran. People said she'd just had a run of it... of cases that *couldn't* be closed for one reason or another, but secretly, she'd begun wondering if everyone was just making excuses for her when the truth was staring her in the face: She'd been doing the job too long. No matter how distinguished a career, every cop knew their last day on the job would come sooner or later. And Charlotte really needed a win before that day arrived. But she'd run out of time and there was nothing else she could do about it.

"Maybe he's right," Charlotte said. "What business did I have running this operation? I should have given it to Diaz or Epps or, hell, even Bartlett." The thought made her wince; Bartlett was half her age. "Any of them would have fit into that place a hundred times better than I did. And they probably wouldn't have cracked under the pressure."

"You didn't crack," Givens protested.

"No, I did," she replied. "He was already on pins and needles. I spasmed. He saw my hand and that was all she wrote."

"You could have tried to explain it away as a medical condition. It's sort of the truth." She glared at him like he was an idiot. "Okay, maybe not. But still, you can't blame it all—"

"Bartlett would have gone in there, looked every bit the part of a twenty-five-year-old player in the game, no physical issues at all, and done the deal. Then we would have had him dead to rights. Now we've got this lawsuit and a possible wrongful death on the horizon. And I'm sure Karkoff already has three witnesses lined up to vouch for him."

"Yeah, three of his own people that no jury would ever believe. You're the good guy here, don't forget."

She shook her head. "I put people in danger. What business did I have thinking I could pull that off?"

The rest of the ride to her house was silent. Givens was a good partner, he always supported her. But he wasn't the best at pep talks. But he was always there for her. They were close to the same age, and maybe on rare occasions Charlotte might have fantasized about there being more between them. Those thoughts were always fleeting, however, because Givens was a devoted husband and father. His daughter was almost out of high school now and he'd confessed to Charlotte that once she was out of the house, he and his wife were planning on taking some time away. Whether that meant retirement or transferring to a less intense job in the department she didn't know, but it served as another reminder that nothing about Charlotte's life was permanent.

"Here, this is fine," she said as they turned onto her street.

"But it's only a few more—"

"Dale, I got it. I need to walk out this crick in my back." He pulled to the side and she opened the passenger door, stepping out into the cold.

"Hey," he called before she could slam it shut again. "Things will be better tomorrow. Whiteside just needs to blow off some steam. You know how he is."

She nodded. "Thanks for the ride." He smiled as she closed the door but didn't pull away. Charlotte rolled her eyes before walking down the row of old brownstones, all packed together like sardines lined up in a can. It wasn't until she was on her steps and her key was in the door that he finally turned around and drove off.

Charlotte shook her head as she entered the warm foyer, shaking off her jacket and removing her boots. She wished she had Givens's optimism. But right now, all she wanted was a long soak in the tub.

.   .   .

The following morning Charlotte was at the station early. She'd put on her best gray suit and pulled her hair back off her shoulders in a tight bun, the way she used to when she first started working the unit. She hoped it would convey that she was still professional and ready to face whatever Whiteside had for her. She wasn't ready to roll over, not yet. A life of fighting had hammered resilience into her head. She could almost hear her dad's voice. *Never give up, even when you're down on the mat, bleeding, Charlie. Don't let them see they've beat you.*

As she passed the department's gym, catching a glimpse of a couple of the others either pressing weights or practicing their martial arts, she felt the same ache in her hand from the other night and flexed it a few times to work out the pain. She'd barely caught the edge of the boxing ring but turned away before she could see if anyone was sparring or not. It would have made her heart ache too much.

Instead, she focused her resolve and headed for Whiteside's office, determined to convince her boss she wasn't up the creek yet. She still had a few good years left in her, but she had to *show* him. Words didn't matter anymore. And that was going to start with an interrogation of Victor's right-hand man from the other night.

When she reached Whiteside's door, it was closed, so she knocked twice before cracking it open. He was on the phone behind his desk, but he motioned for her to come in anyway. She did, closing the door behind her, and took a seat across from him.

"Yeah, I'm sure you're overwhelmed," Whiteside said. Charlotte wasn't one to eavesdrop, but she could barely help it given the man was only a few feet away from her. "It's not something you guys normally deal with."

Her boss glanced at her, then turned in his chair so he was looking out the window on the Chicago skyline as he spoke. Charlotte averted her eyes as he finished up his call, trying to look at anything else in the room other than the back of his head.

"Yeah, yeah, I understand. Well, keep me updated. If you guys need any help, you know I'm here." He chuckled. "Yeah, more than a little. We've seen just about everything. Okay, you too. Take care." He hung up, then turned back to face Charlotte. "How are you feeling this morning?"

"Good," she replied. "A few aches and pains but nothing I'm not already used to."

"Glad to hear it." He reached into a drawer out of sight and pulled out a file folder, placing it on his desk. Charlotte couldn't help but notice her name was on the tab. "Detective Dawes—"

"Before you say anything," Charlotte said, "I wanted to apologize for what happened. You were right. I should have let Bartlett take the lead. It was arrogant, selfish and I put the entire operation in danger."

Her boss sat back, watching her.

"And I'm willing to do whatever I can to make up for it. I have already prepared an interview plan to pit Karkoff's goons against each other. Not to mention I think we can get the fire marshal involved. That club had to have been at double capacity. And I already spoke to Mitchell. Everything they seized from the club definitely came from Dominguez's operation in the Caribbean. I think with a little pressure we can—"

"Dawes, stop," her boss said, cutting her off. "You're off the case."

Deflated, Charlotte sat back. "So that's it? I'm done?"

He grimaced. "I don't want you to think I'm taking this lightly. You have been a stellar detective during your tenure here. But mistakes were made, and the Chief of Police has concerns. Someone must be held accountable."

"I don't guess there's anything I can say to change your mind." She knew this was a possibility, she just couldn't believe it was actually happening.

"Look. We'll have a nice party. You get a gold watch. And a pension. You'll be set and can go out and do whatever you want. Volunteer, open a donut shop. Hell, take a European vacation. You've more than earned it."

She shook her head. He didn't understand. Charlotte didn't want a vacation, and she didn't want to "retire," forced or not. For the last twenty-seven years, this job had been her life. This drive that had propelled her forward to close some of the biggest cases of her career—the Myers Ring, the Don Perlinio case—had come with a high price. Charlotte had been forced to choose between getting the job done, and everything else. And she'd chosen the job. Because it had been the right thing to do. It was a simple equation. If she'd quit, a lot of people would have suffered. Versus the handful that suffered by her staying. The only problem was the handful had included her husband, Ronson... and Haley, her daughter. And now there was nothing left. No one at home, no one other than her colleagues at work. Asking her to retire was like asking her to roll over and die.

"I know it's not what you want to hear, but think of it as a new start," Whiteside said.

Charlotte was desperate, there had to be something she could say to change his mind. And even though it crossed the lines of privacy, she didn't care anymore. What did she have to lose? "What were you talking about on the phone? Was that a new case?"

Her boss narrowed his gaze. "No, it's not relevant. A colleague of mine—it's a small-town thing. Few hours from here."

"They called you about it?" she asked.

He frowned. "Not that it's any of your business, but I'm close friends with the sheriff out there. They've found a body and aren't quite sure how to handle things."

"A body?" Charlotte asked.

"Decomposed one, yeah," he said. "Can't tell if it's been

dumped or been there a while. He was calling for a little advice. I told him if he needed some help—"

"Send me," she said reflexively.

"Excuse me?"

"Send me out to help," she said. "How many corpse cases have I worked? They could use someone with a little experience." She could see him hesitating. "C'mon, Jer, how long do you think it's going to take them to figure out what's going on? Do you think the victim's family deserves to wait even longer because they don't know what they're looking at?" He was continuing to watch her, but she could tell he wasn't dismissing it. At least, not yet. "Plus, it's not like you're losing any resources here. I'm on my way out. Let me at least do one last thing to help. Don't let my legacy hang on Karkoff and that whole mess. *Please.*"

He scowled, then opened his desk drawer and pulled out a half-full bottle of whiskey and a small glass. "*You're* doing this to me, you know that, don't you?" He poured himself half a finger and knocked it back before replacing the bottle and glass out of sight. He pulled his features back as he stared at Charlotte. She could see the war on his face, going back and forth.

"Look, how much trouble can I get into there? I'd be on as an advisory only."

"Goddammit," he said under his breath. "Fine." He pointed at her. "But *only* because I feel sorry for your dumb ass. You stay out of their way and you don't make things worse, you got it? Otherwise, that's it. I yank you back here and you're done. Got it?"

Charlotte nodded. By some miracle, she had just escaped the chopping block. "Don't cause trouble."

"I'll call Sheriff Franklin and let him know you're coming down to assist. You are *not* to embarrass me down there, understand? Franklin and I go way back. You'll be under his command while you assist."

"Thank you, Jer," Charlotte said, standing. "Really. I know I probably don't deserve it. But I appreciate the chance. At least this way I can go out on a high note." She reached out for his hand.

Hesitating, her boss finally took it. "Just don't screw it up."

THREE

It's all predictable.

Detective Mona LaSalle sat at her desk, inputting the last few variables into her computer. She'd spent all morning on this new version of her program and was feeling more confident than usual it would work this time.

Ever since she'd been promoted to the detective unit of Oak Creek's police force, Mona had searched for a way to make a name for herself. Some detectives would dive into cold cases, determined to succeed where the old guard had failed. Some would try taking on as many cases as possible in an effort to get a head start and a few would turn all of their focus on one particularly tough case, hoping to start their careers strong with a solid win.

Then again, Oak Creek wasn't the most exciting place on Earth. In the past thirty years the worst it had experienced was a chain of robberies during the financial crisis that had left a trail of bodies in its wake. But that had been long before Mona's time. She'd still been a kid then and hadn't even lived in Oak Creek. But to hear some of the more experienced officers talk about it, it was Oak Creek's version of the LA riots of the mid-

1990s. Some of them had made their entire careers off those cases, including her current partner. She had happily listened to them spin their yarns while she was still a beat cop, all the while plotting how she could make her mark in a different way once she'd earned her promotion.

That day had come just over a month ago and Mona had yet to work a heavy case. It had been mostly small-time stuff working alongside Sergeant Jack Ramsey, who made no attempt to cover the fact he didn't enjoy Mona's company.

She took it all in stride, however, and the extra time not working on cases gave her the opportunity to focus her energy on what she had determined would be *her* mark on the Oak Creek Police Department.

She was going to be the first person to predict crime before it happened.

As she tapped her foot, her noise-cancelling headphones playing some of her favorite tunes, she inputted the next series of variables into the computer. She'd been toying with this program for a solid year and was close to coming up with a prototype, but the key was making sure it could actually work first. To do that, she'd feed all the variables into the algorithm from certain cases to see if it could end up predicting what had already happened.

Case in point: the robberies from the financial crisis.

Mona figured if she could get the program to "predict" that event, it might be ready for some real trials. But it was tricky. Prediction engines needed lots and lots of data. And even though she had access to more than the average Joe, she worried it wouldn't be enough.

To her, crime was like the weather. It was going to happen, no matter what. So why not take all the data possible to try and figure out what was going to happen before it did? If the conditions for a riot were brewing, her program would give them enough time to warn civilians and to provide an appropriate response, limiting the amount of damage and lives lost. If a career criminal who had a propensity for arson had just been released, perhaps she could predict the most likely locations he would strike again, should the urge come. And perhaps even a timeframe, based on when he was most volatile.

It was all very theoretical at this point, she had to admit. But that didn't mean one day it couldn't have practical applications. After all, every journey had to begin somewhere. And if it proved to be a success, maybe other departments could use it too. Maybe even the FBI. Mona might be sitting on the single-greatest crime deterrent that had ever been created.

She just needed to get it to work first.

Unfortunately, most of her peers—at least the ones she'd shared her plans with—thought it was little more than a waste of time. Some of them even laughed in her face. But they just didn't understand how sophisticated this program was. Mona had been a whiz with mathematics ever since she was a kid. In fact, most of her hobbies involved math in some way, whether it was playing Settlers of Catan—the Robin Hood version—or finding fractal patterns in nature when she was out hiking; numbers just made sense. Her teachers thought she'd end up at an Ivy League; she certainly had the grades to qualify for a scholarship.

But none of that had interested Mona. She wanted to help people, and she figured the best way to do that was to become a law officer. But while she might be smart, she wasn't as physically capable as she needed to be. She'd barely passed the police physical when she'd applied to the academy and if she had to take it again today, would probably fail. She'd always been what her mother had deemed "wiry" and had often been encouraged to eat to make up for it. But that was just because she saw time in the gym as a waste, especially since it was hard to find a workout partner. So she'd rather be here, working on something that could change the world.

Mona ran another round of variables through the system and sat back to watch the program do its work. The song blasting through her headphones finally ended, switching to the next headbanger, but it provided enough of a lull that Mona caught the tiniest hint of a sound from outside the headphones. She turned to see Officer Perez headed straight for her, a serious look on his face.

She pulled off her headphones. "Hey, Hector, how are you?"

"LaSalle, you better get into Franklin's office or he's gonna have an aneurism."

She knitted her brows. "What?"

"He's been calling you over the intercom for the past five minutes."

Mona looked up at the old intercom speaker mounted above one of the offices opposite her desk. "Oh," she said before biting her lip. She'd been warned about the headphones before, but it was the only way she could concentrate. She figured if something vital came up, Ramsey would come find her. "Thanks for the heads up."

Closing her computer and grabbing her jacket, she hustled out of her cubicle and down the hall to the sheriff's office at the end of the building. The door was already open, though she couldn't see all the way inside. She pulled her blazer on, making sure it was straight and wrinkle-free before she slowed her pace and took a few deep breaths as she approached the door.

Sheriff Franklin's office was the largest one in the building, but that wasn't saying much. It consisted mostly of an L-shaped desk which sat against one of the walls and rows and rows of old filing cabinets. A worn yellow sofa sat at the other end of the room, with a small table in front of it, and two chairs took up the space between the table and the desk itself. His jacket lay on top of a stack of files and the trash can was nearly overflowing with Chinese takeout boxes. Every time she came in here, it seemed messier somehow. The room reminded Mona of a college dorm, except instead of books it had been filled with unsolved cases. Though she did spy the latest copy of *Railroad Enthusiast* magazine sticking out from one of the piles. The sheriff was a well-known ferroequinologist, though he never talked about it at work until someone else brought it up. Every vacation the man had ever taken had either been on or to see a unique train of some kind. Word around the office was his ex-wife had divorced him for taking them to Ohio on their anniversary to watch a locomotive retire.

Sheriff Franklin was seated behind the desk, his brushy mustache twitching back and forth as he chewed on the tobacco that was no doubt tucked into his cheek. He'd been the one to promote Mona to detective, for which she was grateful. He'd given her the chance to make a difference.

"Problem with your hearing, LaSalle?" he asked as she walked in.

"Sorry, I was in the middle of... something." Mona looked over to the other occupant in the room, Detective Jack Ramsey, her semi-permanent partner. Instead of acknowledging her, he picked at something in his teeth with a toothpick. Ramsey was eighteen years older than Mona and had been a detective for most of his career. And while she had hoped their different backgrounds and investigative styles would complement each other, her relationship with him had been... strained to say the least. But that wasn't for a lack of effort on Mona's part.

"Probably working on that fucking computer again," Ramsey muttered under his breath.

Mona took the comment in stride and righted the momentary frown on her lips back to a smile. "What can I do for you, Sheriff?"

"Take a seat," he said.

Mona did as she was told, unsure what was happening. Was she about to be reprimanded for being a little late to a meeting she hadn't even known was taking place? "Something has come up," her boss said. "Something I need you and Ramsey to work on."

"Like... a case?" she asked, unable to keep the excitement out of her voice.

"You won't be so peppy when you hear what it is," Ramsey muttered, the toothpick flinging a piece of errant food from his mouth.

Mona turned back to Sheriff Franklin with a confused look on her face. "It just came in his morning," he said, handing over a thin file folder. "A fisherman found the body out by Crystal Creek."

"A body?" Mona asked, opening the file. But all that was in it was an initial report taken from a witness. There weren't even any photographs.

"I've already sent Roberts and Alberhasky out there to secure the scene. But I want you and Ramsey working on this one."

Mona had to work to hide her surprise. "You want me? Working a murder case?"

"Phillips is on leave and I received a message yesterday from Perkins requesting some personal time. Given what he's dealing with at home, I'm not really surprised. Plus, you're due for something substantial."

Ramsey just scoffed, but Mona studied the initial report. "Wait, it says the body is partially decomposed?"

Franklin nodded. "No telling how long it's been out there."

Her heart sank. Some detectives hung their hat on their first dead body case, as gruesome as that sounded. But often how a detective handled this kind of case would determine what kind of career they would have. And as horrible as it was, the fresher the body, the more likelihood there was of solving the case. Bodies that had decomposed were much harder solves. Most of the time any evidence that had been present had long been washed away by the elements, and odds were anyone looking for them wasn't nearly as fervent as they might have been when they first went missing. All of those factors and more made finding out what really happened that much more difficult.

"Do we know—"

"Nothing," Ramsey interrupted. "We know nothing." He stood and stomped out of the room, his hip colliding with Mona's chair enough that it pushed her slightly to the side. She winced but shook it off before turning back to Sheriff Franklin.

"Don't mind him," her boss said. "He's mad because he knows this is probably a nothing case."

"Sir?" she asked.

He shrugged his shoulders. "Jack likes to think of himself as a closer. He's proud of his record here. He considers cases like this beneath him."

"Then why assign it to us?" she asked.

"For you." Franklin appraised her. "I can't keep you behind that desk forever, as much as you seem to be thriving there. I want you out in the field. It'll be good experience. A body is a body, no matter which way you cut it. And who knows, maybe you'll surprise us."

Mona tried not to blush, but it came through anyway. She had tried not to get her hopes up about when she'd finally get a crack at something substantial. This was it, her chance to prove to everyone she wasn't just some wet blanket. She was a force to be reckoned with. "Is there anything else you can tell me?"

"Just to keep an open mind," he replied. "This could be nothing more than a ten-year-old fishing accident that we're just now discovering. But don't let Jack's biases sway you. There's a reason you made detective so quickly. Don't let me down."

Those last words were like sending ice down Mona's back. She had no intention of letting *anyone* down, but for her boss to say it only seemed to further the point. "I won't," she finally said, though her heart was going about a million beats per minute.

Sheriff Franklin nodded. "Keep me updated with your progress. And don't give Jack the satisfaction of pushing you around. Sometimes you just need to push back a little."

Mona stood, nodding, though she generally wasn't the kind of person who "pushed back." Not that she let others walk all over her, but if people tended to get loud and in her face, she usually just blocked them out. Sometimes it worked, sometimes it only made them angrier.

"Thanks," she said as she reached the door. "For this. I know you had other people who you could have chosen."

"Like I said," Franklin replied. "You were due. Just make sure you keep your ears and eyes open out there, huh?"

Mona left with the distinct feeling that this case was more than just a body. The outcome of this case would no doubt define the rest of her career and how her peers saw her. And she was dead sure she wasn't going to screw it up.

Setting her jaw, she followed her "partner" out, Franklin's words echoing in her head.

FOUR

Mona had hoped to drive to the crime scene with Jack so they could discuss the case along the way, but after her meeting with the sheriff, she realized Jack's car was no longer in the parking lot. She tried calling him—then texting, but he didn't answer.

At least with their other cases he had waited for her to join him. But he sure seemed to have a bug up his butt about something on this case. Maybe it was like her boss said, he was pissed because he thought it was a dead end and it would be a waste of time. But how could he know that before they even went to look at the body?

Mona hoped she never became that jaded about the job. Part of the reason she'd wanted to be a detective was to have these new experiences, even though they could be gruesome. But a job like this was full of possibility and she thought it was a mistake to kill that possibility before they even got started.

Before she headed out, Mona went back to her desk and pulled some additional information, such as taking a look at a satellite view of the area around where the body was found, as well as locating all the nearest roads and access points. Branch Road ran parallel to the river, which is how she'd get there, but there were also a few trail roads that ran close to the site. If the body had been dumped, she wanted to make sure she knew every road in and out of that place.

She had to admit she was excited. Her first *real* case. But at the same time she was terrified. What if she screwed something up? What if she missed a key piece of evidence? It was up to her to identify the victim so they could inform the family. And if she missed something, this poor person may never get the peaceful rest they deserved.

As Mona headed out to her car and hopped in, she also considered the possibility of feeding the case information into her program. It was still far too nascent to do any good, but maybe if they got stuck, the computer might be able to help things along a little. She wasn't expecting a miracle, but she believed in the work. One day, her program would be *the* tool departments across the country used to combat crime.

The drive out to Crystal Creek was long, taking her far outside the town boundaries. It wasn't an area she frequented much, though it was an easy drive. The day was overcast, threatening another downpour which would no doubt turn to ice overnight. They needed to get as much done today as possible before they lost any more evidence.

Finally, after following the directions on her GPS, Mona pulled onto Branch Road, driving about two miles down until she saw the group of cars that had blocked off the remaining road. A police cruiser and Jack's Ford sat alongside the road while police tape had been stretched from one side to the other, preventing any traffic from coming and going. Mona pulled up next to Jack's car and stepped out, noting just how much chillier it was out here than in town. An old beat-up red truck sat closer to the water off the road itself, its bed caked with bits of hay and dirt. Mona glanced at the inside and noted the upholstery had been worn away, showing the foam of the seats underneath.

Looking around, she spotted Jack and Officer Alberhasky

standing with another man in a heavy jacket and ball cap, a grizzled beard stretched across his face. Officer Roberts was further down the hill, looking at the water. A mist hung low over the river, obscuring the other shore from view. Above her, the clouds threatened to break open.

"—and you didn't see anyone else here?" Jack was asking as Mona approached, the wind carrying his voice.

"Look, man, I already told you. I went out fishin' and there it was. I drove back in to call you people, then came right back here with your officer over there."

"Hi," Mona said, walking up. "I'm Detective LaSalle." She held her hand out for the man. He furrowed his brow as he took her hand.

"Duane Madden," he said. "How many people you guys sending out here?"

"Mr. Madden," Jack said, getting the man's attention again. "You didn't see any footprints, or tire tracks other than your own?"

"I mean there could have been something else," he said. "This is a common pull-off for fishers. But with the recent rains I didn't notice nothin'. Then again, I wasn't really lookin', was I?" He motioned to where his truck was parked.

Mona tried to ignore the fact her partner hadn't even acknowledged her presence. Instead, she turned to Alberhasky, motioning him to follow her out of earshot of the other two. "What's the situation?"

"Body's over there," he said, pointing closer to Roberts. "We taped off the area, did a preliminary search, came up empty. Took a statement from Mr. Madden after he showed us what he found. Ramsey here arrived about fifteen minutes ago. Asked me to help him question Madden." Alberhasky was closer to Jack's age, so it didn't surprise Mona Jack had asked him to assist him rather than wait for her. He'd been disrespectful before, but it was beginning to bleed over into downright contempt and Mona wasn't sure how to stop it.

"Anything of note?" she asked.

"Just that he came out this morning to do some fishing and almost tripped over the body. Doesn't own a cell phone, so he had to drive back into town to call it in. Which is probably why it's taken so long for everyone to get on board out here."

"Okay, thanks," Mona said. "Jack and I will take it from here. Is the ME on the way?"

Alberhasky turned and spoke into the radio on his shoulder. "Whittle said another thirty minutes."

She glanced up. He better make it quicker than that if he wanted to beat this weather. "Appreciate it."

The officer glanced at Jack, then back at her. "Good luck."

Mona smiled, though she didn't feel it. Jack's constant undercutting was beginning to be a problem. Maybe Sheriff Franklin had been right. Maybe she needed to "push back." She just wasn't sure how to go about doing that. Jack was the kind of person who spoke first and loudest in a conversation. And if he didn't like what you had to say, he just spoke over you until you shut up.

"Okay, Mr. Madden. If you wouldn't mind taking a seat over there in the back of the patrol car while we take a look around," Jack said, flipping his little notebook closed and stuffing it in his back pocket. Mona caught the sound of glass tapping against something when he did but wasn't sure where it had come from.

"Look, I gotta get back," Madden said. "I was supposed to be home two hours ago."

"You can either sit over there quietly or I can put you in cuffs and you can sit there in pain," Jack replied. "Your choice."

Madden huffed and turned, heading for Alberhasky's patrol car, passing Mona as he did and grumbling under his breath. She thought about trying to say something to smooth things over, but the damage was already done. Jack had just alienated their one possible witness.

"Was that really necessary?" Mona asked as Jack turned to head to the river.

"Yes," he replied.

"I don't appreciate your attitude," Mona said. "We're supposed to be partners."

Jack turned on her. "And I don't appreciate being saddled with some wet-behind-the-ears detective who doesn't know a motive from a means."

Mona swallowed a scathing retort. "How would you expect me know if you keep obstructing me every step of the way? Isn't that why Franklin put us together? So I could learn from you?"

"I'm not here to be anyone's babysitter," he said, turning away from her again. "I'm here to do my job."

Mona gritted her teeth, wishing she could just yell at him. But she wasn't that kind of person. She didn't get upset. People had their reasons for being how they were, and it was her job to meet them where she could. No amount of pleading on her part would change Jack's attitude toward her, that much was clear. So she might as well adapt and move forward. It was what she had always done.

"Aren't you even going to look at the body?" she called after him.

"Already did that when I first got here," he said over his shoulder.

Mona took a deep breath, then exhaled, centering herself. This would be a good opportunity for her. She would go look by herself, see what she could find. That way she wouldn't be tainted by any of Jack's... *biases*, as Franklin called them.

As she made her way over through the tall grass, she finally identified the shape of the body which had been marked off by the police tape and stakes Roberts and Alberhasky had set up.

Treading carefully, Mona ducked under the police tape and pulled out her phone, ready to take pictures if necessary.

Upon seeing the body, she noted it seemed to be in advanced stages of decomposition. The skin had begun to rot away but hadn't completely fallen off, and she could only see bits of bone peeking out from the wrists and the neck. The body was prone, one arm laying across its chest, almost like it had been laid there. As far as she could tell there didn't look to be any animal damage yet, but the smell was powerful enough to lead her to believe it wouldn't be long if they left the body much longer.

Squatting down, Mona took a closer look at the condition of the body and the clothes they were wearing. From the shape of the corpse she could reasonably assume it was a woman, but what remained of the hair was cut short. A tan bra peeked out from underneath the knit top and the figure wore shorts that were cut off at the mid-thigh, though they were mottled and specked with mold.

"What do you think?"

Mona jumped, almost falling forward, but managed to right herself at the last second. The voice had come out of nowhere, but when she turned, she saw a shadowed figure standing just outside the police tape.

"Excuse me?" she asked.

The figure stepped forward and Mona realized it was a woman in her late forties or early fifties, wearing a long beige jacket that had been pulled up around her neck. Her dark hair flecked with gray was pulled back into a bun and she wore a serious but curious expression.

Mona's mind immediately went to work. Her face, framed by the collar of the long coat, struck a chord in Mona's memory. She had seen this woman before, but *where*? The connection was just out of reach.

"I'm sorry," she said. "This area is off-limits. We're conducting an investigation here."

The woman nodded, producing a police badge from one of her pockets. Mona read *Chicago Police* emblazoned across the silver shield. "I'm Detective Charlotte Dawes."

Mona's eyes widened as she stood. "Detective Dawes," she said, ducking under the tape again to meet the woman. "I know all about you."

The woman furrowed her brow as she took Mona's hand. "You do?"

"Of course!" Mona said. "I've been studying your cases for years. The Don Perlinio case from oh-six, the Myers Ring in oh-nine and the Construction Worker debacle a couple of years ago. You're practically a legend."

The older woman chuckled as she released Mona's hand. "I think that's laying it on a little thick. I'm just a city cop."

"What are you doing out here?" Mona asked.

Charlotte indicated the body behind her. "I was called in to advise. In case you needed it. Detective..."

"Oh," Mona said, taking Charlotte's hand again, more animatedly this time. "Mona LaSalle. I was just promoted a month ago. Still getting used to the 'Detective' part." She supposed she shouldn't be surprised her boss called in some extra help. Murders of this sort were rare around here, after all. She just hoped Detective Dawes would be more willing to collaborate than Ramsey.

"Congratulations," Charlotte said, taking her hand back again. "You didn't answer my question. What do you think?"

Mona turned, looking at the body again. "Oh, right." She closed her eyes for a second, trying not to focus on the fact someone she'd been reading about for years was standing in front of her, asking questions about the case. "Female victim, looks to be maybe twenties or thirties. Best I can tell, the body has been dead at least a few weeks if not longer, though it's odd there isn't more damage from wildlife."

"What does that tell you?" Charlotte asked.

Mona frowned. If the body has begun to decompose but hadn't been exposed to the local fauna... "That she didn't die here. This is probably a dump site."

"Agreed," Charlotte said. "Otherwise, we'd see a lot more damage at this level of decomp. Someone kept her somewhere else before leaving her here."

"Which means it probably wasn't an accident. Or suicide," Mona said.

Dawes smiled. "And you say you're new to this?"

Mona's cheeks reddened. "Well, I've been studying crime all my life. I've always wanted to be a detective."

"I'd say you're off to a good start," the detective replied. "Does Oak Creek have a coroner?"

"Medical examiner," Mona corrected. "We share one with Poplar Grove and Hebron and a couple other towns. He's on the way."

"Good," Detective Dawes said, ducking under the tape to get a closer look. The wind picked up again, billowing her long coat. Mona had to brace herself against the cold. "You'll want this closed up as soon as possible to preserve any remaining evidence. Though I'm not sure how much you'll find. If someone dumped her here, they probably took their time not to leave any evidence behind." Mona nodded, then hunched down to take a closer look again. She was in the middle of studying the decomposition patterns when she felt Detective Dawes's eyes on her.

She looked up. "Something wrong?"

"For a newbie, you don't seem very disturbed by what you're seeing," the older woman said. "Not your first dead body?"

"Oh, no, it is," Mona said. "I mean, I've seen the cadavers, obviously. And crime scene photos. But this is my first one in person. Am I doing something wrong?"

"No," Dawes said, though she was looking at Mona in a peculiar way. "Some people have strong stomachs. You must be one of them."

"Hey!" a voice shouted, echoing across the river. Both women looked up to see Ramsey storming in their direction. "Get the hell off my crime scene!"

Detective Dawes held up both hands, her badge in one of them. "Detective Dawes, Chicago P.D. I have authorization to be here," she said.

"Then why the hell don't I know about it?" the man said, coming up to the police tape. "Franklin would have informed me if he was calling in assistance." He turned to Mona. "Did you even check with the station?"

"I'm sure your sheriff is getting the call now," Dawes said. "This all transpired this morning."

Sure enough, Mona heard Ramsey's phone ringing in his pocket. He grimaced at both women before pulling out his phone and answering. "Ramsey... yeah. Yeah, she's already here. Uh-huh. Fine." He hung up, his eyes locked on Dawes. "Must have driven pretty fast to get here from Chicago so quickly."

"I know a few shortcuts," she replied.

"Get this straight. This is *my* crime scene. If I want your help, I'll ask for it. Otherwise, I expect you to stay off the site and out of the way."

Detective Dawes held up her hands. "Whatever you say."

"But she can help," Mona protested. "Shouldn't we—"

"And you, you wanna learn something so badly?" Ramsey said, pointing a finger at Mona's chest. "Learn how to shut up and wipe that damn smile off your face. This is a fucking crime scene. There's nothing to smile about." With that, he turned and stormed off back toward the other officers.

Mona winced, trying to hold back her emotions. All she needed to do was take a few deep breaths, keep her cool...

"Wow, what an asshole," the detective behind her said as soon as Ramsey was out of earshot.

Mona turned, unable to help her grin. "Yeah, he's not the best with people."

"He's definitely in the right job, then," she said, ducking back under the tape. "I passed a truck over there. Does it belong to the witness?"

Mona nodded to the police cruiser. "Duane Madden. Claims to have found the body this morning."

"How does he seem to you?" the older woman asked.

"Um... impatient. But I haven't had much time to talk to him."

Dawes nodded absently, looking around the scene, her hands in her pockets. She worked her jaw for a moment. "What was he doing out here?"

"He said he was coming out this morning to fish."

Dawes nodded again, looking in the direction of the police vehicle. "I may be overstepping my bounds here according to your... *partner*, but I wonder what would happen if you went over there and asked him where his gun was."

Mona's eyes went wide. "What?"

"Did you see it? The gun rack behind the seats in his truck? It's empty. I don't know of any farmer who owns a gun rack and doesn't use it. Not to mention the little indentations into the wood where a couple of rifles have worn it away over time."

"You think he might be involved?" Mona asked, kicking herself for not looking closer at the truck as she'd passed.

The detective shrugged. "Won't know unless you ask."

"And you want me..." The question hung in the air.

"It's your case, isn't it?"

Mona couldn't help but be stunned for a moment. Was Detective Dawes testing her? Or was this some kind of hazing ritual, designed to embarrass her? But it was far more than Ramsey had ever trusted her with. *Push back.* She had an opportunity here, and she wasn't about to waste it.

She nodded and headed back over to the cruiser where Madden sat, on the edge of the seat, one leg propped up on the sideboard.

"Mr. Madden?" The man looked up as she approached. "I wanted to ask you a few follow-up questions."

"Can't we just get this over with?" the man protested. "I've got work to do."

"This will just take a minute," Mona said. "Do you own any firearms?"

The man seemed to start, then glared at her a second. "I dunno, maybe one or two somewhere."

"But you don't keep them with you?" Visible beads of sweat broke out across his brow.

"Why would I need to?" he asked.

Mona looked back over at the man's truck. "I noticed you didn't have any fishing equipment with you."

"I left it back at the house," he said. "When I went to call you people."

She nodded but could tell by the slight squint of his eye there was more there. He was exhibiting all the classic tells of a man who did not want to talk about something. His posture was tight and reserved and every answer came out just a bit more forcefully than it needed to.

"Okay, so let's go over it again. What time did you arrive to the scene?"

He huffed. "I already told the other man. It was around seven. Maybe six thirty. Early, before the sun was up."

"And that's when you found the body."

He nodded.

"And you went straight back home to call us."

"That's what I been sayin', ain't it?"

"Mr. Madden, I couldn't help notice you keep a gun rack in the back of your truck."

"So?" he asked, but she could tell she'd hit a closer nerve. Detective Dawes's instincts had been right.

"So why keep a gun rack if you don't keep your firearms with you?" She stared at him, hard, her question pointed.

Madden looked away from her, trying to find someone else —Ramsey maybe—who he could lie to. But Mona was the only one around.

"Okay, look. I was afraid you might think I had something to do with it. I ain't never come across a dead body before."

"What the hell are you doing?" Ramsey asked, walking up.

"Mr. Madden here was just telling me about where he put the firearm he brought with him this morning," Mona said.

Ramsey's eyes went wide, and some of the fury on his face dissipated. "You had a gun with you this morning?"

Madden was clearly feeling the pressure. "I didn't want to get blamed for nothin'," he said, a little too loudly.

"Jesus Christ," Ramsey said. "Where is it now?"

Madden hung his head. "At my house. In the crawlspace."

"So you went home, *hid* your weapon, *then* called us?"

Madden started speaking fast, like he was trying to get it out all at once. "Yeah, I did, but I just didn't want nothin' to happen. My wife was sick last year and that about wiped us out and I didn't have no way to support her if I went to jail—"

"Wait," Mona said. "Why would you go to jail?"

Madden bit his lower lip. "I mean, 'cause... I thought you might think I had something to do with... you know, the body."

"But she obviously didn't die recently," Mona said. "Why would you think we'd assume you shot her?"

"I... I didn't get that good of a look," he protested. "I just saw—"

"Answer the question," Ramsey said. "Right now."

Madden hung his head, cursing. "I was huntin'."

"Without a license," Mona said. He nodded. "Why?"

"It's been a slim winter," the man admitted. "Been cleaning carcasses and selling meat to get by."

"Dammit," Ramsey said. "I should arrest your ass for obstruction."

"I'm sorry," the man said, almost sounding like he was about to start crying. "I'm just tryin' to do what's right here."

"All you've done is cost us valuable time," Ramsey said. "I need to call Franklin." He headed off, his phone in his hand.

Mona couldn't help but feel for the man. She'd heard it had been a tough winter for some of the locals, but she didn't realize just how tough. And people like Madden weren't the kind who asked for help. They often resorted to their own means before inconveniencing others.

"You hunt here often?" Mona asked.

"Every few days," he said, all the fight going out of him. "This is part of a deer trail. They like to stay close to the creek."

"When's the last time you were out here?"

He shook his head. "Probably Thursday. Or Friday. One of the two."

"Which was it, Mr. Madden?" Mona insisted as she crouched down to look him in the eye. "It's important."

He squeezed his features together. "Um. Friday. Came out early, before morning chores. But I went home empty. That's why I figured I'd try again today."

"Did you come to this exact place?" He nodded. "And was the body here then?"

He blinked a few times. "No... no, I would have let someone know. There wasn't anything here."

"Okay, thank you," Mona said, standing back up.

"Listen, I'll quit the huntin' if you'll just let me off with a warning. My wife... she still can't fully fend for herself and if I'm gone—"

"I understand," Mona said. "Give me a minute." Instead of

regrouping with Ramsey who was shouting into his phone, Mona returned to Dawes who stood a few feet away from the scene, looking out over the water. The fog was only growing thicker, nearly obscuring her along with the shoreline. When Mona reached her, she had the look of someone who was completely calm, like she didn't have a bother in the world. Mona wondered if she would ever look so calm and confident in this job.

"Well?" Dawes asked as Mona approached. "Get anything?"

"I'd say I hooked a whopper," Mona replied.

FIVE

Charlotte smiled as the other woman talked animatedly about everything she'd learned from the "fisherman." True to Charlotte's hunch, he hadn't been out here fishing at all, as the creek didn't really seem deep enough for anything large enough worth catching. Still, some people enjoyed the activity by itself and she might have accepted that, if not for the presence of the gun rack in the back of the truck. That, and she thought she'd spotted a few clumps of fur in his truck bed.

As Detective LaSalle talked, Charlotte couldn't help but envy the woman's enthusiasm for the job. Charlotte had been like that once, excited about even the smallest details. Though lately, despite her best efforts, the job had seemed more like a lifeline than something she actually enjoyed doing every day. If she was honest with herself, she probably had more in common with LaSalle's partner than she did with the young woman. But that didn't mean she needed to embrace the cynicism. When she'd first pulled up, she'd been intrigued by the young woman with her nose inches from the corpse, seemingly unbothered by the gruesome form before her. Not only that, but it seemed like she had good instincts when it came to witnesses. Given time, LaSalle was going to be a force to be reckoned with.

It also didn't hurt she seemed to worship the ground Charlotte walked on.

"—probably need to end up issuing him a citation," she was saying. "But I'm not sure he had anything to do with the body."

"Maybe, maybe not. But we should probably have forensics take a look at his truck just to make sure," Charlotte said.

Mona nodded. "I'll make sure they take care of it." She looked over her shoulder at the man who was now talking to Madden again, the hunter shrinking under the barrage of questions.

"What do you think about your partner? Ramsey, is it?" she asked the younger detective.

A slight hesitation. "Oh, he's great. I've learned a lot already," she said. "That's one of the reasons we're partnered together."

"He showing you all the ropes?"

Another slight reluctance. "Yep. Can't complain," she said.

Charlotte had seen that look before and knew what it meant. LaSalle was on the receiving end of the other detective's bad attitude and, given what she'd seen so far, wasn't putting up much of a defense.

As if on cue, the man looked up from his tirade on the witness, his gaze locked on LaSalle.

"Ah, shit," Charlotte murmured under her breath. She'd seen that look more than a few times in her years with the force. The man came stomping back over to them, fury etched across his features. As he came within earshot, Charlotte felt a drop of rain hit her coat.

"Who gave you permission to question the witness without my presence?" he demanded.

LaSalle didn't flinch, either oblivious to his anger or just flat out not acknowledging it—Charlotte suspected the latter. "I didn't realize I needed *permission*."

"When *I'm* the senior detective and you've never worked a corpse before, you do. I don't give a good goddamn how smart you think you are," Ramsey shouted. "You are not to question *anyone* without my approval and authorization."

"But—" she began.

"This isn't some game where you can just do as you please. We have procedures in place, and until you have a couple years under your belt, you don't make any decisions without my say so."

It didn't seem like LaSalle was going to fight back and Charlotte had taken about all she could. "Calm down, Detective," she said, knowing it would only provoke him. "I suggested she speak with the witness about a hunch."

"*You*," he replied, his face going even redder.

"Believe it or not, we can actually make our own decisions when we're assigned to cases. And there is no *procedure* that prevents a detective from speaking with a witness. Not unless you folks have a different set of rules you live by up here."

The rage on the man's face was almost enough to make Charlotte want to chuckle. He was the kind of man who wanted to control everyone and everything around him, and when something didn't follow his specific line of action, it only served to enrage him. She wondered how far she could push him before he cracked.

"You're not even supposed to be here," Ramsey finally said through his teeth.

"I'm just following orders," Charlotte defended. "I'm here as an advisor and I advised Detective LaSalle. And if you would stop blustering and actually listen for a moment, you might learn something." Another drop of rain struck her coat.

Ramsey got right up in Charlotte's face, his mere inches from her own. "You listen here—" he began.

"*No*," Charlotte said with as much force as she could without shouting. She had faced more than her fair share of bullies in her career, and in that area she remained undefeated. "*You* listen. I will not stand here and be pushed around by some self-important tyrant when we have a case to solve. You don't like my methods? Deal with it. You don't like your partner? Too bad. This is the hand we've been dealt, and we can either work together, or you can keep throwing a hissy fit. Which will it be?"

"If you think you can come up here and start throwing your weight around because you're from the city and we're just a bunch of *dumb country cops* you've got another thing coming. Let's see how smarmy you are after I have a discussion with Sheriff Franklin."

If he was trying to intimidate her, he wasn't doing a very good job. "Good luck with that."

Grimacing, Ramsey turned to LaSalle. "And you. I see loyalty means nothing in your eyes. No wonder no one wants to work with you."

LaSalle crossed her features. "I don't understand," she said. "You didn't even want this case when the sheriff gave it out."

That caught the man off guard and he fumbled his words for a moment, causing Charlotte to turn away to hide her smile. But she hadn't done a good enough job as Ramsey caught a trace of it.

"You know what? You two want this thing so badly? Fine. Best of luck. It's nothing but a dead end anyway." More rain began to fall. "Good luck with the weather." He turned and stormed off for his car, driving a line through the tall grass. Charlotte glanced over to the other two officers who had been standing nearby, eavesdropping.

She sighed. Whiteside wouldn't be happy about this.

"Is that true?" she asked. "Did he really not want the case?"

LaSalle turned to her. "Oh... well, yes. He seemed upset about the assignment. At least, that's what I thought..."

"The man has some serious control issues," Charlotte said watching him get into his car and pull out, throwing up rocks as he did. "It's kind of like watching a five-year-old throw a tantrum."

"I guess some people just never grow up," the younger woman said.

Charlotte turned back to her. "You okay running this thing on your own until you get back to the station? I'm sure your boss will iron things out."

"You're not going somewhere, are you?" she asked, and for a brief second, Charlotte caught a hint of panic in her voice.

"No, it's just I'm not officially on the case. It wouldn't be appropriate for me to head it up. In Detective Ramsey's absence, they'll be looking to you."

"Oh," LaSalle said, turning to look at the other officers and the witness still on the scene. "I didn't really think about that."

The icy rain had begun to come down properly now, wetting their hair and sending a chill through Charlotte.

"C'mon, let's see about covering the body until the ME gets here," Charlotte said.

As they turned to grab a tarp from one of the patrol cars, another vehicle pulled up, parking right where Ramsey's car had been. A heavyset man in his forties stepped out, his long hair pulled back into a low ponytail. "That'll be Whittle," LaSalle said. "Just in time." She gave him a quick wave. Charlotte noticed a second of confusion on the man's face as he looked around for anyone else, but it disappeared a moment later. He dug around in the backseat of his car a moment and emerged with two different cases, one over each shoulder as he approached them.

"LaSalle," he said, nodding before turning to Charlotte. "I'm afraid I don't know you."

"Detective Charlotte Dawes, Chicago Police." She

extended a hand, and he took it. "Better get a move on. This weather pattern is moving in quickly."

"Whittle. I cover most of McHenry County. I thought Ramsey was—"

"He went back to the station to... run down some leads," LaSalle said. "I guess I'm your point man."

The bigger man nodded. "Okay. Show me what we've got."

After helping him set up a temporary tent over the body, they spent the next few hours with Whittle as he worked. Charlotte was used to a team of forensics, but Whittle was a one-man show, not only working as photographer but also as examiner of the body and surrounding areas. However, given the weather, there was only so much the man could do.

While they waited for him to finish, Charlotte suggested that LaSalle have the other officers drive Mr. Madden back to the station. While it was possible he might have a hand in this, Charlotte didn't think that would end up being the case. And once Whittle cleared the truck of any human remains, she'd be satisfied to cut him loose for the time being.

Without Ramsey here to be in the way, LaSalle actually took point on her own while Charlotte stood back and watched. She knew she was on thin ice here, and her little spat with Ramsey might be all it would take for Whiteside to yank her right back to Chicago, but she couldn't just let the man bluster. Not to mention, his ego was impeding the investigation, which was already more intriguing than Charlotte had first envisioned.

The body, while somewhat decomposed, presented a unique set of circumstances. As LaSalle had postulated, it looked to be a woman, mid-thirties or so given the style of her hair and what little jewelry remained on her body, though most of her facial features had worn away, leaving little more than a skeletal grin where her mouth once was.

But it was what she was *wearing* that intrigued Charlotte the most. Unless someone had changed her clothes after she died—unlikely—then she was dressed for summer... or at least warmer weather. That wasn't consistent with the near-frigid temperatures of Illinois in February. Which meant someone had kept her for a while before dumping her body. The question was: Why now? It was the middle of winter, meaning she might have died six months ago or more.

Though, that would be for Whittle to tell them.

"Okay," Whittle said, returning to them after hours of investigation. Only Roberts remained on scene as Alberhasky had left with Madden. "That's about all I can do. The blood will take a day or so. The DNA tests longer, if you want them."

"Any immediate cause of death?" Charlotte asked. She was soaked, hugging herself trying to keep warm.

"Nothing that stands out. I'll need to get her back to do a full autopsy. Van is on its way."

"What about her length of time out here?" LaSalle asked. "The witness said he didn't see her three days ago."

Whittle nodded. "That seems consistent. The cold seems to have preserved her for the most part, but I'm not seeing the normal seepage into the ground indicating a long-term situation. I can't nail it down, but I doubt she's been here more than a day or two."

"At least that tracks," Charlotte said. "Any way to tell *when* she died?"

"It'll be tough," he replied. "My gut wants to say she's been dead a month, but I can't say that with any accuracy given the strange conditions. If she died right here, on this spot, I'd say two weeks. But given she was transported and possibly stored..."

"Right," Charlotte said, shoving her hands into her pockets again. The normal hallmarks for determining time of death wouldn't be there, which meant it would be a shot in the dark.

"Thanks, Whittle," LaSalle said. "This really helps. You've

got my number for when the autopsy is done?" For some reason, even though LaSalle was as soaked as Charlotte, she didn't seem to be as cold. Or if she was, she wasn't showing a hint of it.

He nodded. "Appreciate you staying out here, especially with the weather. Most of the time it's just me on my own."

"Of course," LaSalle said, giving the man an affectionate pat on the arm. "Just let me know if you need anything else."

"Will do," he said.

As Charlotte hurried beside LaSalle on the way back to the cars, she couldn't help but reflect on the woman's attitude. "Not much bothers you, does it?"

"What's that?" she asked.

"You just strike me as someone who is practiced in letting things roll off your shoulders. For someone so young that's... impressive." Charlotte hadn't been nearly that even-keeled when she'd been that age. Having just joined the force, coming off what she thought would be a lifelong career that had been cut short, she had been angry, and it showed in every aspect of her life. It took her a long time to control and focus that anger, longer than she would have liked.

"Oh, you mean Ramsey?" LaSalle asked, though Charlotte noticed a nervous chuckle. "He's just gruff. I'm used to it."

"No, he's abusive," Charlotte replied. "But it's good you don't let him get to you. It's probably the best way you could respond."

Charlotte could feel the other woman's eyes on her but didn't match the gaze. She'd already overstepped here, maybe it was better if she backed off. She was scratching the surface of something personal and that might not be her best move. "I think I'm going to find myself a motel in town. Change out of these wet clothes and maybe let things cool down a bit."

"Have you checked in with the sheriff yet?" she asked.

"No, I came straight here," Charlotte admitted. "I wanted to get on site as soon as—"

"I would *love* to introduce you," LaSalle replied, her bubbly personality returning. "I bet most everyone knows who you are; I can't be the only one who's heard of you."

Charlotte shied away from the woman. "That's really not necessary. I should—"

"You have to speak with the sheriff anyway, right? Why not?"

She had to concede the point. Charlotte couldn't put off heading to the station to check in with Sheriff Franklin forever, especially not after her initial encounter with Ramsey. So far, this was not going how she had hoped. But delaying things might only make it worse. Might as well get it over with now.

"Okay," she finally said. "If you insist."

SIX

Charlotte followed Detective LaSalle back across the empty farmlands until they crossed the line into Oak Creek. Due to where the body was found, Charlotte had managed to circumnavigate the town on the way to the site, even though it was further west. She'd never been to Oak Creek before, despite the fact it was only a few hours from the city and had a fair number of bed and breakfast spots she'd often heard Chicago locals rave about. So when they pulled into town she wasn't exactly sure what to expect.

What she found was a quaint little haven that seemed tucked away from the rest of the world. There were no nearby Interstates and thus not a lot of the kind of businesses that survived along those concrete veins. No glut of gas stations or chain restaurants, instead nothing but a series of local businesses all centered around a small downtown area that looked like it hadn't changed much in the past seventy years. There was even a town square, complete with picturesque gazebo where a couple sat drinking coffee as Charlotte pulled into the police station adjacent to the town hall at the head of the square. The station was an old, brick building that looked like it had at least a hundred years on it or more. A far cry from the skyscrapers she was used to.

Detective LaSalle must have seen her looking around at the buildings as she stepped out of her car. "Most of these buildings are original to the town," she said, approaching. "The station here used to have the town jail in the basement, but we just use it for storage now. Jail's a block that way." She pointed northeast, where Charlotte caught sight of a commuter train pulling up to the small station on the far side of the square.

"I didn't realize the Metro came all the way out here," she said.

"Yep, most people just park and ride the train in," LaSalle replied. "Less traffic."

Charlotte turned back to her. "You spend much time in the city?"

LaSalle shrugged. "A little. But I like it out here better. It's quieter."

"That's true," Charlotte replied, just now noticing that even in town, there was barely a noise other than the crossing gates for the train that were down. A couple of people walked the square, but it seemed to her like most of the businesses were either closed or had gone bust long ago. Most of what was left were bars.

"Lead the way, Detective," Charlotte said. They might as well get this over with.

"Oh, you can just call me Mona," she replied. "I'm not sure if I'm comfortable with people addressing me formally yet."

"Okay, then, Mona," Charlotte replied. "I'm in your capable hands."

The younger woman's eyes flashed as bright as her smile. "I still can't believe you're here. C'mon." She led the way from the small parking area in the back of the building around to a side entrance. Charlotte noticed rows of small rectangular windows just barely above the sidewalk with bars behind the glass plate.

Prisoners back in the day would have been able to watch all the traffic walking by, the world going on without them. A window could be a cruel reality sometimes because it separated you from everything else. Charlotte couldn't help but think of her own future situation, retired, sitting alone, in her home, watching life go by out the window.

Once in the station and past the security checkpoint, Mona started pointing out all the different departments and their department heads, not that there were a lot of people in the station to begin with. Contrasted to the mob-like crowding of her own station, this was like walking into a ghost town.

But that didn't stop Mona from introducing Charlotte to every person they crossed paths with. The first few times Charlotte tried to be gracious, but by the sixth Mona was introducing her as *Detective Dawes, the woman who solved the Myers Crime Ring*, it had begun to grate on her nerves. She didn't like being in the spotlight, never had. And this was the most attention anyone had paid her in years. Would they still think she was so great if they knew she'd just botched a massive drug case that cost the city and the state hundreds of thousands of dollars?

As they climbed the stairs, heading for the sheriff's office, Charlotte caught wind of a familiar voice. And there, at the top with three other people surrounding him, was Detective Ramsey, sitting on the edge of one of the desks.

"—and then this bitch just shows up and starts pretending like it's her own show, like she knows this county better than—" An errant glance from one of his listeners drew his attention to Charlotte and Mona standing not more than ten feet away. "Speak of the devil."

"Thanks, Ramsey," Charlotte replied. "*This bitch* appreciates the warm welcome."

"Hey," he said, standing. "I wasn't the one who barged in on someone else's crime scene. Is that something you would have stood for if it had been one of your cases?"

Immediately she knew the answer but wasn't about to give him the satisfaction. "I didn't barge. I'm here on an advisory basis only."

"Sure didn't seem that way when you sent the puppy dog over there to do your work for you." He motioned to Mona.

"That's enough," Charlotte replied, stepping closer.

"Yeah? You gonna show me how tough city cops really are?" he asked, and she detected a faint trace of alcohol on his breath. He must have come right back and had a drink to settle himself down. But it had only had the opposite effect.

Ramsey looked over Charlotte's shoulder at Mona. "Did she tell you she hasn't closed a case in over two years?"

Charlotte winced but didn't break her eye contact on the man. He turned his attention back to her. "That's right. I looked you up. You're a has-been. This the best Chicago could send us? A used-up cop with only a few weeks left in the job?"

Charlotte's hand reflexively formed a fist. The urge was there, all she needed to do was step into it and one solid hit would take the man down. The muscle memory of that kind of punch surged through her system, commanding her to take up the position and strike.

"That's enough!" a voice called across the room.

Charlotte—and everyone else—turned to see a gruff man with a brushy mustache approaching. "Ramsey, go pull your head out of your ass and sober up," he said.

Charlotte's hand relaxed, but when it did, the ribbons of pain shot up her forearm, just like they had that night at the club. She had to hide it behind her back to keep anyone from seeing it tremble.

Ramsey grumbled something under his breath but finally turned away, pushing past one of the people he'd been talking to earlier.

"Okay, break it up. You all have better things to do than sit around here and gossip," the sheriff said to the other people in the office.

Mona stepped forward. "Sheriff, this is—"

"I know who she is," he replied, sizing Charlotte up. "I want both of you in my office, right now."

Fantastic, Charlotte thought to herself. *Way to keep a low profile*. Whiteside would have her head for sure.

She followed Mona across the room until they were in Sheriff Franklin's office. Boxes of marked cases stood stacked along the edges of the office, looking like Franklin was in the process of moving in. But there were also plaques and dedications on the wall behind him, and above all of that, a large, framed photo of an old train locomotive, looking majestic with the sun shining over the mountains behind it. Charlotte found her eye drawn to it as it seemed to dominate the small office. Franklin rounded the desk but didn't sit down, so neither did Mona or Charlotte. Instead, the three of them stood there, watching each other for a moment. "Is this how you make a good impression, Dawes?" he finally asked. "Nearly getting into a physical altercation with one of my detectives?"

"I'm sorry, sir," she said. "I wasn't thinking." She noticed on one of the shelves to her right a small model of a train. Apparently, the sheriff enjoyed his trains.

Mona cleared her throat. "Sir, Detective Ramsey was—"

"I know what he was doing," Franklin said, cutting Mona off. "He was being an ass, per usual. He already came in here complaining about you once. But I told him you were a professional, highly recommended by your commanding officer in Chicago. Was that an incorrect statement?"

Charlotte stiffened. "No, sir."

"Good. Because Whiteside promised me you wouldn't be a problem. And I've known Jeremy a long time. He doesn't make promises lightly." Charlotte gritted her teeth. Despite her recent screwup, her boss had gone to bat for her. And she'd repaid him by almost punching someone.

"Won't happen again, sir," she said. "It was a long drive."

Franklin eyed her for a minute before finally sitting down. "Long drive. That's creative. Look, I know Ramsey isn't the easiest person to get along with, but you were just walking into the lion's den."

He was right; if Charlotte had thrown a punch, she would have been gone in an instant, which was exactly what Ramsey had wanted.

The sheriff sighed. "It's a... pleasure... to meet you. I'm Sheriff Franklin." He held out a hand and Charlotte took it, giving it a hearty shake.

"Charlotte Dawes." She detected a hint of chewing tobacco as she leaned in closer to the man.

He nodded. "Take a seat, both of you." He turned to Mona. "Don't tell me she managed to get under your skin too."

Mona shook her head. "Not at all. In fact, Detective Dawes was instrumental in breaking some information about the case."

Franklin arched an eyebrow. "Well? Give it to me, I don't have all day here."

"Right," Mona said, and then launched into everything they'd learned so far about not only the body, but the witness, Mr. Madden, who was downstairs at this moment awaiting his fate. While he listened, Franklin kept shooting glances at Charlotte, who allowed Mona to give all the details without interrupting. There wasn't much she'd be able to add anyway, the woman had it all covered.

"Sounds like you have already been of some help on this one, Dawes," he replied once Mona was done.

"Thank you, sir. I'm eager to help in any way I can."

Franklin worked his jaw for a moment before laying his hands on the desk before them. "Look, I won't lie. We've had our fair share of bodies pop up in Oak Creek over the years, but usually they're either drug-related, or domestic abuse victims. This... this looks like something else to me. And since my usual team is out of commission, I was grateful Whiteside offered to send you down here." He paused a moment. "Seeing how you two seem to be working well together already, I'm assigning you both as leads on the case."

"What about Jack?" Mona asked.

"There are more than enough cases to keep everyone busy," Franklin said. "But I'll reassign him. I don't need ego getting in the way of this case, and seeing how he already left the scene of the crime before you'd finished gathering evidence, he and I need to have a long discussion."

"I don't want to cause any issues," Charlotte said, sitting forward. "I had just planned—"

"Do you want the case or not?" Franklin snapped.

"No, of course. I do, thank you, sir," she said, sitting back, glancing at the picture above him again.

"Word of advice, Dawes. When someone offers you a gift horse, don't spit in its mouth." She nodded. "I'm confident if LaSalle has a question about something, you'll have the answer, given your experience in the field." He turned to Mona. "It seems I should have let you out of the pen sooner. Some people are just naturals at this job, so let's see what you can do."

"Thank you, sir," Mona said. "We'll get to work right away. What do you want to do about Madden?"

"Issue him his citation and cut him loose," he said. "We'll come back to him if anything shows up from the truck, but I'm not holding him because he lied about hunting."

"Got it," she said.

"Given what we now know, I want the two of you to start with local missing persons. We need to figure out where this woman came from."

Charlotte leaned forward again. "I'm sorry to say, I don't think she's local. She's not dressed for the weather. And according to your ME she hasn't been dead long enough to have died when it was still warm enough for shorts around here."

"Still, let's eliminate everyone we can before we go looking for a nomad. Maybe you'll get lucky."

Or it could just be a big waste of time, Charlotte thought.

The sheriff relaxed back into his chair while still giving them both a pointed gaze. "LaSalle, get with Michaels and get Dawes a desk. I have a feeling she's going to be here for a while."

"Yes, sir," Mona replied. It might have been Charlotte's imagination, but she thought she saw the grin on the woman's face widen.

Finally, Franklin stood, holding out his hand again. "Best of luck to the both of you. You're gonna need it."

SEVEN

It took about twenty minutes to get Detective Dawes set up with a desk and a computer as well as login credentials. The station only had one tech services guy, a young officer around Mona's age named Michaels. He had always been reserved, yet friendly. But to Mona's disappointment, he'd never heard of Detective Charlotte Dawes. She'd had to explain to him how lucky they were to have someone with her record working in their small corner of the world.

Ever since she had arrived, Mona had been doing everything she could to restrain herself. *The* actual Charlotte Dawes was here, and now they were working on the same case together. Mona never would have believed it had it not actually happened. It seemed like all her hard work was finally paying off, in more ways than she could have ever expected. She barely even noticed she'd almost completely dried out from being out on site half the day.

While Michaels helped Detective Dawes, Mona went deep into the archives and pulled all the missing persons cases for the past five years for all of McHenry County. In total there were about seventy files for missing women, which would take some time to pore through. By the time she reached Detective Dawes again, Michaels was showing her how to log in to the department's system.

"Thanks, I can take it from here," she told Michaels.

"If you run into any trouble, I'm right downstairs," he said. "Welcome to the unit." He nodded before leaving them to it.

"Here you go," Mona said, handing her half the stack of files. "I figure if we work straight through, we can have a lot of these eliminated within a few hours."

"You don't waste any time, do you?" the older woman asked, taking the files from Mona.

"Why waste time?" she asked. "There's probably a family out there, looking for her right now. We can give them closure."

"I remember running hot all the time too," she said, setting the files on her desk. "That's a good way to burn out. This job is a marathon, not a sprint. You need to give yourself time to process. We still don't have a definitive report on how she died yet."

"Well, no," Mona admitted. "But I figured while Whittle is working on the body, we could at least eliminate all these possibilities." Mona found the other woman watching her carefully. She'd seen her do that a couple of times already. What was she looking for?

"Okay, sure," she finally said after a moment. "Let's go ahead and start looking."

"Is it because you don't think she's from around here?" Mona asked.

Charlotte sat back in her chair, watching Mona again. "I don't. And I think this is a waste of time. But it won't hurt to make sure. If it makes your boss happy, let's go ahead and go through them. If for no other reason than for you to get to say, 'I told you so.'"

That was the second time the woman had given Mona credit for something she'd thought up. Why did she keep doing that? Was it because she wanted to bolster Mona's confidence? Ramsey never would have given Mona credit for anything, even if she *had* found something on her own. In fact, she was sure it had been Detective Dawes's endorsement that had convinced the sheriff to put her as a lead on this case.

"LaSalle, you okay?" her new partner asked, eyeing her closely.

"Yeah," Mona said too quickly. "Just looking forward to poring over these."

Dawes chuckled. "No one looks forward to sifting through missing persons cases." She leaned forward. "You look like you need to get something off your chest."

"Nope," Mona chirped. "I'm good."

The newcomer watched her again for a few moments; Mona could practically *feel* her eyes appraising her. She just smiled, hoping she wouldn't ask any more questions. With Ramsey it had been easy. The man had never been interested in what she had to say and thus had never paid her any attention. That went for most of the people in the office. Detective Dawes was the first one to take a close look at Mona, and she wasn't sure she was ready for it.

Finally, the other woman turned her attention to the files. "Okay, let's get started. I think we can eliminate anyone over the age of fifty. You don't usually see people that age in that kind of attire." She started opening files, flipping through and tossing them aside.

"Good idea," Mona said, thankful the attention was finally off her. She really was looking forward to focusing on the case; she just had to tamp down the nervousness of working with someone so closely—someone way out of her league. Dawes wasn't like the others—she didn't shut Mona down with every other word, and that was new. In fact, she agreed with Mona's suggestion they also eliminate anyone under the age of sixteen. But as they worked, something gnawed at Mona's subconscious.

She kept wondering if she should bring it up or not, given they would be working closely together for who knew how long. But then again, this was Charlotte Dawes; what right did Mona have to question her? The woman had almost been in the job as long as Mona had been alive. Unlike Jack, Charlotte was silent as she worked, and finally Mona found she had to say *something*.

"What got you interested in police work?" she blurted out.

The other woman looked up. "What?"

"Sorry," Mona said. "I don't work great in silence. I usually have my headphones on." She indicated to the device sitting next to her computer.

"You can listen, I don't mind."

"No, no, that would be rude," Mona said.

"How does it work when you're working on other cases? With Ramsey?" Mona hesitated a beat too long and realized the seasoned detective had already come up with the answer. "You're not used to working with others, are you?"

Mona gave a pinched smile. "It's okay. I've always been good on my own. I'm an only child, so I'm used to it." *Shoot.* She shouldn't have said that. Now she was going to think Mona was some kind of *weirdo* who didn't know how to act in the real world. Why did she have to open her mouth? Why did she always have to *volunteer* information? That was one of the things that got her in trouble.

"That's good," Dawes said, surprising Mona. "You're going to need to work on your own a lot in this job. While you'll collaborate a lot too, many times it's just you."

"What about your partners?" Mona asked, strangely feeling a little better.

"Partners come and go," Detective Dawes said. "Don't hang your hat on them." Though as she said it, there was a slight crinkle of her mouth that Mona couldn't read. Surely, she didn't operate on her own all the time?

The phone on Mona's desk rang, breaking the tension. "LaSalle," she said.

"Detective. It's Whittle. I have news."

They had to drive over to the ME's local office, which was about ten minutes away, just outside the town limits. They'd agreed to take one car, though Mona hoped Detective Dawes didn't ask her any more personal questions. It was becoming more difficult to deflect. She hadn't realized when they started working together that the other woman would actually be interested in her. In an effort to stave her off during the short drive, Mona instead peppered Dawes with questions about her time as a police officer.

"You never did tell me what made you want to become a cop," Mona said as the discussion had begun to run dry.

"It's not a very interesting story," Dawes replied. "My other career didn't work out, so I found something that I thought I'd be good at. Turns out I was."

"What was your other career?" Mona asked. "Wait, let me guess. Military?"

"Close," Dawes replied. "No, I was a kickboxer. Practiced for eight years, got pretty good too. Almost good enough to qualify for national competition."

"What happened?" Mona asked.

The other woman sighed. "Bit off more than I could chew."

An uncomfortable silence stretched between them as Mona waited for more, but she could tell this was not a subject Detective Dawes was used to discussing.

"As in—you lost a match?"

"As in I broke both my hands," she admitted. Mona noticed she flexed them as she said it, though she wasn't sure Detective Dawes knew she was doing it or not. "Stupid mistake."

"Wow, I didn't realize kickboxing could get that violent. Shouldn't the referee have stopped it before—"

"It didn't happen in the ring," she replied. "I'd rather not talk about it."

"Sorry," Mona said. "I didn't mean to pry."

"It's okay," the woman replied. "But they were pretty messed up for a while. I had to teach myself to write and type again. There was no way I could go back to the sport."

"That must have been hard," Mona replied.

Detective Dawes got a faraway look in her eyes. "Yeah. But the police training wasn't as rigorous as kickboxing and by then my hands had healed enough that I could qualify, so I started out as a beat cop and worked my way up."

"I'm glad you did," Mona said, pulling into the parking lot of the one-story building and killing the engine. "I mean, I'm sure you would have made a good kickboxer, but you made a great detective."

The woman scoffed as they got out. "I'm not so sure everyone would agree with you. This the place?"

"Yep," Mona said, leading the way to the doors. Inside she showed her badge to the man at the desk who just nodded to them both.

"Not a lot of security here," Dawes commented.

"I guess it's a lot different than what you're used to." She made her way down the familiar corridor to the ME's office. She'd been this way a few times before, usually following Ramsey as he walked ahead of her. This was the first time she'd ever been in the lead.

Whittle didn't keep an office in this building; instead, he had one at the next closest office over in Hebron. So it was no surprise to find him in the examination room, typing away on a computer which was mounted on a standing desk.

"Detectives," he said as they came in, removing his glasses

and setting them aside. "I appreciate you coming all the way over here."

"All the way, it was a ten-minute drive," Detective Dawes said.

"Still, it would be more convenient for me if it were connected to the local hospital instead of in a stand-alone building off the beaten path." He waved the thought away. "But that's neither here nor there. Let me show you what I found." He headed over to the five cold-storage drawer units, opening the first one. On it lay their victim, though she looked a bit different than she had this morning. Her clothes had been removed and her chest cavity had been opened to allow access.

"You're quick," Dawes commented. "It usually takes my coroner a good day to finish an autopsy."

"This is my first autopsy in twelve days," Whittle admitted. "Other than this, the only call I've had was for a nursing home patient they wanted to make sure hadn't been poisoned. Turned out she hadn't been. Just had a lot of lithium in her system." He returned to the recently found body.

"I was able to confirm she died about a month ago"—he moved his hand over the open cavity in the middle, indicating what little remained inside—"given the rate of decay of the internal organs. However, as I speculated at the crime scene, the victim didn't die there. There would have been a lot more trace evidence in the surrounding grass and soil. I also picked up some debris that I can't identify; more than likely it came from the original site where she died. But since then, the body has been in relatively cold and clean conditions. Which is why she's as intact as she is."

"Cold as in... a freezer?" Dawes asked.

"Perhaps. But probably not long-term," Whittle said. "I know I said she hadn't been exposed to the elements as long, but there are instances of freezer burn on parts of the body, which indicates rapid thawing and refreezing."

"She was moved around?"

"I'm just telling you what I found. I also found ligature marks here and here," he said, pointing to the upper arms and mid-thigh area. "There wasn't enough to pull a pattern, but it would indicate some kind of restraint was used *after* she died."

"She was restrained," Detective Dawes said.

"Restrained?" Mona asked. "Why restrain her after she was dead?"

The other woman grimaced. "Probably for easy transport. Did you find any fibers not belonging to her clothes?"

"You mean like a blanket or something similar?" Whittle asked. "No, I suspect if a cover was used, it was probably a tarp. Cleaner, easier to handle."

"But why cart her around for a month, then dump her?" Mona asked.

"I wish I could tell you," he said. "But more importantly I found this, around her jugular." He pointed to what was left of the skin on her neck. "You can't see it very easily because of the decomposition, but I was able to determine, based on the dislocation of the bones as well as remnants of bruise marks, that this woman was asphyxiated. I believe it was the cause of death."

"Someone strangled her?" Mona asked.

"Someone strangled her, then kept the body for a month before dumping her in the woods for whatever reason," Dawes added. "Not something you see every day. What about prints from the marks?"

"If they existed, they're gone now. Or they used gloves," Whittle replied. "I wish I had more, but I thought you'd want this information as soon as possible."

"Thanks," Mona said. "This is... it's a lot. Anything else that might help us with an ID?"

"I have the dental work up, but without something to compare it to—"

"Any tattoos?" Dawes asked. "Or other identifying marks?"

"Unfortunately not. The full report will be in the system within the hour."

Dawes nodded before turning back to Mona. "Looks like we have our work cut out for us."

So it *was* a homicide after all. It hadn't been a hundred percent clear if that was the case out where they found the body, but now there was no question. Which meant they had a killer somewhere in the area. It was possible they just used the creek as a dumping area on their way to somewhere else, but Mona wasn't convinced. It bothered her that whoever dumped the body had kept it for so long. Why release it now? What was special about Oak Creek?

On the drive back to the station, Mona felt the pressure of the case building. Could she have predicted this, given all the variables? If Detective Dawes was right and it was someone from out of town, that would make predicting their behavior much more difficult. But at least they had a lead. Maybe she could find a way to track the killer down using some of her algorithms.

"You're quiet over there, LaSalle," the older woman said, breaking Mona from her reverie. "Deep in thought?"

She gave a weak smile. "Yeah, I was just thinking about what you said. And I was wondering if there was a way to predict our killer's next move."

"Predict? How?" Dawes asked.

"Oh, well..." Mona hesitated, heat rising in her cheeks. Every time she'd brought this up to someone in the field, the response... well, it hadn't been great. But so far Detective Dawes hadn't been like the others. Maybe she'd understand. "I've been working on this program, running simulations of how to predict crime. It's kind of... a pet project of mine."

"*Predict* crime?" she asked.

"Yeah, you know, kind of how meteorologists can predict weather? It's not an exact science, and it won't be for years to come, but I believe with enough information and variables, certain types of crime can be accurately predicted."

Dawes furrowed her brow. "I'm not sure about that one," she said. "The human element is the most unpredictable force on the planet. Weather doesn't get mad when it finds its wife sleeping with another season."

Mona had heard this argument dozens of times before. But people just didn't understand the nature of large data sets. That, at scale, *everything* became predictable. It was just they didn't have enough information or a way to collate what little they did have to make it effective. "It's just a theory," she said, deflated. Apparently Detective Dawes wasn't so different from the rest of them after all.

She pulled into the station parking lot again, worried she might have alienated the older officer. The last thing she needed to do was make Detective Dawes think she wasn't competent— she was the only person who had actually shown Mona any encouragement.

As Mona contemplated how she could get back on Detective Dawes's good side, she found herself face-to-face with Officer Burketty. He'd positioned himself in their way as they headed back into the station.

"Detective LaSalle?" he asked, looking from her to Detective Dawes and back. In his hand was a thin manila folder.

"Oh, hi," she said, a little unnerved. As far as she could recall, Burketty had never spoken to her before. "What can I do for you?"

"They told me you were pulling all the missing persons cases?" he said.

"That's right," Mona replied. "They're upstairs. Were you looking for one in particular?"

The bigger man shook his head. "No, I need to add one to your pile. Just came in this morning." He held the file out for her.

"Oh, thanks," she said. "We'll look into it right away."

Burketty excused himself as Mona opened the file. Perhaps their luck was changing. A missing persons case called in just this morning was a hell of a coincidence. What were the odds that it could be for the same woman?

But when she looked at the name written across the top, her stomach dropped.

"What is it?" Detective Dawes asked. "Is it our Jane Doe?"

"No," Mona said, her throat suddenly dry. "No, it's someone else."

EIGHT

"I don't understand," Charlotte said. "You know this woman?"

They'd returned to the office upstairs, though the entire time, Mona had worn a smile that never reached her eyes. It was like she was trying to be artificially happy at the realization that someone she knew—and possibly cared about—had gone missing.

"I... yes, well, I know her," Mona said, taking a seat but not meeting Charlotte's eye.

"*How* do you know her?" Charlotte asked. She'd already noticed Mona wasn't big on offering up personal details. In that way they were very much alike. But it meant, unlike Givens, Charlotte needed to push to get the answers she was looking for. Mona had an uncanny ability to mask herself, a skill Charlotte hadn't seen in some time. It might explain why she was so unbothered by the corpse. The woman was something of an enigma, and Charlotte was having a difficult time figuring her out.

Mona hesitated for a long moment. "We were friends... for a long time. But we haven't been in contact much recently." She ran her fingers down the report in the file, almost as if the act of doing so would give her more insight into the case.

The gesture caused Charlotte to think back to Mona's theories about crime prediction. She had heard of people attempting the feat before—it was a field under study by the FBI and, of course, had been the subject of many books and movies. But she had never really put much stock into the idea. People could snap on a whim, and there was no predicting that. Mona was too young and inexperienced to understand the full nuances of human behavior, but after a few more years in this job, she would come to appreciate that some things just couldn't be accounted for. Though Charlotte was sure she had already received a fair amount of criticism, and she wasn't about to pile on to the woman, especially not now.

"I'm sorry about your friend," Charlotte said. "But if someone just reported her missing, then she's obviously not our victim. I'm sure she'll turn up somewhere."

"Yes," Mona said, nodding and blinking rapidly at the same time. Was she blinking away tears? Charlotte couldn't tell. "You're right." She was about to close the file when she stopped, leaning in for a closer look.

"What is it?" Charlotte asked.

"When did Whittle say the body was dumped?"

Charlotte turned to her computer, using her new login credentials to get into the system and look up the ME's report on the body. The full autopsy wasn't in there yet, but the preliminary report was. "He says here the body was most likely left at the location between Friday evening and Saturday afternoon. And given what we know from Madden, the body definitely wasn't there on Friday morning. Why?"

"Because my friend went missing Friday night," Mona said, her voice slightly softer. "According to the report."

The hair on the back of Charlotte's neck stood up. She walked over and examined the file over Mona's shoulder.

"Robin Bellinger. Twenty-six, operates an art gallery here in town?"

Mona nodded. "Actually, it's right across the square over there." She pointed toward the windows. "I see her sometimes, on her way into work in the mornings. She usually opens the shop around ten or eleven."

Charlotte read the rest of the file. The report had been made by Robin's mother when Robin failed to call her on Friday night. After repeated attempts to get in contact with her, speaking to her colleagues and friends with no results, they had notified the police this morning.

"It's probably just a coincidence, right?" Mona finally asked. "It's like you said, she'll turn up."

It had already been two days. If no one had heard from her in that long, then there might be something to worry about. Charlotte couldn't quit thinking about the body at the creek. There was no way it was the same person—their Jane Doe had been dead too long. She didn't want to jump to conclusions, but given the proximity of both events, she didn't want to discount it either.

"Do we have any other missing persons cases for that particular day?" she asked.

"I'm not sure. We'd have to go back and look at the ones we discounted," Mona said. "All the men and children."

Damn. That's right. They'd set those to the side.

"Are you saying you *do* think it's related?" Mona asked.

Charlotte stepped back. "Let's just... let's get through the files first. You up for it?"

"Of course," Mona said. "I'll get started right away."

It took them another two hours, and by the time they were finished, the sun had set and the office had mostly emptied out. Also, Charlotte's stomach was rumbling from lack of food all day. All she'd had was a bagel and two cups of coffee on her way to Oak Creek this morning. Beyond that, they'd been working straight through. She noticed that Mona hadn't said anything about eating either. Whether that was because she was like Charlotte and was too distracted, or because she didn't want to be the one to suggest it, Charlotte didn't know. But they needed to get some sustenance soon otherwise her stomach was going to turn inside out.

"I think that's all of them," Mona said, setting aside the last file. "I didn't see any with report dates close to Robin's."

"Neither did I," Charlotte said, gathering her things. "C'mon. I need to eat. Bring the Bellinger file with you. We're going to make this a working dinner."

Charlotte didn't have a problem letting Mona choose a place to eat or drive because she needed time to think. What had seemed like a straightforward case had already had more than one unexpected element and it was starting to make her nervous. She'd dealt with her fair share of dead bodies, and dumps, but nothing quite like this. Usually, the person had been killed and left where they died. But it was this aspect of moving the body that confounded her. *Why?* What was the point in moving the body around for a month and *then* dumping it? Could it be a crude attempt at trying to hide the true identity of the victim? If that were the case, why not drive further out into the wilderness and dump her? Why do it close to a town where someone was bound to find it? Did the killer want the body found?

There were so many questions surrounding this case it was making her head hurt. One thing was for sure, this wouldn't be a quick one. She'd have to let Whiteside know she'd be here more than a few days.

"Here we go," Mona said. "Ronnie's Café. I think you'll like this place. You're not a vegetarian, are you?"

"No," Charlotte said, looking up at the neon sign next to the low-slung building. The sign not only advertised the name of the place, but the fact that it had a casino attached. But given it was Monday, the parking lot only had half a dozen cars. "You eat here often?"

"*Everyone* eats here at least once a week," Mona said. "It's kind of like the unofficial restaurant for the town." Just as she said it, the door to the restaurant opened to reveal a woman in an expensive-looking beige coat with a small container in one hand.

"Oh," the woman said in a soft-spoken tone. "Hello, Mona."

Mona gave the woman a quick nod. "Hi, Dr. Pekannen."

The woman, who had a short haircut and bird-like features, didn't even acknowledge Charlotte. "How are you doing?"

"Pretty good," Mona replied. "What's the special tonight?"

"Meatloaf," the woman said in what should have been a casual way, though to Charlotte, her tone seemed slightly off. She kept shooting inconspicuous glances at Mona, almost like she was looking for something. LaSalle, for her part, seemed oblivious.

"Thanks, good seeing you," she replied as she made her way past the other woman into the restaurant. Charlotte only caught a brief look from the doctor as she followed Mona in.

"You too," Pekannen said, and headed out to the parking lot.

"Who was that?" Charlotte asked.

"Oh, shoot, I'm so sorry," Mona said, turning to her. "I forgot to introduce you. That's Dr. Pekannen, local psychiatrist. I'm so hungry my stomach is making me loopy."

"That's okay," Charlotte said. "I don't need to meet your entire town." Inside the place looked like it hadn't been updated since the mid-80s. Beige booths dominated most of the restaurant, while a glass case at the front with the cash register held a bevy of pies and cakes, all advertised as freshly baked.

"Ah, Detective LaSalle," a booming voice said. Charlotte looked over to see a thin man in his sixties approaching, his salt-and-pepper hair trimmed close and a pleasant look on his face. In his hand he held a set of menus. "Brought a friend with you this time, I see." He held one arm out in a welcoming gesture.

Mona smiled, clearly looking for an opportunity to make up from her misstep before. "Ken, this is Detective Charlotte Dawes. She's here with us from Chicago to work on a case."

"Ah, welcome," Ken said, holding his hand out for Charlotte, which she took. "Big case? Important? Of course it is!" He had a jovial nature about him which Charlotte was sure was good for business. "Here, let me get you seated. The usual seat?"

"That'd be great," Mona said.

"What are you working on this time?" Ken asked, leading them to a booth near one of the windows. Charlotte spotted a glass door at the back of the room which advertised the attached "casino," which was little more than a room full of electronic slot machines. As far as Charlotte could tell, the room was empty.

"Let me guess," Ken continued, showing them the booth. "Robbery? Must be pretty big to have someone come in from Chicago." He handed Charlotte a menu as she slid into the booth. It was at least four pages thick, each of them packed to the brim with options.

"Well," Mona said, "we're not entirely sure what we're dealing with yet."

"You'll figure it out," Ken said. "You're one of the best. Now, I already know you'll take a water with ice. What about you, what can I get you to drink?" he asked Charlotte.

"Whatever you have on tap," she replied.

"Be right back," he said with a smile.

Charlotte watched Mona's reaction for a moment. "You know everyone in town?"

"Oh," she said. "I guess so. Small towns, you know. I'm sure it's a lot different to Chicago. Here everybody's connected to everybody else in some way or another."

Charlotte pushed the Bellinger file over to Mona, noticing the woman wince as she did. "I need you to tell me everything you can about your friend Robin."

"So, think it's related?" Mona asked.

"I have my suspicions," Charlotte replied. "I know you said you two haven't been simpatico for a while, but in all the time you knew her, was she prone to disappearing like this? Did she ever just take a break and cut herself off for any reason? Even if it was just once?"

Mona shook her head. "Never. Robin is super close with her family. She wouldn't leave without telling them. At least, not willingly. What are you thinking?"

"I'll be honest with you, LaSalle. I don't like where this case is heading." Charlotte's brow formed a deep V. "One anomaly is enough to make me pay attention. Two is a problem."

"I don't understand," Mona said.

"In most cases like this, where a body is found, decomposed out in the wilderness, you're looking at a standard killing. Generally, people don't move the bodies. They either panic and hope no one will find the person, *or* they're confident that the person will never be identified due to how they've... handled things."

"You're talking about mutilation," Mona said.

"Yes. But in this case, you have neither. While we don't have an ID on the woman, I believe we will eventually find out who she is. We have enough clues that it's only a matter of time and effort. Which seems to indicate whoever did this doesn't care about us finding and identifying her. In fact—I hesitate to say this—but it may be what they want."

"Why would anyone want that?" she asked.

Ken returned with the drinks, setting them down between the women. Charlotte didn't say anything else until he was out of earshot. "That's the problem. There's no way to know. It's like I was saying, people are unpredictable and we have someone out there whose behavior is way off the norm." She sighed. "And now we have a missing woman whose timeframe happens to line up with the crime. I don't want to jump to conclusions, but my fear is this person who dumped our Jane Doe may have taken another victim."

The small smile on Mona's face momentarily faltered. She took a drink of water, then reset herself. "But... we can find them, right? With your experience—"

"I'm not a miracle worker," Charlotte said. "But if I'm right, we're dealing with a very dangerous individual. And we need to be extremely careful."

Mona nodded. "So, what do we do?"

Charlotte tapped the file with her index finger. "We need more information. And we need it fast."

NINE

Thankfully, Mona's relationship with the restaurant owner meant they were able to get a quick meal. Even though it was already evening, Charlotte didn't think investigating a possible connection between the two victims could wait until morning and wanted to get moving as soon as possible. With some food in her system, she and Mona decided to speak with Bellinger's family to make sure they didn't leave anything out of the report.

Even though Mona had agreed wholeheartedly, Charlotte had enough experience with difficult relationships to tell from her body language that speaking with the family wasn't at the top of her to-do list. Whatever had happened to the relationship between her and the Bellinger woman had some long-term repercussions. But she didn't have time to tiptoe around the situation. They were on the clock now and Charlotte suspected in her gut that if they found Robin Bellinger, they would find the answers they needed about their victim.

"I just hope this gives us something," Charlotte said, getting out of the car and glancing at the house. It was a modest two-story that sat in an old residential neighborhood in town. The house was nothing special, but it looked well-kept and clean on the outside. An old Pontiac sat in the small driveway in front of the garage.

"So do I," Mona said. "But part of me hopes it isn't connected. We already have one victim. What if—"

"Don't worry about that right now," Charlotte said. "Focus on what we're here to do. Find out if Robin's disappearance could be related to our victim. That's it." She looked at the door. "Do you want me to handle this?"

"No, I'll do it," Mona said, flashing that now-familiar smile to Charlotte.

Charlotte narrowed her gaze but decided to let it go. Her goal was to get as much information about Bellinger as possible, and given Mona hadn't spoken to the woman in a few years, the next best option was the family.

When they got to the front door, Charlotte noticed Mona take two deep breaths before she rang the doorbell. She was steeling herself for something, though it was tough to tell what. Almost as soon as the doorbell rang, the door flew open to reveal a woman in her mid-fifties, her short hair cropped to frame her face, though it looked like it hadn't been brushed in a while. Her face, while frowning with lines and creases, had a kind nature about it with soft features.

"Mona?"

"Hi, Mrs. Bellinger," Mona said.

"*Ohmygod.* What's happened? Did you find her?"

"I'm sorry, no," she said. "But I was hoping—" Her question was cut off by the bear hug Mrs. Bellinger wrapped her in, burying her face in Mona's shoulder.

"I had hoped you'd be the one working the case. We've been so worried"—the woman's voice was muffled—"I don't know what to do."

Mona patted the woman's back, shooting a quick glance to Charlotte. "It'll be okay," she said. "We'll find her."

Finally, Mrs. Bellinger let go. "I don't understand. What are you doing here if you don't have any information?"

Mona stepped to the side. "This is Detective Charlotte Dawes. She's here from Chicago helping us."

"Ma'am," Charlotte said, taking the woman's hand and giving it a quick shake. Her skin was clammy, most likely from nerves or crying. Or both. "May we come in? We'd like to ask you some follow-up questions about your report."

"Of course, of course," Mrs. Bellinger said, stepping to the side. "Please, make yourselves at home."

Inside the house smelled like patchouli, no doubt from a candle burning somewhere. It was a modest home, but much like the outside, the inside was clean and well-kept. A small living room sat off the hallway. Mona led the way.

"Can I get you anything?" Mrs. Bellinger asked. "Coffee?"

"We're fine, we just ate," Charlotte said, surveying the room. Photographs and art covered the walls. "But thank you. When was the last time you spoke with Robin?"

"Thursday," Robin's mother replied. "She called asking if I'd picked up tickets to the Icehogs game yet. We were supposed to go on Saturday." She took a seat in one of the single chairs, while Charlotte and Mona sat across from her on the couch.

"Do you know if she went to work on Friday?" Mona asked.

"She did," Mrs. Bellinger replied. "We went over there to check the place had been locked up. I asked the man who runs that game store beside the gallery if he saw her on Friday and he said he saw her eating lunch. She was definitely there."

"What time does Robin normally close on Fridays?" Charlotte asked.

"Around seven. She keeps consistent hours but sometimes will close early if it's a particularly slow day."

"And she's an artist, is that correct?" Charlotte pulled out a small notepad from her blazer, jotting down a few details.

"She always has been. She sells her own works in addition to some other local artists' work. It's not great money, but it pays the bills."

Charlotte took a quick glance at the pieces of landscape art. She guessed they came from Robin, gifts, or maybe just a proud mother showing off her daughter's work. "And when did you first suspect something was wrong?" Charlotte added.

She saw the hint of impatience on Mrs. Bellinger's face. "I already went over this with the man who took my report," she said. "It was late Friday night. She normally calls to let me know she's home safe, and when I didn't hear from her, I grew worried. So I tried her number, but it went straight to voicemail. I figured she was on the phone with someone." Mrs. Bellinger winced and her emotions threatened to come breaking through, causing her to pause and look up at the ceiling for a brief moment. "I tried again Saturday morning, but it was the same thing. That's when I *knew* something was wrong.

"I called all her friends—at least all the ones I knew and asked them if they'd heard from her. But none had."

Charlotte glanced over at Mona, narrowing her eyes. "Why didn't you call Detective LaSalle?"

Mrs. Bellinger dropped her head. "Well, after... everything, I wasn't sure she would take my call."

"Of *course* I would have," Mona said, reaching forward and taking Mrs. Bellinger's hand. "I still care about Robin."

"It was stupid of me," the older woman said. "I'm sorry. I just called the police instead. I wasn't sure who they might send out to speak with us."

"I didn't find out until just a few hours ago," Mona said. "Otherwise, I would have been here sooner."

Charlotte caught a movement out of the corner of her eye. Through the foyer, at the stairs that led up to the second floor, a person was standing just below the landing. She leaned over to get a better look, though when the person saw he'd been spotted, he continued down the stairs like he'd been intending to do that all along.

"Adam?" Mrs. Bellinger asked, leaning to match Charlotte's movement. "Mona's here. She's going to help us find Robin."

The kid, whose face still held the round features of a teenager while his frame was that of a young linebacker, didn't even acknowledge the trio, instead, he made his way right past the living room and headed into the kitchen.

"Adam!" Mrs. Bellinger called, straining her voice. A door slammed somewhere further in the house. "I'm so sorry. He's been on edge since Robin's disappearance. We both have."

Charlotte made the connection to the photographs in the room. Most were of Adam and who she presumed to be Robin when each of them was little. There were also a few awards with Adam's name on them—accolades for his academic performance. A few more recent pictures showed Mrs. Bellinger, but she didn't see any with a father in the picture. "How old is your son?" she asked.

"He's seventeen now, a senior in high school." She turned to Mona. "Can you believe it? It seems like just yesterday you and Robin were that age."

Mona gave the woman a supportive smile. "Those were some good times."

Mrs. Bellinger shook her head. "I'm so sorry for what happened. I'd hoped the two of you would have patched things up."

As much as Charlotte wanted to follow this thread, she didn't believe it would help them track down Robin. "Are you and Mr. Bellinger..." She let the question hang in the air as it was obvious *something* had happened between them.

"He passed away," the woman said. "A few years back."

"I'm sorry," Charlotte replied. "Is there anything else you can tell us? Anything you might have thought of since you made the initial report?"

The woman shook her head. "I've been going through it over and over in my head, and I keep coming back to the fact that something must have happened to her. She's *never* gone this long without letting someone know." That wasn't good. Given the proximity to their first victim, Charlotte had a sinking feeling that time was running out for Robin, wherever she was. Not that she could voice those concerns aloud.

"What about your daughter's home?" Charlotte asked.

"I've already been over," the woman said. "There's no one there."

"Does she live alone?"

"Yes," Mona said before Mrs. Bellinger could answer, causing both women to turn to her. "Unless... that's changed recently."

"No, no," Mrs. Bellinger replied. "I've tried to convince her to at least get a pet, but she's always refused. I worry about her so much, all alone over there all the time."

"Do you have a key?" Charlotte asked. "We'd like to check it out."

"Of course," the woman said, standing. "Let me go find it for you."

"While you look," Mona said, "would you mind if we spoke to Adam? I know he and Robin were close. Maybe he could add something."

"Be my guest," Mrs. Bellinger said. "He told me he didn't know anything else, but you're more than welcome to try. He's probably in the garage. You remember the way?"

Mona nodded. "We won't be long." She led the way through the house like someone who had the experience of spending a lot of time here. Two doors sat at the other end of the kitchen, past the refrigerator. Mona opened the one directly in front of them, which led into the garage.

A long workbench ran the back length of the garage, filled with metal parts from what had to be a hundred different objects. Charlotte could make out remnants of old televisions, clocks, stereo equipment, pretty much anything powered by electricity. At the far end of the table stood Adam, hunched over the workbench as he shoved a screwdriver into something he was holding.

"Hey, Adam," Mona said softly. "How've you been?"

The boy didn't say anything, just continued working on his project.

"I'm really sorry about Robin. We're going to do everything we can to find her," Mona added. "I was hoping you might—"

"You don't care about her," Adam said without turning around. "I heard you when you got out of your car. You're looking for someone else."

Mona shot a quick look at Charlotte. "Yes, we're trying to solve another case, but we think Robin's disappearance—"

"Look," Adam said, turning around and giving Charlotte her first good look at him. For seventeen, he had a decent bit of muscle on him, the kind that came on quick with puberty. His dusty blonde hair was cropped short on the sides, longer on the top in the kind of style she'd seen popular with other kids of his age. His dark green eyes were alight with fire—though, pointed and accusing, which seemed reserved for Mona. "I know how cops work. You say one thing and you do another. You don't care about my sister. Never have."

"That's not true," Mona said. "I care about your sister very much."

"Then where did you go?" he asked. "It's been over a year."

Mona flashed the same smile she'd used with Ramsey. "It's not that easy, Adam. Your sister and I had... well, we just needed our space."

The boy scoffed. "Yeah, space. Doesn't matter what you say. You'll find the person you're really after and leave my sister behind. Just like you did before."

"That's not true," Mona said, again.

"Adam," Charlotte said, needing to wrangle this situation. "We're going to do everything we can to find Robin."

He looked at Charlotte for a moment, distracted from Mona, before he turned back to his table. "Uh-huh."

"When was the last time you spoke with her?" Mona asked.

"I didn't," he said, his back still to them. "Mom did. I already told her everything."

"What about a text message? Have you—"

"How many times do I have to tell you? I haven't talked to her, okay?" His voice was full of anger and fury, a scared and hurt kid who had put up more barriers than they could hurdle.

It was clear he wouldn't be cooperative. Whatever Mona had hoped to accomplish by coming out here, Charlotte was pretty sure it was a dead end. She made a motion with her head for them to leave. Mona waited, watching Adam for a moment before she finally relented.

"I'm sorry," Mona said once they'd retrieved a spare key from Mrs. Bellinger and were back at the car. "I had hoped they could give us more."

Charlotte had left her card with the woman in the event of her thinking of any additional details, though she suspected that was unlikely. The family was in a panic, and they were no doubt racking their brains for anything they might have missed. She looked up to the second-floor window which was cracked open. Adam had been sitting there listening in the dark as they'd pulled up. "Clever kid."

Mona nodded. "Back when... well, he was always at the top of his class. It got to be a problem for his mom after a while, because he started to get so bored during school that he'd act out. It turns out that he's got a very high IQ. He'll probably end up at an Ivy League with a full scholarship. If he can stay out of trouble."

He was angry, that much was obvious. But he was also scared and had tried to mask his fear with accusations and bravado. But Charlotte had seen behavior like that before. It was nothing more than a cover for someone who was deeply concerned. He was trying to process the disappearance of his sister. She wasn't sure if there would be a situation where they *could* get him to talk.

"Did they have a good relationship?" she asked.

"You know how little brothers are," Mona said. "But I guess for the most part, yeah. Why?"

"No reason," Charlotte replied. "Just curious." She checked the time, noting it was closing in on 10 p.m. "I think we should check out Robin's shop and her home, but we'll have to do it tomorrow." It had been an extremely long day, and Charlotte needed a few hours of shut-eye. "Can you recommend a good motel in town? Preferably something cheap?"

"I have an extra bedroom if you'd like to stay at my place," Mona said. "Wouldn't cost you a dime."

Charlotte shook her head. "That's generous, but I wouldn't feel right. A motel will do fine."

"Try the Blue Bird Inn over near the highway. It usually has rooms. Unless you want a bed and breakfast. There are more than a dozen or more in this area alone."

The thought of someone fixing Charlotte breakfast—working away in a kitchen downstairs while she was in a bedroom somewhere trying to get some sleep—sounded like a special kind of hell.

"I'm not about to press my luck. Just do me a favor and drop me back off at my car."

TEN

The diner was bustling with the hum of clattering dishes, muffled conversations, and the occasional bark of laughter. From his spot in the corner booth, John had a clear view of them. His gaze was trained on the two women sitting at a table by the window, their heads tilted together in conversation, unaware of the invisible eyes watching them.

John's fingers drummed lightly on the table beside him as he watched the younger of the two. She was sitting on the left, dressed in the same outfit she'd been wearing earlier in the day —a simple jacket and jeans, hair frazzled and falling in waves to her shoulders. Her movements were quick, precise, like she couldn't afford to waste time. He admired that about her. She had all the tools she needed to complete her tasks, were she left alone to do it. She had the intelligence and instincts to figure out what he wanted her to, if only she'd been left to do it on her own.

But the other woman—the older cop sitting with her, the interloper—*she* was the problem.

They brought someone else in. Unexpected, he thought, his lips pulled into a tight line. *No outside help.*

He chanced a hard look, honing in on the face of the stranger. She was in her early fifties, with sharp eyes and a no-nonsense demeanor. Her movements were slower, more deliberate, but there was something about her that rubbed John the wrong way. Something he didn't like.

The nearly full cup of coffee cooled in front of him as he pondered. Everything so far had required precision. Just like pieces on a chess board—you had to think ten steps ahead. Once he made sure the other detectives were out of the way, LaSalle had been assigned the case along with that blowhard of a partner of hers, as he'd predicted. Things had been going swimmingly. John had been ready to make his next move.

And then *she* showed up. The older one.

There wasn't supposed to be anyone else on the case. Detective LaSalle was supposed to work it with Detective Ramsey. Ramsey would eventually try to take over, to use that brutish and overbearing nature of his to push LaSalle out— which was where the next part of his plan would come in.

But that was all out the window now.

A new player has entered the game.

John was no stranger to research. In fact, it was the bedrock of everything he did. How could he expect to win if he didn't understand *all* aspects of the contest? He needed to know the field, the players and their abilities. And this *woman* was not part of the equation. From what little he'd found so far, she was a Chicago cop. But this wasn't a Chicago case. So what was she doing so far from her department? It changed the entire dynamic of the situation.

How to handle this? As he stared at the pair of women he contemplated his next move. He was nothing if not adaptable; he'd just have to change tactics. What had begun as a simple game of find and seek was straying into more complicated territory. A rogue thought crossed his mind, causing him to sit back unexpectedly. He could just call it all off right now. He could just get up and walk away. Things weren't working out like he'd thought, and there was no way he could move forward with his original plan.

But that would mean quitting. It would mean *giving up*. Admitting he'd been beaten before he'd truly even been able to play. And maybe if he were a lesser man, he'd actually consider it. But John had always been what some might call unrelenting. And if fate was going to slip him a trick card, he'd just have to rise to the challenge.

You want to change the rules? Then prepare to accept the consequences.

He watched them a moment longer, his mind twisting and turning. How to incorporate this new player into the game? If this was how it would be, they needed a new kind of challenge. This required the precision of a surgeon, not a bumbling oaf. He'd been too myopic before, trying to cut corners—to get to the end quicker. Which had been why he had failed last time.

Don't get impatient. By introducing this new element, they had inadvertently shown him his own weakness.

He grinned, almost laughed but stopped himself. This countermove had nearly unseated him and they didn't even realize it. But he'd remained steadfast. And now it was time for his response.

Sliding out of the booth, John pulled on his jacket and shoved his hands into the pockets. He left a few crumpled bills on the table and made his way to the exit, the bell above the door chiming softly as he stepped out into the cold evening air. Neither woman looked up as he left.

As he crossed the street to his car, his mind whirled with thoughts of how to regain control. *Countermoves... how to adapt,* he mused, slipping into the driver's seat.

He started the engine and glanced at the passenger seat, where Robin sat, her eyes downcast, her body rigid. She looked tired, worn out, as if she'd been through hell. Her lips were pale, her face drawn, but she didn't say a word.

"I was right, they are working together," John said, his mind ablaze with possibility and promise.

"You sound disappointed," she replied, her voice meek and small.

"Disappointed, my dear woman? Perhaps for a fleeting moment," John admitted, staring out the windshield at the diner as the two detectives remained inside, hunched over the table as they discussed the specifics of the case. "But no. I am *excited*. What was going to be a simple test needs to be something much more... *involved*." Where before he had been content to keep the body count low in order to draw LaSalle out, it was obvious something much more intricate was needed. Without Ramsey there to lose his cool and isolate her, John needed something... unique. Something... *personal*.

He turned to his companion, his eyes dark and hungry. *She* was the key.

The artist and her art.

Robin's gaze turned to him, her eyes wide and alert. "What are you going to do?"

A smile spread across his lips like a shadow as John studied her. "I need more from you. And we both know you have more, don't you? Many, many more."

Robin didn't move, didn't blink.

"You can't hide from me. Where do you keep them?"

She lowered her gaze. "In a storage unit. Off Wilkinson."

"*Good girl.*" There was a risk pushing things this far. But without risk there was no reward. "We're going to show them something they've never seen before."

He shifted the car into gear, pulling away from the curb and heading toward the edge of town. His mind was already working out the details, swirling through the permutations. It would require even more precise moves, impeccable timing and constant observation. Yes, he could see it now, the possibilities expanding like light hitting the horizon.

"Strange, isn't it? The two of us in the car like this? I bet you never expected this." Robin remained silent beside him, staring blankly out the window.

The road wound through the edge of town, the trees casting long shadows in the fading light. John's hands were steady on the wheel, his thoughts focused. Ideas swirled and clicked into place, forming a coherent plan. Time was of the essence. He had to act fast.

They reached a small, nondescript row of buildings on the edge of a rundown neighborhood. It wasn't much to look at, just a storage facility tucked away behind a row of decaying houses. But inside... a hidden treasure trove.

John parked the car and stepped out, glancing over at his passenger one last time. "Combination for the lock."

"Three-one-six-nine," she whispered.

He grinned. "Would you like to come? It is your work, after all," he said softly.

Robin didn't move. She knew her place. So much better.

"Suit yourself." John moved quickly, slipping inside the building and making his way to the back. The storage units were stacked with old furniture, boxes of forgotten belongings, relics of lives that had moved on without them. But he wasn't interested in trinkets or clothes.

Moving aside the false wall along the back, he revealed the cache, all lined up, in perfect order. Right where they were supposed to be. He took his time sorting through them, picking the perfect ones, each macabre and disquieting. He hadn't realized the depravity with which she worked. The woman was a true artist. Her work reflected someone reaching for salvation but never quite grasping it.

After a few minutes of searching, he found the perfect depictions. He took a step back, examining each of them in turn. Yes, these would do nicely. A message that couldn't be ignored. Robin had provided the pieces; all she had needed was someone to position them—a *gamemaster*. A title he relished.

John smiled as he stacked them together and replaced the false wall, obscuring the larger cache from view. "First you set up the board, then you lay out all the parts. And once the players are ready..." He tucked the items under his arm and headed back to the vehicle.

"You really do have a gift for this kind of thing," John muttered once he was back to the car, placing the items on the back seat. "You know, you could have made a killing with these. So many sick and twisted minds out there and these... these would have provided solace to those in pain. But you kept them all for yourself, didn't you?"

As he slid back into the driver's seat, he glanced at Robin, who hadn't moved an inch. She only stared out into the night.

"We've got a lot of work to do. But you'll help me with that, won't you?" John said, his voice calm, methodical. "All it'll take is a little elbow grease."

Robin didn't answer, but John didn't need one. It was as if something had taken hold of him—a fervor. What had been just a spark in his mind twenty minutes ago had grown into a mission. It would be the most important thing either of them would ever experience. And at the end of all of it, when he finally had what he wanted, it would all be worth it.

"You should be honored," he continued, starting the car again. "Who else leaves a legacy the world will talk about for years to come?"

He grinned as the car rolled down the dark, empty streets, the items secured safely behind him. "When they find it— when they finally understand what's happening, *then* and only then will we come out of the shadows. You just watch. This is going to be my magnum opus. And it's all because of you."

And with that, he drove off into the night, a smile spread wide across his face.

ELEVEN

Mona couldn't stop her foot from tapping as she waited patiently at her desk for Detective Dawes to arrive. She hadn't gotten much sleep and, as a consequence, had downed more coffee this morning than she probably should have. And now all that energy had to go somewhere.

How could Robin be missing? The possibility that her disappearance was connected to their current case was almost enough to make her sick. Maybe they hadn't talked for a while, but that didn't mean Mona didn't still think of them as friends in some way. Robin might not feel that way anymore, and that was fine. But Mona wasn't the kind of person who cut people out of her life. If Robin appeared today and told her all was forgiven, Mona wouldn't hesitate to rekindle their friendship.

But it never worked like that. Some things couldn't be forgiven... or forgotten. And here Mona was, looking at a dire case with virtually nowhere to go. She wondered if they should inform Sheriff Franklin about the possibility of the cases being connected. Though, if she did that, he might remove her from the case—given her personal connection to Robin. Detective Dawes had effectively given her the lead on this case, which meant the decisions were her call. A responsibility she wasn't entirely sure she was comfortable with.

No, she would rather have something concrete to give to her boss before going down that road. Presenting a bunch of suppositions and assumptions wasn't the hallmark of a good detective. But what had surprised her was how willing Detective Dawes had been to link the two cases. She didn't think Jack would have done that. Then again, he probably would have shoved this case back in the cold cases already, given what they'd learned about the victim. As she was thinking about how likely he would have been to cut Mona out entirely given the chance, she heard footsteps coming up the stairs to the office.

"Ah, you're here early," Detective Dawes said as she rounded the corner, spotting Mona.

Mona was on her feet, the caffeine doing its job. She handed a still-warm cup to Detective Dawes. "Morning!" she said, too enthusiastically—especially given the specifics of the case, but she couldn't help it. "How was the motel?"

The bags under Dawes's eyes told the story well enough, but the woman didn't flinch. "Hm. Any new developments?"

"Nothing so far," Mona said. "I followed up with a few mutual acquaintances this morning, but they haven't heard from her either. If she's not in contact with her family, I doubt she'll be in contact with anyone else." Like Mona, Robin was something of a loner and didn't have many close friends. It had been something they'd shared together.

The detective took a sip from the coffee, though from the look on her face Mona could tell she was doing her best not to show her distaste. "Then we pick up where we left off. You said her place of business is right across the square?"

Mona nodded.

"Let's start there. Then we can take a look at her home. Lead the way."

Mona took a final sip of her drink before gathering her coat and throwing it on. As she led them outside and through the square, she couldn't help but see Adam's face over and over in her mind. He'd looked so... disappointed. Could she really blame him? Then again, it had been *a year* since she and Robin had spoken. Mona wasn't in their lives anymore—so why did she still feel like it was her responsibility to resolve this?

"Hey," Detective Dawes said as they passed the gazebo in the middle of the square. "You okay? You look distracted."

"Nope," Mona said. "Just thinking about the case."

"You do that a lot, don't you?" Dawes asked.

"What?"

"Hide your pain," the woman said. "I've seen it a few times now."

Mona stopped, turning to face her. "What do you mean?"

Dawes grimaced. "I don't mean to be so blunt, but if we're going to work this case together, I don't want to be walking on eggshells around you. It's obvious something happened between you and Robin. Can you divest yourself of that, or is it something we need to talk about?"

Mona found her heart was hammering in her chest. Her mind flashed back to that night one year ago when things fell apart. She'd done everything she could to block it from her mind —to never think about it again. It had been painful enough once, and she had no desire to revisit it ever again.

"Oh, I guess, some people just drift apart, you know... nothing... specific." She realized she was doing it again—smiling—and wiped her face of emotion, hoping Detective Dawes wouldn't pursue the subject.

The older detective watched her for a moment before sighing. "This isn't going to be a problem, is it? Given your... proximity to—"

"No, of course not," Mona said, waving the issue away. "It's not even worth mentioning."

But that wasn't true. It had been one of the most heart-

wrenching nights of her life. And she still didn't quite understand exactly what had happened. Those moments seemed to be par for the course for Mona. People just kept leaving her. Her father when she was young, then eventually her mother—in a way—and finally Robin. But now was not the time for self-examination. They had two cases on their hands that might very well be connected, and they had a killer to find before it was too late.

As they reached the other side of the square the wind picked up, gusting down the sidewalk and nearly pushing Mona into Detective Dawes. Thankfully she righted herself and pointed out the storefront with the darkened window. "It's this one." She looked inside the art studio, but since the lights were off it was difficult to see anything beyond her own reflection in the glass.

Detective Dawes tried the door, but it was locked and didn't budge. "It would have been helpful if Mrs. Bellinger had a copy of this key too. Back entrance?"

Mona nodded. "This way." She led Dawes around the corner, down a side street, until they came to an alleyway that ran behind the art studio and the other businesses connected to it. The alley was probably only fifteen feet wide and featured pavement that had seen better days. The city hadn't done any maintenance back here in years and it showed. It was a claustrophobic space, with the buildings rising two or three floors on either side of them, making the space seem narrow and enclosed. Detective Dawes led the way, passing the first door which led to the business on the corner.

The second door, the one leading to Robin's studio, was two steps below the pavement, due to the slope of the alley. Just as Mona was about to point it out, Dawes's hand shot out, holding her back.

Mona looked over, noticing the door to the back of Robin's studio stood slightly ajar—though it didn't look like the lock had been broken. Detective Dawes unclipped her weapon and drew it from its holster, holding it down while she made her way forward, nearly silent. She turned to Mona, pointing with two fingers for Mona to check the rest of the alley.

Nodding, it was like a switch flipped in Mona's head and everything she'd been thinking about Robin was immediately tossed aside as her instincts took over. She drew her weapon as well and made a cursory check of the blind corners in the alley, the ones created by the large dumpsters or stacks of old crates from the other businesses.

Clear, Mona mouthed as soon as she'd made sure no one else was hiding in the alley.

Dawes stepped up to the door, keeping her back against the wall as she crept forward. Mona, taking up the other side of the door frame, watched Dawes for a signal. There could be anyone in there from a homeless person trying to get warm to a thief about to make off with thousands of dollars' worth of art.

Finally, Dawes motioned for Mona to take the lead. For a second Mona thought she was doing that thing again where she was stepping back and letting Mona take the credit, only to realize she was doing it because Mona would be more familiar with the inside of the studio.

She nodded, holding her weapon up as she leaned around the door frame, checking it quickly. Unfortunately, it was almost pitch-black inside the back of the studio. Unlike the front, there were no windows here, which resulted in poor visibility. Mona retrieved a small flashlight from one of her coat pockets and clipped it to the top of her weapon. She nodded at Detective Dawes as she used the light to sweep inside the doorway.

Nothing but a couple of crates as far as Mona could see, but there could always be someone hiding behind them. She swept the inside again, this time more thoroughly. "Police," she called out. "Show yourself."

There was no response.

Dawes nodded for Mona to take point, which she did, rounding the door as she continued to sweep the space. A second later, the room was flooded with light as Dawes found the light panel near the door.

Mona dropped her weapon, taking a breath. An easel stood on one side of the room, covered in old splatters of paint, though there was no canvas. Additionally, paint dotted the floor and walls, mostly reds and blacks, but also mixed in with whites, blues and greens. On the far side of the small space stood a few boxes full of office supplies and what looked to be blank canvases. Another door stood open in the corner of the room, which led to a small hallway, restroom and the front of the store. Mona flattened her back against the wall beside the door, then went through the same motions, checking the corner, sweeping the area, and finding nothing.

Detective Dawes flipped on more lights until the entire studio was lit. And after a quick check to make sure no one was in the restroom, both women holstered their weapons.

"Her mother said when they came over here, the place was locked up tight. Would they have checked the back door?" Detective Dawes asked.

"I don't know," Mona replied. "Maybe. Probably. Mrs. Bellinger is thorough. The whole family... they aren't absent-minded." She began looking around the space for anything out of the ordinary, but as far as she could tell, nothing had been stolen. All the paintings hung in their respective spaces and other than a little dirt on the floor, everything looked to be in order.

"What is your robbery rate like in Oak Creek?" Dawes asked as she rounded the counter to take a look at the register, which was little more than an iPad on a swivel. As far as Mona was aware, Robin only took digital payment so there wouldn't have been any money to steal. And even if there had been,

Robin would have no doubt deposited it on the last day she'd been at work. The bank was less than a two-minute walk across the square.

"We get the occasional car theft, sometimes a home break-in, but they're rare," Mona said. "Why?"

"Because if this had been Chicago, you can bet this place would have been cleaned out within an hour," Dawes said, looking around. "I have a hard time believing that door's been ajar for three days and no one has noticed. And by that, I mean this probably happened recently. Is anything missing?"

Mona made a cursory study of the art on the walls. As far as she could tell, there were no empty spots. Nothing looked like it had been moved. "Nothing out here, I don't think. I know she used to paint in the back, but why would a thief just take that? Why not the finished pieces out here?"

"No cameras," Detective Dawes said, looking in the corners. "No way to tell *what* happened."

"We should talk to the neighboring businesses. See if they've noticed anything out of the ordinary over the past twenty-four hours," Mona replied.

Dawes nodded, though her brow creased. Mona followed her gaze to a chess set that had been set up on the only small table in the room. Mona knew that Robin had sometimes used that table to have a cup of coffee when the shop was slow. "Is your friend a chess player?"

Mona took in the sight of the set, which looked to be brand-new and not the cheap kind either. The pieces were all made of what looked like alabaster, set up on a large marble field. But what really drew her attention was the red tablecloth under the chess set.

"I don't think so," Mona said. She'd never known Robin to play chess in her life. But then again, maybe it was a hobby she'd taken up in the past few years. "I guess she could have started playing after I was out of the picture." But something about that didn't feel right. Mona loved chess, always had. And she'd tried over and over to get Robin to play; but her friend had never had any interest in it, always preferring books to games.

Detective Dawes walked over to the chess set, studying it closely. "Who do you assume she was playing with?"

Mona observed the pieces. She found the game of chess to be a thrilling sport with an unlimited number of outcomes, a game of moves and countermoves, adjustment and variation. Though she realized now she probably hadn't picked up so much as a pawn in at least five or six years.

"No one," Mona said, pointing to the arrangement of pieces. The pawn at E2 had been moved forward two places. "It's just an opening move. No countermove."

Dawes squatted so her view was level with the chess board. "Why would she do that?"

"Maybe she was just trying it out? Or maybe it's décor... for the shop?"

"Maybe," Dawes replied, though Mona could tell from the tone of her voice she was deep in thought. After a few moments, she stood back up, looking over the rest of the room. She took some time to examine the paintings on the walls, though Mona wasn't sure what she was looking for. When she reached the door, she stopped. "Detective."

Mona paused, then joined Dawes by the door. There, in a small frame, was a picture of Robin with Mona, their arms around each other in front of the art store. Mona remembered Mrs. Bellinger taking the photo, it had been the day Robin had signed the lease. She'd been so proud of her. A well of emotion threatened to overwhelm Mona, but she managed to swallow it back down. Why had she kept this picture up? Especially after everything that had happened?

"That's you," Detective Dawes said.

Mona nodded.

"Did you know she had this picture here?"

"I had no idea," Mona replied, which was the truth. It had only been a few short weeks after the picture had been taken when things had fallen apart. They'd been celebrating how well the opening had gone. And maybe Robin had too much to drink... and...

Mona shook the events of that night away. Reliving them now wouldn't do her any good. But after that night, Robin never wanted to see her again. So then why would she still have a picture of the two of them in such a visible place? It had to be a daily reminder of the pain Mona had caused.

The other woman made a small guttural noise in the back of her throat, and Mona wasn't sure if it was intentional or not. Finally, she turned away from the picture.

"C'mon. Let's speak with the neighbors."

TWELVE

Nothing about any of this smelled right to Charlotte. A missing woman, last seen at her place of business. A place of business which had been broken into, but presumably with nothing missing. A Jane Doe, found out by the river in a state of advanced decomposition and not a clue to work with. None of these details were adding up and it was beginning to frustrate her. Usually, her cases made sense. Maybe not at first, but after some level of investigation, Charlotte could normally begin to piece together what was happening.

That wasn't the situation here. All she knew was something was very wrong and the further they dove into this investigation, the more anxious she grew.

It didn't help matters that she hadn't gotten much sleep. She'd spent about twenty minutes on the phone with Whiteside last night informing him of what little progress they'd made and giving him a heads up that she may be here longer than they thought. After enduring some good-natured ribbing about making up details so she wouldn't have to come home to face the fire, Charlotte had tried to get some rest, only to find her mind wouldn't shut off. It kept coming back around to the fact that there would be no more meaningful work after this case. No more investigations. No more life-and-death situations. Charlotte would be relegated to a life of mediocrity—of doing work that didn't matter. And that filled her with a sense of dread and foreboding. Because without this, she had the very real sense that she would just waste away, forgotten.

At least while she was working for the police department her life mattered. But once that was all over, what would she have left? She'd seen her colleagues leave and get other jobs such as selling homemade candles or volunteering with the SPCA. But that wasn't her. She was a cop, through and through. There was nothing else. The thought of sitting around all day doing menial, unimportant tasks sounded like someone's sick idea of forced prison. And Charlotte had already had enough suffering for one lifetime.

Beyond that, she was beginning to suspect something else was going on with Detective LaSalle. Despite her repeated denials, Charlotte had been in the game long enough to know when people were pretending, and pretending was Mona's default setting.

Whatever was affecting the woman, it was something dark, hard and painful. And that made Charlotte just a little bit nervous. She knew firsthand how quickly things like that could get out of control, and what would happen if you couldn't fully trust yourself to react appropriately. Whatever was eating at Detective LaSalle could rear its head at the worst possible time, putting both of their lives in danger. Just the thought of it was enough to make Charlotte flex her hand almost nonstop, as if doing so would prevent another situation like the one at Victor's club. The fact was, Charlotte had permanent nerve damage in both hands, and a lifetime of hard police work coupled with the injuries of her youth had brought on arthritis early. She could barely rely on herself; if she couldn't rely on LaSalle, they were both up shit creek without a paddle.

After calling in a black-and-white to secure Bellinger's art studio, they decided to start with the upstairs neighbor, which was accessed by a staircase from the front sidewalk beside the door to the art studio. The stairs led up to a small landing with a door and a sign that said read, *Olivia Pekannen (LMFT). Hours: Monday to Friday, ten to four or by appointment.*

"Huh," Charlotte said, reading the sign. "I assume that's the woman we crossed paths with last night?"

Mona nodded. "I didn't realize she'd moved her office here. This used to be a dentist's office."

Charlotte checked the time. It was barely nine. They'd have to wait around another hour at least.

"The store next door is already open," Mona suggested. "I think that's the one Mrs. Bellinger mentioned."

Accepting they'd have to come back, Charlotte followed her new partner back down the stairs to the store set up to the left of Robin's. The sign hanging off the building advertised *The Dragon's Hoard*, with a purple dragon sporting blood-red fangs wrapped around the words. It looked to be about the same size shop as Robin's studio, and as they entered, a little chime went off above their heads.

Charlotte had seen places like this before; she'd just never been in one. Neat shelves ran along all the walls, holding hundreds of different types of board games, none of which Charlotte had ever heard of before. She had last played board games as a child, but there was no trace of Monopoly or Sorry anywhere in sight. Instead, the games all had intricate art on the boxes, each promising a different type of challenging adventure with interesting names such as Mystic Expedition: Beyond the Veil or Dawn of the Lost Kingdoms. She didn't realize board games were such a big business.

"Morning," a voice called from the back. Charlotte glanced past all the games to see a bearded man wearing a screen-printed T-shirt and a blazer sitting in the middle of a U-shaped counter area. The glass counter was full of cards of all types, many in acrylic cases with little price tags on them. "Let me know if you're looking for anything in particular," he said.

Charlotte pulled out her badge, walking up to the counter. "We're looking for information about your neighbor, Robin Bellinger. I understand you spoke with her mother a few days ago?"

"Yeah, she came in asking about Robin. I guess she didn't call... or something?"

"When was the last time you saw Robin?" Charlotte asked.

The man screwed up his face. "It's like I told her mother, it was lunch on Friday. I know she wasn't in Saturday or yesterday. We had tournaments both days and I never saw her lights on."

"Tournaments?" Charlotte asked.

The man pointed to his back room. It mirrored the room where Robin kept her crates, except his was full of fold-out tables and the walls were plastered with posters advertising dozens of different products. "We hold them in the back on Wednesdays, Saturdays and Mondays."

"Does Robin ever join in?"

The man gave her a rueful smile. "I've tried to get her to play a few times, but she's not much of a gamer. Prefers to read. Hey, everyone's got their thing, right?"

"What time on Friday did you see her?" Charlotte asked.

"Around lunch," he said. "I closed up for a few minutes to run across the square to grab some tacos. She was sitting outside under the gazebo when I passed."

Charlotte glanced back through the store to outside to the gazebo in the middle of the square. "In the cold?"

He shrugged. "Yeah, I guess she likes it. I've seen her out there a few times. Me? I prefer to eat in the warmth of my shop."

Sensing this was nothing but a dead end, Charlotte nodded

at the man, tapping the top of the cabinet absently. Mona stood just over her shoulder, listening, but apparently didn't have anything to add. Did it bother Charlotte that Mona's story about her and Robin's relationship wasn't making much sense either? Especially considering the latter kept a framed picture of the two of them together in her place of business?

She was starting to feel like she'd bitten off more than she could chew on her own here. "Okay, thanks for your help." As she began to make her way to the exit, Charlotte noticed along the bottom of one of the display racks were stacks of chess sets, ones that looked almost exactly like the one that had been set up in Robin's store. She motioned for Mona to grab one of the sets as she returned to the proprietor.

"Are these alabaster?" Charlotte asked as Mona brought the set to the counter.

He nodded, his face lighting up. "They are. And the bases are pure marble. They're a nice collector's item, especially if you enjoy long play. Durable, but also aesthetically pleasing."

"Did you sell one of these sets to Robin?" Charlotte asked.

The man frowned. "No, I don't think she's ever bought anything in here. Not that I'm aware of, anyway," he said.

"Does anyone else locally sell these sets?" Mona asked.

"I doubt it," he replied. "They were a special order from a manufacturer in France. This isn't something your average Walmart is going to carry. Like I said, it's a *collector's* item." He seemed almost insulted at the insinuation.

"How many of these sets have you sold in the last week?" Charlotte asked, her pulse picking up speed.

The man turned to his computer. "Let me check. I remember selling one myself, but I'm only here four days a week. Another might have gone out when I was off." He typed a few letters before the result came back. "Nope, just the one in the past week. On... Friday. Man came in and paid cash."

"On Friday? What time?" Charlotte asked.

"System shows it was just before closing. About nine thirty."

Charlotte turned to Mona to make sure she understood the implications of this. And for the first time, that smile was gone from her face. "What did he look like?" the other woman asked. "Did he say anything?"

"I'm trying to remember," the man said. "We were busy on Friday—"

Charlotte leaned forward. "You said he paid cash?"

The proprietor nodded. "I remember that much. I mean, it's a two-hundred-dollar chess set. Not a lot of people are in the market for them, and when they are, they don't often pay cash. He was friendly, I remember that much."

Charlotte looked into the corners of the store but didn't see any video cameras. "Do you have surveillance in here?"

He shook his head. "Never needed it. Sorry. Why, what's this all about?"

Charlotte turned to Mona. "Do you have a sketch artist in the station?"

Mona nodded. "Jackson. She's pretty good."

"Get her down here, we need to take a statement. And we'll need Whittle. I want a full forensic workup on the art studio."

"Wait," the game man said. "What's going on?"

"What are you thinking?" Mona asked.

"That there are too many coincidences here to count," Charlotte replied, ignoring the proprietor. "And that makes me nervous."

An hour later Charlotte stood with her arms crossed as Whittle worked on dusting the chess set sitting on Robin's table for prints. Jackson had worked with the game-shop owner to get a rudimentary sketch of the man they suspected might have had a hand in Robin's disappearance. Whoever this man was, they needed to find him and find him quickly. He might be the only one who could give them answers. Unfortunately, the game-shop owner admitted he'd never seen him before. And Jackson didn't recognize him either, based on the sketch.

Mona stood beside her, watching Whittle work, though Charlotte couldn't read her face. It had been a complete blank since they learned a man had purchased the set that now sat in her friend's empty store. The open door in the back may explain *how* the set got in the store, but not why.

Finally, Whittle stood and began putting his tools away. "I hate to say it, but it's clean. No prints anywhere."

"That doesn't make sense," Mona said. "Even if Robin had moved one of the pieces—"

"She never touched them," Charlotte said. "*He* did. Whoever *he* is. And he wiped them clean before leaving." She turned to Whittle. "Nothing on the board itself. Or the edges?"

He shook his head. "Sorry. Whoever they were, they were thorough. But this is just one area. I still need to check the rest of the store."

They'd been able to confirm the chess set was the exact one sold by the store next door due to a limited-edition number that had been engraved along one of the marble edges. It matched up with the log of editions the game store owner had received in his shipment. So, they knew the game was purchased at that particular store by a man that no one seemed to recognize, then set up here in Robin's store. But that couldn't be all.

Charlotte turned to Mona. "What is that move?" she asked. "The pawn out like that?"

Mona shrugged. "Nothing. It's just an opening gambit. You're allowed to move the pawn two spaces on its first turn."

"Nothing special about it?" Charlotte asked. "Like a partic-ular strategy?"

Mona shook her head. "No. It's very common. Why?"

"Because it's a message," Charlotte said. "And if I'm right, it's one we're *meant* to interpret. This is no random move by a passerby. Otherwise it'd have prints all over it. It's deliberate. Whoever this man is, he *wants* us to pay attention to this."

"Feel free to examine it all you wish," Whittle said. "I'll get started around the counter."

"So... what? This is some kind of game?" Mona asked as he headed for the back door.

Charlotte approached the chess pieces, examining them for any kind of clue, but as far as she could tell, they were all arranged correctly. "Maybe I'm reading too much into it. But the fact is we have a dead body, a missing woman—and this chess set is the first possible clue that could link to both. Or neither."

"Well, whoever set it up at least knows the rules," Mona said. "See? White always goes first." She pointed to the pawn.

"Opening move," Charlotte said, staring at the set. In kick-boxing, the opening move set the tone of the entire match. How you responded could spell victory or defeat. But what did it mean? Was Robin's disappearance the opening move? Or was it the body they'd found? Or was it neither and Charlotte was reading into something that meant nothing at all? Maybe some guy had decided to set up a game in Robin's art shop with a friend and they'd never showed up. Unlikely, but possible.

As Charlotte was about to lift up the velvet tablecloth to check under the table, she felt a soft tap on her shoulder. Looking up, she realized Mona had brought her attention to Sheriff Franklin, standing at the front door to the store, speaking with Jackson. Finally, the sketch artist nodded and took off in a trot back to the station. Franklin opened the door, signaling to the two detectives.

"Sheriff," Mona said. "What's going on?"

He paused a brief moment as he met her eye. "I need you two to come with me. We've got another body."

THIRTEEN

The stench hit Charlotte before her eyes even registered the scene. A coppery tang of blood that hung thick in the barn's stale air, mingling with the musty scent of old hay. It was the kind of smell that clung to your skin and clothes, the kind that would linger days, even weeks later.

She stepped through the barn doors, her eyes adjusting to the dim light filtering in through the wooden slats. The beams overhead creaked with age as she looked up and saw the body suspended high in the rafters.

Charlotte's stomach twisted at the sight. The victim was splayed out, her arms spread wide, wrists bound tightly to the beams. Her legs were tied together, dangling below her in a grotesque parody of a crucifixion. Blood soaked her clothes, the dark red stark against the pale skin that was still visible. What was left of her, anyway. Her torso had been flayed open, and her innards had spilled out, resting in the hay below.

One of the officers on the scene was retching violently off to the side, his hands braced on his knees as he struggled to regain composure.

"Is it her?" Charlotte asked as she and Mona stared up at the body.

"Yes," Mona replied, completely emotionless. Her eyes were flat and her lips drawn in a relaxed line. Charlotte figured the shock of it all must have caused Mona not to react as they watched what remained of Robin Bellinger swing ever so slightly above them.

The ropes holding her had all been tied off on a nearby hitching post inside the barn. Two other officers were working to release the ties so they could lower her down. No doubt Whittle would need to call in help for this one. A decaying body by the river was one thing. This... this was something else entirely.

Charlotte found she had to turn away from the body to think straight. But as she did, Mona continued to stare up at the scene, like a woman transfixed. Finally, Charlotte took Mona by the arms and physically turned her around. "Give yourself a moment to process this," she said.

"It's horrible," Mona said. "But I'm okay. I can handle it." And when Charlotte looked into the woman's eyes, she saw no physical discomfort—no emotion at all. A tiny crease of the brow was all that told Charlotte she wasn't looking at a robot. Mona was feeling the pain of this moment, but she was doing everything in her power to hide it. Maybe because she didn't want to look weak, or maybe for some other reason, but her mastery over her emotions was impressive. Downright scary, if Charlotte thought too long about it. "You take a minute if you need to," she added. "I'll stay in here and make sure they get her down safely."

Charlotte wasn't sure what to do with Mona's behavior, so she tucked it away for the time being. Maybe the woman just had an uncanny ability to compartmentalize. She'd already seen hints of that with their first victim. But it was different when it was someone you knew rather than some stranger. A majority of officers could handle examining a random body if they absolutely had to. But people who could assess that kind of mutilation to someone they cared about—or once cared about—were rare. It hit differently. Many people couldn't stomach it.

Even Charlotte, who had been trained to take an indifferent approach to the work, found herself grappling with her emotions. She had met Robin's family, spoken with her mother. And now they would have to meet again to deliver the bad news. Where the first body wasn't personal, Charlotte couldn't help but feel this one was.

She strode back out into the cool air outside, taking a few deep breaths. The weather wasn't any better today, and dark clouds hung low over the scene. The officer she'd seen puking earlier stood off to the side, his complexion pale. Beside him stood a man she presumed to be the owner of the house, a man in his late fifties wrapped up in a heavy woolen jacket and a hat, his hands shoved into his pockets. A pipe hung out of his mouth, but he didn't seem to be smoking from it, just using it to chew on as another set of officers set about restricting the barn with police tape. They stood about halfway between the house and the barn, about thirty yards away.

Charlotte approached the man, nodding to the officer. "Afternoon," she said, showing her badge. "I'm Detective Dawes. You're James Gentry?"

The man with the pipe nodded.

"I'm told you're the one who found the body."

"Shouldn't nobody have to find somethin' like that," he said. His eyes were glassy, like they weren't quite seeing her. Charlotte couldn't imagine what kind of a shock that must have been for the man.

"Can you tell me what happened?" she asked.

"Wasn't nothin' special," the man replied. "Jus' comin' out to check the barn like I always do. Make sure nothin's fallen down or gotten screwed up. Supposed to start seedin' in a few weeks, gotta make sure everythin's ready." He had the kind of accent that told Charlotte he'd been a native to this area his whole life. If she was willing to bet on it, she'd say his entire family had been farmers going back to the Civil War.

"How often do you come out to check your equipment?" she asked.

"'Bout once a week," he said.

"Always on the same day?" she asked.

"Usually. Unless there's a storm or somethin'. We got another front moving in tomorrow, thought I'd do it today instead. That matter?"

Charlotte was thinking back to the chess board. And their first victim. Jane Doe had been dumped in an area known for fishing, almost guaranteeing someone would find her sooner rather than later. And now they had Robin Bellinger, left in another place that might have seemed remote on the surface but was checked regularly. It was a little thing that may or may not connect the victims, but Charlotte couldn't ignore it.

"Did you happen to hear anything out here in the past few days?" They'd need Whittle to tell them how long Robin had been suspended up there, but if Charlotte's hunch was right, it wouldn't have been long. But what bothered her was the state of the body. Their Jane Doe hadn't been in nearly that condition, did that mean they were looking for *two* killers?

"Nope," the farmer said. "Been quiet. I would'a come out to see if I'd heard anythin'."

Charlotte looked back at the red building. "Do you keep your barn unlocked?"

"Course not," he said. "Last thing I need is someone settin' up camp in there thinkin' they run the place. Lock was broke when I came to check," he said.

"It's over there, by the house," the officer said, pointing at the back steps that led up to the door into the home. Charlotte headed over to inspect the lock. Bending down she could see it had been cut clean through with something sharp, more than likely a pair of bolt cutters. From its position it had probably fallen off when the barn door had been opened.

"You live alone, Mr. Gentry?" Charlotte asked, returning to the man.

"I got a couple of hands that come help durin' the season," he said. "But otherwise it's just me and Gus."

"Gus?" The man leaned back, giving Charlotte a perfect view of the porch banister to where an old hound dog lay, his muzzle gray and his eyes closed. "And he didn't hear anything either?"

"He's deaf," Gentry said. "Wouldn't hear a train whistle goin' off right beside his head. Not good for much other than eatin' and sleepin' but he keeps me company."

Charlotte didn't like the growing sense of unease forming in her stomach. If her hunch was correct, it meant they were working with someone who wanted their victims to be found. Where there was some question with the Jane Doe, this was as clear as crystal. Whoever killed Robin Bellinger wanted her discovered. They wanted their work displayed. Almost like a piece of art.

"Detective?"

Charlotte turned to see Mona walking up. "They finally got her down. I didn't know if you wanted to take a closer look or not."

As much as she didn't, it was important to examine the body to see if she could determine any similarities between her and their Jane Doe. If this *did* turn out to be the same killer and they had a double homicide on their hands, this was about to get very messy.

"What's your take on this?" Charlotte asked as she excused herself from Mr. Gentry and headed back toward the barn.

"I'm not sure I have enough information to make a conclusion yet," she said. "We just found the body."

Charlotte turned to her, one hand on Mona's chest stopping her in place. "I know people process pain and grief differently, but I have to be honest. The way you are so... measured with the death of your friend is something I've never seen in my twenty-plus years. I don't know how you're doing it, but it's off-putting."

Mona flinched before looking down at the ground and for a brief second, Charlotte thought she saw something else there. "I've heard that before."

"You have?"

"It's part of the reason people don't like working with me," she said. "When I first started, I got the nickname *Tin Man*, because—well, I'm sure you can figure it out. I guess I wasn't... emotional enough for them? But I've never heard of a man who goes to a crime scene and doesn't break down crying as 'not emotional.' And frankly, it was upsetting to know people still hold those kinds of biases."

Charlotte had to admit she'd been on the receiving end of those kinds of prejudices her entire career. And here she was committing the same sin against someone who very well could have been her twenty years ago. "I know how that goes."

Mona nodded. "I just find that things go a lot smoother if you remove emotions from the equation. It's something I learned a long time ago." She paused. "I was bullied a lot when I was younger. I guess people don't like newcomers when you move to a small town. But I realized that half the time they were just trying to get a reaction out of me. And if I just turned everything off, they couldn't hurt me. At least, not in the way they wanted to."

"I'm sorry," Charlotte said. "I shouldn't have assumed anything. These situations are just... well, they can be stressful." She glanced back to the barn. "I'm sorry about your friend."

"Thank you," Mona said, her voice a little smaller. "So am I."

As they returned to the barn, Charlotte steeled herself. Nothing about this would be easy, but she didn't want the reality of the situation to overwhelm her. Entering the barn again, she saw they had lowered what remained of Robin Bellinger onto a blue tarp, so she was lying on her back. The grotesque nature of what she'd endured was evident by the massive gash across her midsection, though Charlotte could see no reason for it. Obviously, the body had been staged to make a statement, but what kind? What could the killer be trying to communicate?

Her immediate thoughts went to religious iconography. Obviously, since Robin had been in a "crucifixion pose", it made sense. The body by itself might not be enough to tell the whole story. But she took a moment to examine it. Obvious bruising around the wrists and the feet where she was bound, her toes and fingers purple from being out in the cold for so long. Could she have been strung up while she was still alive, then opened? Unless she was under some heavy sedation, Charlotte didn't think so. She would have no doubt let out a scream that would have alerted the owner. Which means she was probably already dead by the time he hauled her up there. The gash opening her up had been for show.

"Fuck," she said under her breath.

"What's wrong?" Mona asked. Charlotte turned to her, her expression incredulous. "I mean... beyond the obvious."

"He's too confident," Charlotte said. "I don't like it when they're so sure they won't get caught. It means he's probably going to escalate."

"Escalate how?"

"That's the problem. We don't know until he does it." One thing was for sure, Robin Bellinger wouldn't be their last victim. Whoever was doing this wanted to make a statement. Charlotte's mind returned to the chess set. He'd made the first move. And they had responded. Robin was another piece of the puzzle. So now it was their turn again.

"Have you checked the rest of the barn yet?"

Mona was staring at Robin's body but pulled her attention away, blinking. "No, why? Is there something we should be looking for?"

"I have a hunch," Charlotte said. Frankly, she wasn't sure how long she could stomach looking at the remains and needed a distraction. Whoever was behind this, they were deliberate. The chess set had been a message. Maybe there was another one. She began examining the dark corners of the barn.

"Are you thinking they left some evidence behind?"

"Maybe," Charlotte said. "But I don't think we're getting a complete picture here. She was up there like that for a reason. I want to know why." She used the light on her phone, shining into the empty horse corrals in the barn, the dirt floor with only a light layer of hay covering it.

"Maybe they don't have a reason. Whoever did this might just be crazy," Mona said.

"They're definitely crazy, but this feels more nuanced than that. More measured. I don't think this is someone just acting out whatever they feel. I think they're following a plan."

"Why is that?" her partner asked.

"Why else would he leave her in that condition if not to send a message? Why take the time to set that up if it doesn't mean anything?" As she swept her phone over the darkened areas, she thought she saw something peeking out from beneath some old boards. Charlotte crept closer, causing a rat to skitter away from the corner back into the safety of the darkness.

Charlotte paused, grimacing. She really didn't want to deal with a rat's nest. But there was definitely something there. Reaching forward carefully, she moved the boards aside, revealing a dark rectangle that had been set against the back of the barn.

"What is it?" Mona asked from behind her.

Charlotte retrieved a glove from her pocket and snapped it on before gingerly taking the rectangle and removing it from behind the pile. As she turned it around, she forced herself to hold in a gasp.

"It's a painting," she finally said. "A disturbing one."

FOURTEEN

Perched in the tall grass more than five hundred yards away, John watched through the scope of the rifle. From here he had a clear shot of the entire barn, including the old man's house. But the safety on the rifle was engaged and there wasn't even a round in the chamber. He was much more interested in what he could view through the scope.

And as the two women emerged from the barn with the painting in hand he had to hold in a shout of excitement. Out here sound traveled, and even though he was a safe distance away, he didn't want to risk giving it away too early.

But there they were, Detectives Dawes and LaSalle with the clue in their hands.

Clever girls, he thought, harkening back to a line out of one of his favorite movies. He flipped the dial on top of the scope which magnified the image five times, giving him an almost perfect view of their faces. Detective Dawes's face was drawn tight, worried and in anguish. However, LaSalle seemed less affected by the discovery. Much less.

Interesting.

He suppressed a smile. "Not bad, huh?"

He turned to the side, glancing over at his companion. She laid beside him in the grass, her skin pale and features sickly. Her eyes were sunken, her lips blue and cracked. The ropes had left dark bruises around her wrists, the marks still fresh in his mind. "I'll admit I was a little worried when they missed the first clue. But they came through."

She didn't respond, just looked out across the plain in the direction of the barn. John resumed his position, watching the detectives through the scope. "You didn't think I could do it, did you?"

I never said that.

"But you thought it. Don't worry, I'm not mad. I just want you to know you're wrong." There was a buzz of activity at the site now, other officers coming over to look at the painting. Taking his eye away from the scope it looked like nothing but a swarm of ants all moving around a newly discovered piece of food. This was sure to kick them into an absolute frenzy.

"Look at them all down there. Action and reaction, cause and effect. And they have no idea why. It's funny that way, isn't it? So often we go through our lives not really knowing why we're doing what we're doing and then something comes along to change all of that."

You've freed them.

He turned to her, appraising the woman for a brief moment. "Thank you. I appreciate you saying that, Robin, I really do." He turned back to the scope to watch. "We've always understood each other, haven't we?" He continued to watch for another ten minutes in silence before he finally set the weapon to the side and sat up. His back cracked as he did. He'd been in this position for a few hours now, waiting and watching. And it had all been more than worth it.

"Time to go," he said, removing the kickstand on the rifle and folding it back together. Beside him, Robin's form sat up as well, though she kept her eyes turned to the distance.

"Don't worry about them, they're on the right track now. They're smart. They'll figure it out."

What if they can't?

He grimaced as he zipped up the case around the rifle before slinging it on his back, standing all the way up. "Then they don't deserve to continue, right? No extra lives in this one. No do-overs." He patted the rifle case as he took short steps back down the hill to the truck waiting at the bottom. Behind him his companion lingered on the hill for a few moments before following behind.

"You know, I think you're proud of me," he said, his voice low as he placed the rifle in the truck bed. "I've managed to pull this whole thing together in less than a day and have given them a case the likes they've never seen before. I can't wait to see what happens next." He paused, glancing at her dead, hollow eyes, and his grin widened. "You know, it's all thanks to you."

No. It's because of us.

He smiled. "You're absolutely right. I would say we should celebrate, but unfortunately there's no time. They've found the clue. We can't delay. The next pieces must be set up."

He opened the door and got in, and by the time he pulled on his seat belt, she was in the seat next to him. "Did I ever tell you I used to be in the creative arts myself?"

Tell me about it.

He turned over the engine, grinning. "Back in high school— I was one of the smarter ones. Always finished my work early. And I got bored. Bored kids get in trouble." He glanced over to see if she was smiling, but her lips only sagged under their own weight. Oh well.

"Eventually, they assigned me to the library, where they kept all the computers. I think they hoped they'd keep me busy, and they were right. You can learn anything in a library. And I learned how to build things. Specifically, homemade rockets. I got so good, I managed to build one that actually launched hundreds of feet into the air using nothing but a few household items you can find anywhere.

"But were they impressed? Of course not. I came back one day to find they had forbidden homemade rockets from school grounds. The excuse was it was too *dangerous*. Not only that, but they'd confiscated and destroyed the rocket I'd prepared for our school's science fair, because they were afraid it would go off unexpectedly. Now, you tell me, does that give someone the right to just destroy your work?"

They didn't appreciate what you'd done.

"Damn right they didn't," he said, smacking the steering wheel as he drove. "That's when I learned not to waste my time on permanence. Instead, I turned to games. First the board games in the library, then more complex ones later. I figured if I learned how the games worked, I could learn how to bend the rules... or rewrite them." He shot a smirk at Robin. "Of course, they didn't like that either. But they couldn't just confiscate what I'd learned. Not this time. They couldn't take what was up here." He tapped his temple a few times. "And that's when I figured it out. Everything we do, everything in the world is a kind of game, each with its own rules. And as long as everyone follows the rules, everything works. While you know this, not everyone does. Some people make their own rules. Some people just flat out break them. Some people cheat."

And cheating isn't allowed.

"Damn right it isn't," he replied. "Which is why I make my own games. It's the only way to beat the system. You either prove yourself worthy, or you fail. And so far, no one has won. But these two women... I have faith they can do it. I'm *rooting* for them, if you can believe it." He thought back to Detective Dawes, with that intensity she showed out in the field. She was a sharp one. Since she'd come into the game, he'd done a few background searches on her. The Perilino case, the Myers Ring. She was an established detective with a stellar track record. The perfect opponent. Without her, the game wouldn't have been nearly as thrilling. But now... now it was art.

And LaSalle... if anyone could solve this puzzle, it was her. She had a reputation for being extremely clever. Someone who thought outside of the norm, someone who could see things other people couldn't. The two of them together—how could they lose?

But it couldn't be too easy. He might be laying bread-crumbs, but they still had to put it all together. They had to figure out the game *as they played*. There was no manual. No rule book. And just as before, if they broke the rules, there would be punishments.

You're giving them a beautiful gift.

He grinned again. "You're right, I am, aren't I? But let's not get ahead of ourselves. We can't just jump to the end." Gods, how could he have ever thought Carol was a good companion for him when someone like Robin had been out there. Ever since they'd gotten together he hadn't even had the urge for a beer. No, his head was clear for the first time in *years*. She had been just what he'd needed. He reached over to place his hand on hers, but it rested on the armrest instead.

"Thank you, for being here with me."

Where else would I be?

He chuckled. "I guess that's true. Still, we're going to get your friend over the finish line together, aren't we?"

She didn't respond, but then again she didn't have to. Robin had been instrumental in this puzzle, and even though her role was mostly over, he wasn't about to let her go. "Don't worry, I'm never going anywhere. We're together... forever."

For a brief second, he thought he saw something flicker across the woman's hollow eyes, her dead lips twisting in a peculiar fashion. But it came and went so quick he decided he'd imagined the whole thing.

As he pulled up to the house and killed the engine, he took

a minute to breathe in through his nose and out through his mouth. Everything was in motion now, there was no going back.

As he stepped out of the truck to face the darkening sky, the cold air biting at his skin, John felt a surge of exhilaration. He was still one step ahead. And it was up to him to make sure it remained that way.

Until the very end.

FIFTEEN

The drive to Robin's family home was punctuated with a thick silence. Charlotte had grown used to silence in the car during investigations, but this was different. It wasn't the usual focus-before-the-storm kind of quiet. It was something else entirely—something unsettling. She kept stealing glances at Mona, hoping to catch a glimpse of any reaction, any sign of the woman beneath the hard shell. But there was nothing.

The subject of the painting had been a nude woman, draped across a crimson chaise longue in a relaxed fashion. It might have been beautiful were it not immediately apparent the woman was dead, with two red *X* marks on each wrist. A pool of blood mirrored the chaise longue below her, the only other color on the dark background which seemed to stretch into noth-ingness.

No one had known what to make of it, least of all Charlotte. She'd been exposed to graphic art before, but there was some-thing about this piece that made it feel intensely personal. There hadn't been a signature, but Mona had been the one to surmise that it belonged to Robin—that it was painted in her style. But when Charlotte pressed for more information, she got nothing in return.

The only other mark on the painting had been across the back, a strange pictogram that Charlotte didn't recognize. Still, they had categorized it and catalogued it for evidence after Charlotte had taken some pictures with her phone. As the evening had waned on and darkness fell at the barn, they decided it was best to inform the family before waiting for Whittle to arrive. Jackson had informed them Whittle had contacted backup from the surrounding counties to come in and assist.

Mona's hands gripped the wheel with the same precision and steadiness she'd shown back at the barn. Her face was still, her gaze fixed ahead on the road, as though they were simply heading to a routine interview and not about to break the worst possible news to Robin's family. There was no way to tell what was going through the woman's head. But whatever it was, she wasn't sharing it with Charlotte. Maybe it was better that way. Best not to get too close. Still, they had a job to do.

"I'm happy to take the lead on this," Charlotte finally offered, her voice quiet but cutting through the hum of the engine.

Mona's eyes didn't leave the road. "That's okay," she said, her tone calm.

"I've done it more than I'd like to admit," Charlotte pressed. "Telling someone their loved one's dead... It's not something you ever get used to, especially when you knew the victim."

"I was her friend. It's my responsibility," Mona said.

Charlotte sat back, chewing the inside of her cheek. The puzzle that was Mona seemed to grow more complicated with every passing hour. She should be sweating bullets, or at least be on the edge of panic at the thought of what they were about to do.

But no, that impenetrable wall was back up.

Charlotte thought back to their conversation at the barn. Was she really being prejudiced in how she saw Mona? Just because the woman wasn't reacting like she would react didn't mean she wasn't affected. But still, something felt... off.

The thoughts swirled in Charlotte's mind as they pulled up to the modest house. Staring at it, Charlotte couldn't help but consider the strange juxtaposition of the calm setting with the cacophony of emotions they were about to unleash on the family. If only they were here to deliver better news, news that wouldn't tear Robin's family apart and be the source of years of grief and torment. That was often the worst part, knowing that the families would never be the same after learning the truth. Some people never moved past it, and in the worst-case scenarios, it ended up destroying even more lives, whether through substance abuse, or worse, suicide.

Mona turned off the engine and sat there for a moment, staring at the house. She took a deep breath, but it seemed more like a formality than a need for composure. Charlotte watched her, trying to decide whether to push further. But before she could, Mona was out of the car, walking up the driveway at her usual brisk pace. Charlotte followed, feeling the knot of unease growing in her chest.

The door opened before they reached the front porch, Mrs. Bellinger standing on the front steps with hope and worry fighting for dominance across her face. For the flash of a second, Charlotte saw herself standing there, her hands wrung together as she waited for them to get closer, her eyes pinched and red-rimmed as she waited to hear some unspeakable news about Haley.

She pushed the thought away as Mona stepped forward, taking a deep breath.

"Here, please, come inside," Mrs. Bellinger said as she almost stumbled over herself to get them into the house. The hint of hope in her voice just about broke Charlotte's heart. Just as before, the house smelled faintly of coffee. The woman probably hadn't stopped drinking the stuff since their last visit.

Mrs. Bellinger didn't speak. She didn't ask questions. She just held herself as if she might shatter at any moment. The world seemed to stop, the only sound the ticking of the clock on the mantel.

Mona let out her breath. "I'm so sorry."

The woman's knees buckled, and Charlotte instinctively shot forward, grabbing the older woman and helping her down into the nearest chair where she slumped to the side, a vacant expression on her face. She'd seen this so many times before, she'd anticipated it—the loss of all hope and thought as the mind goes into shock. Mrs. Bellinger stared into space, her eyes unfocused, like she couldn't bear to process what she'd just heard.

"What happened?" The sharp question came not from Mrs. Bellinger, but from the person Charlotte hadn't realized had been standing at the edge of the kitchen. Adam rounded the corner to face them, his face red and his fists clenched tight at his sides.

Mona turned toward him, her expression still unreadable. "She was found in a barn not far from here. We're still investigating the circumstances, but—"

"I knew it," he snapped, stepping forward with an anger and intensity that surprised Charlotte so much she almost reflexively went for her weapon. "I knew you couldn't help her. And now my sister is dead because of you."

Charlotte stepped in, putting a hand in front of Mona. "Adam, I know this is hard," she said gently. "But we're doing everything we can to—"

Adam shoved past them both, his eyes blazing with grief and rage. "Keep your bullshit excuses to yourself. Robin was never your priority, and now she's gone because you were too busy to find her. I told you—" His voice cracked, and he turned, storming away. The sound of the garage door slamming echoed through the quiet house.

Charlotte sighed, rubbing her temple. She'd seen reactions like this before. Anger, blame—it was a common way for people to cope with loss. Especially teens. But it never made it easier to deal with. Adam was running at full temperature, and it would take him a while to cool off.

Mrs. Bellinger still hadn't said a word, just stared ahead as if Robin's death had hollowed her out from the inside. Charlotte knelt beside her chair, speaking softly. "Mrs. Bellinger, I'm so sorry. I know this is overwhelming. But we need to ask a few more questions, anything that could help us understand what happened to Robin."

The woman blinked slowly, turning her head just slightly toward Charlotte. "Why... what happened to her?" she whispered.

Charlotte pressed her lips in a line. "Someone... displayed her. It's better you don't know the details. But this was no accident."

Mrs. Bellinger squeezed her eyes shut, as if blocking out the truth might make it less real. In Charlotte's experience, she would eventually press for the details of what happened to her daughter, and they'd be compelled to tell her, making all of it that much worse. But for now, she hoped she wouldn't force the issue. Because as much as she hated to do it, they still needed information from the woman. She pulled out her phone, scrolling to the picture she'd taken of the painting they'd found in the barn.

"I know this is hard," Charlotte continued gently. "But I need to ask you if you've ever seen this painting before." She turned the phone, handing it to Mrs. Bellinger. "Do you recognize it?"

The older woman stared at the picture, confusion mingling with the sorrow on her face. "It... it looks like it could be one of

Robin's paintings. But I've never seen anything like that before. It's so... dark. Not like her at all."

"That's true," Mona added, her voice calm, almost clinical. "As far as I know, Robin only ever painted landscapes... but it does resemble her style."

Mrs. Bellinger shook her head, her brow furrowing. "She stopped showing me her work. She used to show me every piece —she was proud to do it. But lately... I don't know what was going on with her. She'd become so withdrawn."

"Do you know why?" Charlotte asked gently.

"I don't," she replied, looking at the painting above the couch. "*That* was my Robin. Not whatever the hell this is." She pushed the phone away.

"It's good," Charlotte remarked, and she wasn't just being polite. It was clear Robin had real talent. "Did she ever mention anyone when talking about her work? A boyfriend, someone she was close to? Someone she might have confided in?"

"No," Mrs. Bellinger said softly. "Robin was always... private about her personal life. She always has been, ever since she was little." Her breath caught in her throat as tears fell down her face. "I don't even know if she had a boyfriend."

"She didn't," Mona said softly.

Charlotte narrowed her gaze. "How do you know?"

But the other woman just shook her head. "Mrs. Bellinger. When did Robin start to... withdraw?"

"I—I'm not sure," she replied. "Maybe a year or so ago." Mona nodded but didn't say anything else.

Charlotte asked a few follow-up questions, but Mrs. Bellinger didn't have much else to offer. Robin had kept her secrets well hidden, even from those closest to her. After making sure she would be okay until one of her friends could arrive, they turned back to the door. Mona paused, glancing toward the hallway where Adam had stormed off. Going after

Adam would only make the situation worse, and thankfully she headed outside instead of pursuing it.

As they stepped outside, the cold wind hit Charlotte's face, making her feel as though she could finally breathe again. The air inside the house had been thick with grief and guilt, suffocating in its sorrow. Mona walked beside her with a forced cheerfulness, but it was obvious from how tight she was holding herself that she was masking her true feelings.

"Mona," Charlotte said, trying to keep her tone even, "I know you said you process stuff like this differently, but I just want you to know that if you need to talk to someone, I can be a great listener."

Mona turned to her, confusion on her face. "What's there to talk about?"

Charlotte blinked as if she'd been slapped. The way this woman could cut off her emotions like a switch was something she'd never encountered before. But that didn't mean she wasn't human. "I'm just saying, if you need to vent to someone, I can help."

Mona's eyes flickered for a moment, the forced happiness slipping away. She shrugged, her shoulders tight. "I appreciate that, Detective, I do. But I'll be fine."

Charlotte gritted her teeth as she was forced to follow the woman again. It was as if she had a singular mission and wasn't about to stop and process what had happened. "Maybe you should talk to Franklin about taking some time off. No one would think less of you for it."

"I'd much rather find out who did this to Robin, wouldn't you?" she asked, matter-of-factly, as they reached the car.

"Of course, but—"

"Great," she said. "Then we should get started. He's out there somewhere. And he's getting further and further away by the second."

Charlotte had to admit getting Mona to open up was like

trying to pry open an oyster. It was going to be painful for everyone involved and more than likely someone was going to crack if she pushed any harder. She'd have to let Mona process this in her own time; she just hoped it wasn't at the expense of the case.

As she slipped into the car a text came through on her phone, from Whittle. She glanced at it, along with the photograph he'd attached.

"Shit," she said.

Mona glanced over. "What is it?"

"We missed something," Charlotte said. "Something big."

SIXTEEN

"*Two* paintings."

Mona stood beside Detective Dawes as they examined the two canvases side by side. They were exactly the same size, and both featured similar subject matter, the primary colors being black and red.

After they'd left, Whittle's backup had arrived to help him process Robin's art studio. And the team happened to find the second painting—or maybe they should consider it the first painting—hidden under the tablecloth that held the chess set.

That painting had featured a subject very much like how they found Robin Bellinger—a figure suspended high in the air, arms splayed to the sides and her midsection sliced open, spilling out and on the ground. Obviously, the intention had been for them to find that painting first, then Robin, before uncovering the second. Like the one found at the barn, this one featured strange symbol on the back that no one could make head nor tail of. For the moment, Detective Dawes assumed it was some kind of signature of Robin's, though Mona had never known her to sign her name in that way.

Since they were the only two pieces of evidence that had

been recovered, both had been brought back to the station where they'd been kept in the evidence locker overnight until Mona and Detective Dawes could take a proper look. After last night, neither woman had felt like investigating Robin's home address.

Mona couldn't express how thankful she'd been when Detective Dawes agreed they should start again in the morning. For the first time in *years*, she'd almost lost control at Mrs. Bellinger's house. Learning about Robin's circumstances had been heart-wrenching. She'd been up almost all night mulling it over, going back and forth. And in the end, she could only come to one conclusion.

Whatever Robin had been through, the cause of all her darkness and despair, it was because of Mona. Because Mona hadn't been there when Robin needed her most.

Mrs. Bellinger had said Robin had begun to withdraw into herself a little over a year ago, which had been right after Mona had stopped coming around. Robin, like Mona, never had many other friends and must have turned her pain inward. Mona almost couldn't contain the guilt that threatened to burst through her chest at any given moment. It was a miracle she was even standing here, looking at the paintings. Somehow, she managed to compartmentalize it and focus on what her new partner was saying.

"I can't believe we missed this," Detective Dawes said, fury tinting her words. "We were *right* there."

"To be fair, it was hidden," Mona said impassively. She knew her particular style of investigation was beginning to grate on the detective—eventually, it grated on everyone—but Mona couldn't help it. It was just how she was. And did it really matter? She saw her protections as a benefit; they allowed her to do her job without the messy emotions that got in the way of other detectives. The only problem was no one seemed to trust her. That had been one of Ramsey's complaints. But then again, he was just a jerk. She had hoped her relationship with Detective Dawes could be different.

The door behind them opened, revealing Sheriff Franklin, his hair tousled and dark circles under his eyes. Apparently, he hadn't gotten much rest either. "You two, in my office."

Mona didn't even bother protesting; she knew she was on shaky ground due to not informing her boss of her possible connection with one of the victims. She should have told him right away, when they realized Robin went missing the same day the Jane Doe was dumped. But Mona hadn't been sure then, and things... things had gotten a little out of control since.

She and Detective Dawes followed her boss back to his office.

"Close the door," he said, rounding his desk and taking a seat. The air in the room had a heavy musk of tobacco to it, like Sheriff Franklin hadn't opened the windows to let it air out in a while.

Franklin glared at the two of them. "Excuse my language, but what the *fuck* is happening out there? I have you two on a dumped body and the next thing I know I have a woman hanging from the rafters like something out of a horror movie and now we've got these damned *paintings*. Can one of you tell me just what the hell is going on?"

"We believe the cases are related, sir," Dawes said as Mona found herself studying the edge of a new railroad magazine on the edge of his desk. Should she have gotten him a present for promoting her to case lead? Nothing big, maybe just a token of gratitude? He'd already done so much for her, and Mona hadn't reciprocated very well.

"Robin Bellinger went missing the same day the Jane Doe was dumped in the woods. We think the killer may have taken her as a victim after disposing of his last," her partner continued.

Franklin looked down at the information that was already strewn across his desk. "MOs don't match."

"No, sir. They don't."

"Then how do you know they're connected?"

"Because the odds of Oak Creek having two killers at the same time are near astronomical," Mona said, finally looking back up. "You look stressed, chief. Can I get you some coffee? Or some tea?"

The sheriff pinched the bridge of his nose. "No, LaSalle. I don't want a coffee. I want you to tell me what connects these two cases other than coincidence."

"We're working on that," Detective Dawes said, shooting Mona a suspicious glance. "But we think this is all part of some deliberate plan on the killer's part. We think he's trying to speak to us... to tell us something."

"As in?" Franklin asked.

Dawes leaned back. "We're not sure yet. But you can obviously see that the body of Robin Bellinger was arranged in the same manner as the person in the painting found in her art studio. That's *not* a coincidence. That's as deliberate as anything I've ever seen."

Franklin picked up a photograph of the first painting, examining it. "So... what's the point of the paintings?"

Detective Dawes and Mona had been trying to decipher the implications of the second painting all morning. And they could only really agree on one reasonable conclusion. "We think the killer is using them to tell us where his next victims will be," Mona said.

Detective Dawes leaned forward again. "See this one, how the light is illuminated behind her? You could almost make the argument that had we found it—we might have surmised that Robin was being held up somewhere high. Then again, we didn't know it was her at the time. We just thought—"

"Detective," Franklin said, working his jaw. "You may get

some strange cases back home, but this is a lot to swallow. Even for me."

"I know it's a lot, but we think we were *supposed* to find that first painting with the chess set, which would have led us to Robin—"

"Then what?" he interrupted. "This second painting is supposed to lead to another victim?" He pointed to a photograph of the second painting. The same one Detective Dawes had shown Mrs. Bellinger.

Detective Dawes sat back again. "Yes, we believe that could be the case."

"You have got to be kidding me," Franklin said under his breath, but it seemed more to himself than to them.

"Consider, chief," Mona said. "There hasn't been any evidence left at any of the three scenes. Whittle and his people did a thorough check of the woods, the art studio and the barn. There was no trace evidence left behind. Whoever is behind this, they are meticulous."

"Which means they're also experienced," Detective Dawes added. "It wouldn't surprise me if you were dealing with a career killer here. One who is very good at not getting caught."

"Why now?" the man asked. "Why *here*? What is it about this place that's ignited this psycho all of a sudden?"

"Who knows?" Detective Dawes said. "It could be anything. Maybe he's just bored. Or maybe something specific here set him off."

"Something such as..."

Dawes glanced at Mona again. After speaking with Mrs. Bellinger, they had realized that their victim had been keeping more secrets than anyone thought. "It might have been Robin herself," Mona said, her voice wavering slightly. "After all, she is the one who we believe created the paintings."

Franklin furrowed his brow. "You think when he saw these paintings they... what, triggered him in some way?"

Dawes nodded. "And he set out to recreate the scenes in real life."

"But how would he have even seen them?"

"He must have seen one when he came into her studio on Friday," Mona replied. "She liked to paint in the back, and we found that empty easel."

The man paused a moment, staring at the pile of information in front of him. "Why didn't I take that job down in Slateville?" he muttered before returning his attention to them. "Okay, fine. Keep working this angle. But if you're right and these paintings are pointing to victims, then does that mean we already have another body out there we don't know about?"

"Impossible to tell," Dawes said. "The killer may want us to think there is a chance to save them, or he may not actually kill them until we're on the trail, but we're going to do everything we can to find out."

"Make it quick," he replied. "Because as soon as this hits the media, we're going to have a frenzy on our hands. I can see the headlines now. They'll start calling him *The Artist* or some other bullshit." Dawes nodded, standing. Mona made a motion to follow her out.

"LaSalle, a minute." Franklin motioned for her to stay. Dawes gave her a considered look before heading out, closing the door behind her. "You knew the victim?" her boss asked.

"I did. We were friends... once. Years ago."

He leveled his gaze at her. "Are you okay to continue working this case?"

"Yes," she said, stiffening. "Of course."

"You're sure," he said. "Because I can reassign someone else to work with Dawes. I'm not sure I like you being so personally connected to what's happened."

Mona pinched her features. This was one of those times when she thought her particular style would be a benefit. She was free from becoming too emotional on the job because she could shut things off where other people couldn't. "Sheriff, there is nowhere else I would rather be. Robin was—*is* my best friend. She's the only person who ever really understood me, who accepted me for who I was when I first moved here. I need to do this for her, to discover what happened. No one else in this office will work harder for that. I'll grieve in my own time. But not while he's still out there."

Her boss scrutinized her, and Mona knew if she even flinched, it would all be over. But she remained completely solid until he finally relented. "Go on, get out there."

"Thank you," she replied, and headed back out to join Dawes.

"Everything okay?" the older detective asked.

"Yep," Mona replied. "Right as rain. Where do we go next?"

"Next we figure out where we're being led," she replied. "And find a way to get ahead of him."

SEVENTEEN

The pieces were finally starting to fall into place. And it had all been because of that second painting. If not for that discovery, Charlotte was sure they'd still be spinning their wheels. But now she'd clocked the killer, and she had a working theory. If they were lucky, they could reach the next victim before he could take this any further.

Charlotte wasn't sure, but the fact he was leaving deliberate clues for them meant he wanted to be caught, in some perverse fashion. It also meant they needed to be particularly careful, as he was no doubt unhinged. Every scene they approached from this moment on had to be considered a trap, because in her experience, psychopaths like this didn't just sit around waiting to be found. They were always working behind the scenes, creating new angles and new obstacles. To them, this was nothing more than a big game. A game they were intent on winning.

But Charlotte was going to put an end to it. No matter the cost.

After their discussion with Franklin, Charlotte had given Whiteside a call and informed him of their progress... and the unfortunate circumstances of discovering Robin Bellinger's remains. He'd offered to send Givens down to assist, but Charlotte had immediately rejected the offer. Not that she didn't think Givens could help, but because the rest of the Oak Creek unit was already on edge with her there. Adding another Chicago cop would only make the situation worse.

Plus, she could handle this. There was only one wild card: Detective LaSalle.

But Charlotte didn't have much of a choice. She *had* to keep working with the woman. She was a good detective, and she was sharp. If not for the way she could turn her emotions on and off, she would probably have had Charlotte's full trust by now. And Charlotte couldn't deny it might be her own hang-ups keeping her from fully appreciating her partner.

Still, she wasn't about to drop her guard.

"I want every officer in the entire department to have a copy of this image," Charlotte told Michaels as she strode into his small office in the back of the station. She turned her phone to show it to him.

He immediately recoiled. "What the hell?" He looked as though he might go green. Charlotte hated to think what would happen if he caught a glimpse of Robin's actual body.

"It's evidence," she said. "We believe the painting may reflect a real-life location here in town. I want as many people looking at this as possible. I want to know where it is."

"Yeah—yeah, okay," he said, regaining his composure. "Send it to me and I'll distribute it to the troops."

"Thanks," Charlotte said. "I owe you one." She headed back to the evidence room where Mona had set up shop, studying the two paintings. "Anything?" she asked, sticking her head in the door.

"It looks vaguely familiar," Mona said. "But I can't nail it down. Then again, it could be anywhere. Just like Robin could have been in any number of barns in the county. There was no way to tell which one. We may not be able to find the next victim until he wants us to."

"I refuse to accept that," Charlotte replied. "There has to be a way to get ahead of him. He's leaving us clues, let's find a way to hang him with them." She winced at her choice of words, but they didn't seem to bother Mona in the slightest. "C'mon, we need to do some recon."

Mona joined her at the door. "Recon?"

"If these paintings are what set the killer off, I have a feeling they aren't the only ones. We still need to check Robin's house—though now we'll need to treat it as a potential crime scene. I want to learn as much about your friend as possible."

"That makes sense. Should we get Whittle over there?" Mona asked.

"Not yet," she replied. "This killer seems to know a lot about her. It's possible he's been there—or maybe that's where he's set up. Either way, I want to see it for myself first." Though she wasn't sure that was the answer. Maybe Robin became involved with the killer without realizing it. There was a possibility he might have left something at her home.

As they headed out and down the steps of the precinct, a small crowd of people had gathered at the nearby gazebo in the center of town. "What's that?" Charlotte asked.

"I don't know," Mona replied. "There aren't any get-togethers or rummage sales scheduled today. Sometimes they'll set up a farmers' market, but that's only in the summer."

The gazebo itself was slightly elevated on a platform, almost large enough to work as a stage for musical acts. But it was also rotting in certain places and didn't look as strong as she would want. And up on that stage was Ken, the café manager they'd met the other evening. Charlotte took a few furtive steps closer, trying to catch what the man was saying.

"—an important part of this community. If any of you have anything you'd like to say, please come up and speak." It was then that Charlotte caught sight of the bunches of flowers that had been left at the base of the gazebo. A couple of balloons and stuffed animals were interspersed with the flowers as well.

As Charlotte and Mona drew closer, Ken stepped down from the gazebo as another woman took the "stage," bundled tight against the cold. She was probably in her sixties and began speaking about how much she enjoyed going into Robin's art shop once a week. As soon as he was off the stairs, Ken made a beeline for Mona.

"Detective," he said, his voice somber yet urgent. "Have you made any progress?"

"You know about Robin Bellinger?" Charlotte asked.

"Of course," he said. "Word travels fast in this town."

"Where did you hear it?" Charlotte asked, perplexed at the lack of security in Oak Creek. If this had been her department, this thing would have been buttoned up tight. But obviously someone had leaked the information overnight.

"One of the customers told me this morning," he replied. "Have you spoken with her mother? Some of us thought about perhaps preparing some meals—"

"We informed her last night," Charlotte said, flustered. Her mind immediately went to Ramsey.

But apparently Ken thought her irritation was at him as he turned to Mona. "Detective LaSalle, you understand, don't you? People are scared. Do you have any idea of who could be behind this?"

"Not yet," Mona said, shooting looks at Charlotte. "But we're working on it."

"What can we do to help? Robin—she was an important part of this community. I just can't believe something like this could happen here."

"We're taking care of it," Charlotte said. "It's best you let us do our jobs."

Ken grimaced again, his attention returning to Mona once

more. "You were friends with her, weren't you? Would you come say a few words?"

"Oh," Mona said. "No, I better not."

Ken seemed taken aback. "But—"

"We need to get going," Charlotte said. "Detective." She turned and headed back toward the station as Mona caught up with her.

"They're worried," Mona said. "And they want to help."

"We need to stay focused." She glanced back at the crowd. Dozens of pairs of eyes were watching them. Maybe even the eyes of the person who had killed Robin Bellinger. Whoever was doing this a complete unknown, moving silently through the community, like a rat through a sewer. Anyone could be a suspect. She pointed to the crowd. "And they need to stay out of the way. Don't go giving out information about the case. It'll only come back to bite us in the end." Whatever game this killer was playing, Charlotte didn't want to do anything that could egg him on. No doubt he was enjoying watching them flounder.

"It was just—"

"I assume you know where Robin lived?" Charlotte interrupted.

Mona nodded. "I do."

"Then let's go. We're losing time."

EIGHTEEN

Charlotte couldn't keep her mind from racing through the details of the case as she drove. The paintings, the mutilations, the careful staging—it all pointed to something much deeper than a simple murder. But the question that kept gnawing at her was *why*. Why had Robin painted those images, and why had she been the target of such a gruesome game?

Beside her Mona was quieter than usual, and Charlotte couldn't help but think it was because of what had happened at the gazebo. Perhaps she had been harsher than she should have been, but there had been a serious breach of security, one that could compromise the integrity of the case. Not to mention that now word was out, it would make their job that much more difficult. She had come here hoping for an easy win to hang her hat on and had ended up with something much more complex and sinister. And it was beginning to test Charlotte in ways she hadn't been tested in years. The puzzles, the bodies, it all pointed to something, and she was getting more frustrated by the hour that they weren't coming up with any answers. As much as she didn't want to admit it, this case might not go as she'd hoped. There was a very real chance she could leave Oak

Creek with more questions than when she arrived, and the last case of her career would end up a colossal failure.

As they pulled up in front of Robin's home—which bore more than a passing similarity to her mother's house—Charlotte forgot all about the gazebo. Something was off. The front door was closed, but the faintest glimmer of movement inside caught her eye. One of the curtains swayed back and forth as though someone had been standing there. She slowed the car to a stop, glancing over at Mona.

"Did you see that?" Charlotte asked, her voice low.

Mona looked up, having been lost in thought herself. "What?"

"Someone is in the house," Charlotte said, her thoughts returning to when they had found the door to Robin's studio ajar. Maybe they weren't as far behind this killer as she had initially thought. "Get ready."

Mona snapped to attention, her face full of determination as Charlotte killed the engine.

They exited the car in near silence, their movements smooth and practiced. Charlotte drew her gun, holding it close to her body as she moved toward the door. Mona followed, her own weapon at the ready, covering Charlotte's back. Whoever was inside, they couldn't afford to lose them. This might be their only chance to shut this thing down right now. Charlotte took a deep breath, steadying herself. A ribbon of pain shot up her arm, as if to remind her she couldn't count on herself in situations like this. She was too frail.

Stop it, she told herself and tried to regain her focus. It wouldn't do either of them any good if she couldn't keep it together. *Victor was a fluke. You can do this.*

Ignoring the pain, Charlotte carefully tried the doorknob, finding it unlocked. That was a relief. She wasn't confident she had the power to kick the door in if necessary. She exchanged a glance with Mona, who gave a small nod. With a quick motion,

Charlotte pushed the door open, slipping inside with her gun raised.

It wasn't immediately evident that something was wrong until she saw the cushions on the couch had all been upturned. And the console that held the TV had been pulled away from the wall near the curtains. That must have been what she'd seen from outside. Sounds of rustling came from somewhere deeper in the house.

Charlotte moved through the front hallway, her heart pounding in her chest. "Cover me," she whispered to Mona, who nodded and took a defensive position by the door.

As Charlotte rounded the corner into the living room, she saw a dark form standing over the dining room table, their back to them. His hands were spread in front of him and he was hunched over the table. The only light in the room was from the flashlight sitting on the table beside him, providing only a small glimmer of light from which to read. But given his position, he was backlit, and Charlotte couldn't see his face.

Her instincts kicked in. "Freeze!" she shouted, leveling her weapon at him.

The figure turned and stumbled back at the same time, knocking over the flashlight so it hit the floor, rolling away. The lights above them came on and Charlotte blinked in surprise to find Adam staring back at her, his eyes wide as he took short, panicked breaths.

"Bellinger?" Charlotte said, lowering her weapon. "What the hell?"

Beside her, Mona lowered her weapon as well, but she was staring straight at him. "I may not have been here for a few years, but I still remember where the light switch is."

Adam's gaze darted from Charlotte to Mona, his expression a mix of anger and desperation. "Are you going to shoot me?" he spat, his voice trembling.

Charlotte hesitated a moment before holstering her

weapon. "Depends. Tell us what you're doing here." Teens could be unpredictable. She'd had her fair share of run-ins with them over the years. It was hard to tell on which side they might fall. Those who had been hardened early were the most dangerous and she didn't have a good read on Adam. Not yet.

Some of that anger she'd seen before returned as soon as the guns were away. "I told you I wasn't going to just sit around," he said. "I'm doing what you should have been doing in the first place. Trying to find out who took her. Who... killed her."

Mona stepped forward. "Adam, this isn't the way. You can't just break into her house and start tearing it apart. You need to leave this up to us."

Adam's face twisted with emotion, his hands clenching into fists. "Because you really came through on your promise and found my sister before they killed her, right?" He moved to take a step forward, then seemed to think better of it. "You don't understand."

Charlotte could feel the tension crackling between them. Not only had someone leaked the information about Robin, but here was her brother, actively contaminating what could be considered a crime scene.

"I do," Mona said.

"No, you don't," he yelled. "You didn't live in the same house with her. You didn't get angry with her or call her names when all she was doing was trying to help." A tear welled and fell down his cheek. "You weren't the one who pushed her away because you figured she'd always be there and you could apologize later. Don't you get it? I can't tell her I'm sorry. Not ever!"

He was working himself into a frenzy, which only made him more unpredictable. Charlotte needed to put a stop to this, right now. "You're under arrest," she said, pulling a pair of handcuffs out of her back pocket. The boy's eyes went wide as soon as she approached.

"Wait, what?" he shouted.

"Put your hands behind your back," Charlotte said.

"Mona!" Bellinger protested.

"Detective, maybe we should—"

"He's compromised a potential crime scene," Charlotte replied, her voice hard. Adam's outburst had reminded her too much of Haley. Of how they'd left things. "Which makes him a suspect."

"Suspect?" Bellinger shouted, his voice higher. "She was my *sister*. All I'm trying to do is find out what happened to her."

"Did you tell anyone about what happened?" Charlotte asked.

"No, why would I?" he replied. "It took me half the day to find the freaking key to this place buried in my mom's junk in the garage." Tears had begun to fall freely down his cheeks. Finally, he exhaled and sank into the nearest chair, much like his mother had done in her own home the night before. "Fine. Do whatever you have to do." He held out his hands.

Charlotte paused. Part of her wanted to cuff him and haul him in, but that wouldn't do them any good. Bellinger was just looking for answers. Maybe in the worst way possible, but still, Charlotte couldn't help but feel pity for the boy. Maybe because she didn't want to cause him more pain. He wasn't her daughter, and she couldn't let her personal feelings interfere with the investigation. "You said you needed to find the key. So the house was locked when you arrived?" He nodded. "And was anything out of place when you got here?"

"I—I don't think so. I haven't been here in a while. But it was all very neat."

She put her handcuffs back in her pocket. Bellinger stared at her for a long moment, his breathing heavy. "I had to do *something*," he mumbled. "I can't just sit in that house... with my mother... Do you know what it's like to listen to someone who won't stop wailing?" All the hardness in his face disappeared, and for a brief moment he looked no older than twelve.

He was nothing but a child, and he'd suffered an unimaginable loss.

"I'm sorry," she replied. It wasn't Bellinger's fault they couldn't keep a lid on this case. "But do you realize you may have compromised evidence that could have been left by the killer? You've obstructed this case, intentionally or not."

"I swear I was just trying to help," he replied weakly.

Charlotte surveyed the damage. "A lot of that going around, apparently." This was exactly what she was afraid of. The more people that knew about this, the harder it would be to track down their killer. "Did you at least find something useful?"

He shook his head. "I thought maybe if there was something she was hiding... like some money or... I dunno. I started looking behind the furniture..." He trailed off, his eyes unfocused.

Charlotte exchanged a glance with Mona. The boy was fragile, and the subject matter wasn't exactly pleasant, but in her experience, teen boys didn't have a problem with grotesque things. And they needed answers. She pulled out her phone, showing him a photo of the painting they had found. "Do you recognize this?" she asked gently.

Bellinger looked up, his brow furrowing as he studied the image. "No," he said, shaking his head. "Is that one of hers? It looks familiar... but I've never seen that one before."

"Did you know she painted things like this?" Mona asked.

"Why... does it have something to do with what happened to her?"

Charlotte sighed, her frustration bubbling beneath the surface. "Perhaps. But we don't know why she would have painted just these two in such a... macabre manner."

"Sometimes she took commissions," he offered. "Maybe someone paid her to paint them."

Before Charlotte could respond, Mona left the dining room. "Where are you going?" Charlotte asked.

"To check her computer," Mona replied from further in the

house. Charlotte followed along while Bellinger picked up the slack behind her. The short hallway led to a bedroom that had been turned into an office. It didn't appear that this one had been touched yet, and Charlotte pulled out a pair of gloves, slipping them on before flipping on the nearest light.

On the right side of the room, bookshelves filled the entire wall, full to the brim with books of all shapes and sizes. Not only were there fiction titles, but also a lot of art books, most of them with little stickers on the spines, indicating they probably came from the library or a thrift store.

"A reader, huh?" Charlotte asked, glancing at the titles. Mona was already in the only seat in the room, which sat in front of a desk holding a small laptop.

"She always had her nose in a book," Mona replied, typing a few of the keys to wake up the computer.

"Gloves," Charlotte said.

Mona stopped, her hands frozen in the air above the keys. "Shoot. I'm sorry, I just got so excited—"

"Here," Charlotte said, handing her a pair.

She slipped them on before continuing. "Detective, I—"

"Just keep going," Charlotte replied. "Do you even know how to get into that thing?"

"I think so," Mona replied.

"How?" Bellinger asked from the doorway. "Even I don't know her password."

"It's oh-eight-two-seven-oh-six," Mona said as the computer unlocked. "It always has been."

"How do you know that?" Charlotte asked, her attention pulled away by the mood board hanging above the bookshelf. All of the images were of a darker nature. A woman reaching out from the shadows; a dark, wooded area with a person standing in the distance; the crescent moon; two hands almost touching; and finally, a knife being used as a pen, carving words into a wall. In fact, all of the décor in this room was of a darker nature. The curtains were purple velvet and despite the lights being on, the room had a heaviness about it that Charlotte couldn't explain.

"It was the date she adopted her first dog," Mona replied. "Biscuit."

"Oh yeah, Biscuit," Bellinger said, his voice a little lighter.

Charlotte turned to him, remembering herself. "I think it's time you left," she said, her tone firmer now.

"I can't leave," he protested. "I haven't finished looking yet."

"You can either leave here on your own, or I pull out the handcuffs again. It's your choice," Charlotte replied.

Bellinger's eyes flashed with anger, but he didn't argue. "Fine." Charlotte escorted him to the front door. "By the way, thanks for nothing."

Charlotte grimaced. "We're going to find out who did this."

The boy scoffed. "Sure. Just as soon as you solve your other murder."

"Adam—"

"Save it," he replied. "You cops are all alike. Just a bunch of bullies who can't be counted on." He stormed out the door and away from the house, headed in the opposite direction of their car.

Charlotte sighed, watching him skulk away. Nothing she could say would ever make it better for him; she just hoped he found a way to deal with his anger. Her own daughter had left in much the same way, full of anger and resentment. If he continued down this path, Adam would lose the one family member he had left.

Once she closed the door, she decided to take in the rest of the house before returning to Mona. The kitchen was clean and tidy, not a utensil out of place. Bellinger's refrigerator was mostly bare, indicating she didn't do a lot of cooking at home. Across from the office was the woman's bedroom, which was similar in décor to the office. Her bedside drawers didn't reveal much other than a few personal items, and nothing that would indicate anyone else had been there. Though there was a photo tucked inside, of her and Adam, both a few years younger, arms around each other and smiling for the camera, both of them soaked from head to toe and in swimsuits. In the background stood a waterfall and a natural pool, the environment lush and green. It had obviously been taken by their mother, probably recording a rare moment of joy.

Charlotte took a picture of the photo. As she replaced it she noticed a pen near the small lamp. When she opened the drawers again, she shuffled through the items inside, but there didn't seem to be anything to write on.

"Mona," she said, returning to the office. "Did Robin keep a diary or journal?"

Mona turned in her seat. "She used to. Back when we were younger, she always had one with her. She liked freewriting. Always said it helped her clear her mind."

Charlotte examined the room again. "Did you see one anywhere? It's not in her bedroom."

Mona shook her head.

Charlotte pinched the bridge of her nose. They'd have to notify Whittle he had another scene they needed to examine. If there was even the possibility her journal had been stolen from this house, then whoever stole it might have left some trace evidence behind.

"This is taking forever," she muttered.

"What?" Mona asked, her attention back on the computer.

"We are never going to catch up to him if we keep getting bogged down like this. Please tell me you've found something useful."

"Nothing yet," Mona said. "I have access to her email, but I don't see anything about any secret commissions. There was one from the mayor a few months back, to have her do a mural in the high school auditorium. And there was another by a well-known philanthropist—but he lives in Denver. It says here she shipped his paintings to him. It's possible she was in contact with someone through a message board or private website. But something like that will take time to find. It wouldn't necessarily show up in her email."

Charlotte looked over the woman's shoulder as she went through email after email. "Dammit. I don't know, this feels... wrong. Like we're looking in the wrong place."

"What makes you say that?" Mona asked.

Charlotte returned to the bookcase, looking through all the titles. "I just don't like feeling as though I'm being yanked along like a puppet on a string. Someone is out *there*, orchestrating all this, and I don't think we're going to find the answers we need *here*." She stared at the mood board again. Along the edge, something looked to be peeking out from the back. She furrowed her brow, then pulled the board off the wall, turning it over.

"Oh my God," Mona said behind her.

On the back was a completely different "board" of sorts. Except all these images were much darker, much more graphic than the ones on the front. If those had been dark, these were downright *scary*.

"These have to be from the dark web—where else could she have found images this... disturbing?" There were photographs of mangled body parts, of people who had been in accidents, or who had hurt themselves in different ways. It was enough to turn Charlotte's stomach.

"They look like those two paintings," Mona said.

"Inspiration, perhaps?" Charlotte asked.

"Look, there are numbers on the bottom," Mona said.

"They're years." Each one was marked by a specific date. "This isn't something recent. Did you know about this?"

"No, never," Mona replied. Her face was drawn in worry,

almost anxiety. For the first time, that mask of hers had begun to slip. But it was enough for Charlotte to notice.

"What was she painting these for?" Charlotte muttered, frowning at the board.

Mona's brow furrowed in thought. "Robin always expressed her feelings through her art. When she was happy, she would paint bright, colorful scenes. Beautiful landscapes. When she was sad or angry, her work would be more muted. Darker."

Charlotte studied the board. "Then what was she feeling when she painted the images we found?"

"Despair," Mona said. "Anguish."

"Did she have a therapist that you know of?"

Mona hesitated. "Perhaps Dr. Pekannen? It would have been convenient, since she was right above her shop. There are a few others in town we could check with, but we'd never—"

"No, doctor-patient confidentiality, I know," Charlotte replied. Even if they found Robin's therapist, they'd never be able to access her files. "Let's go back to the paintings. We think he took at least one from the studio. I haven't seen anything that would indicate she kept them here. She must have other works that aren't on display. So if they're not here and they're not at the shop, where are they?"

"Hang on," Mona said, turning around in the chair again and typing away. "Let me check something." A few seconds later she hit the enter key. "Yep, here we go." She smiled as she pulled up a specific email.

Charlotte leaned over her shoulder to get a better look.

On the screen was a rental contract for a storage unit.

NINETEEN

Charlotte and Mona arrived at the storage facility just as the sky was turning a dusky gray. The ominous clouds had obscured the sun, threatening the bad weather that was sure to be approaching. The facility itself was small, no more than a collection of corrugated metal units surrounded by a chain-link fence with a single gate set behind an old neighborhood of homes. The kind of place no one really paid attention to.

Charlotte's fingers drummed impatiently on the steering wheel as she stared at the office, a run-down shack with a blinking neon *Open* sign. Inside could be the answers they'd been looking for. Or just another dead end. She was growing more frustrated by the second by the lack of answers on this case and her unease surrounding Robin was only growing. What they'd found at her house had been disturbing to say the least. There was no telling what Whittle and his team would unearth, as soon as they caught up to their backlog. She could feel time running short. If they didn't figure out the location of the second painting soon, they'd have another body on their hands.

Thankfully, Franklin had obtained the warrant for the

storage unit quickly, and Charlotte's gut told her that whatever was inside was going to bring them closer to the truth about Robin. She just didn't know if she was ready for what they might find. She flexed her hand out of habit.

"Everything okay?" Mona asked from the passenger seat, her eyes scanning the facility.

"Yeah," Charlotte muttered, cutting the engine. "Let's get this over with."

They stepped out of the car and made their way toward the office, the gravel crunching under their feet. As they approached, Charlotte noticed a figure lounging on a chair just inside the doorway. The storage unit manager.

He was a thin, wiry man, probably in his sixties, with a thick, scraggly beard that looked like it hadn't been trimmed in years. His face was deeply lined, like a road map of bad decisions, and he wore a trucker hat that had seen better days. His name tag, haphazardly pinned to his shirt, read *Elmer*.

"Afternoon, ladies," Elmer drawled, barely glancing up from his newspaper. "Y'all here to rent or what?"

Charlotte pulled out the warrant, holding it up so he could see it. "We're here to search one of the units."

Elmer squinted at the paper, then let out a long, low whistle. "Ah, shit. Guess it had to happen sometime."

"What do you mean?" Mona asked.

"Figured one of these assholes would do somethin' illegal eventually," he said, opening a drawer and removing a set of keys and a pair of bolt cutters. "Just wish it'd happened on my day off. Y'all gonna need records?"

"No, we know the owner," Charlotte said. "We just need access."

Elmer checked the map he had pinned to the wall. "Unit 34, right?" Charlotte nodded. "Follow me."

They followed him across the gravel lot to the unit in question. "Here, hold this," he said, pushing the bolt cutters into

Charlotte's arms. He then went to work fishing out the right key from the ring of fifty. Trying three different keys before he found the right one, he finally popped the lock on the unit and removed it. He then took the bolt cutters back. "Thank'ee. Have at it."

"What were those for if you didn't have to cut the lock?" Mona asked.

"Sometimes owners don't leave a copy of their key. Or they use the kind that only has a combination, no key. Paranoid, I guess. But they forget all it takes is a clip from ol' Betsy here to open their units. Ain't no more secure than a cow pasture, really. Anyway, lemme know if you need my help. I'll start drawin' up the paperwork to close the unit." He turned and ambled back toward the office.

Charlotte shot Mona a glance as the other woman shrugged. She then pulled open the heavy metal door, revealing the contents inside. At first glance, the storage unit seemed to be what someone would expect. Dusty furniture, boxes labeled *Kitchen* or *Winter* along with a few other odds and ends set up on a storage rack. The air smelled faintly of paint thinner and dust.

"Doesn't look like much," Mona said, stepping inside.

"Keep a sharp eye," Charlotte replied, scanning the space. It was clear someone had been here recently as there were marks in the dust where boxes had been scooted around. But had that been Robin? The front office didn't have any cameras, neither did the units, so there was no way to tell. Charlotte rolled her eyes. *Small towns.* The fact was she'd gotten used to seeing cameras everywhere in the city. She'd come to rely on them. Not having them in this case was a growing problem, and could even be part of the killer's agenda.

They split up, each taking a different side of the unit as they started sifting through the shelves and boxes—and this time, Charlotte made sure both of them were wearing gloves before getting started. But as she searched through box after box, finding nothing more than old clothes or knick-knacks that had more than likely been forgotten, she couldn't help but feel that same sinking feeling that it was another dead end. Robin's house had been immaculate, but all of these boxes were filled with clutter. Was that because Robin couldn't bear to throw it all away? She didn't want it in her home, but she couldn't bear to discard it either. The more she learned about this woman, the more intrigued she became.

Charlotte was about to give up and move to another section when she heard a faint, hollow *thunk* from Mona's side of the unit.

"Detective," Mona called out.

Charlotte approached Mona to find her crouched near the back wall, running her fingers along the seam of what looked like an ordinary shelving unit. But as she knocked on it again, the sound was off. Hollow.

Charlotte moved closer, her pulse quickening. "A false wall?"

Mona nodded, her face tight with concentration. She pushed against the shelving unit, and after a bit of effort, it slid aside, revealing a hidden compartment behind it. The sight that greeted them took both women by surprise.

Dozens upon dozens of canvases were stacked inside, crammed together like forgotten memories. Each one was more disturbing than the last. Dark, twisted figures. Grotesque, nightmarish scenes. Images of pain, suffering, death.

Mona stood frozen for a moment. Her eyes were wide as she took in the sheer number of paintings. "They're like the others... and the board in her house... You were right, she's been doing this for years."

Charlotte's breath caught in her throat. "There are so many," she muttered, stepping forward to pull one of the canvases from the stack. The painting depicted a figure, arms outstretched, surrounded by a sea of red, as though it were drowning in its own blood.

"These definitely aren't commissions," Charlotte said quietly. "Robin wasn't painting these for anyone. This was something else."

Mona's hands trembled as she reached for another painting, this one even darker, more grotesque. "Look," Mona whispered, her voice barely audible. "Each slot has a number."

She was right. Below where each painting was being stored was a small four-digit number, all of them sequential. "They're dates." It seemed Robin was meticulous. Just like she'd dated her images, she'd dated each of her works in an efficient catalog system.

Charlotte's mind raced. Robin had been hiding these paintings from everyone—her family, her clients, maybe even parts of herself. She must have been using them as some kind of outlet, a way to deal with whatever pain or darkness was consuming her. What could have caused her so much torment? Whatever it was, Charlotte couldn't imagine something so terrible that the only way to process would be to paint such disturbing images. And that still didn't explain who had taken such an interest in them now. Or why.

"None of them have the markings on the back like the other two," she said, inspecting one painting after another.

"It wasn't her signature," Mona replied, though she was staring at the stack of paintings, as if she was trying to divine something just by looking at them.

"We need to call Franklin. All these need to be catalogued and entered into evidence."

The other detective didn't respond.

"Mona?" Charlotte asked, her voice softening.

Mona shook her head, her lips pressed into a thin line. "It wasn't me," she whispered, her voice thick with regret. "Her pain... I never saw it. I was her friend. I should've been there for her."

Charlotte watched her carefully, noting the way Mona's shoulders slumped, the way her hands clenched and unclenched at her sides. This wasn't the same Mona who always had a smile plastered on her face, the one who could turn her emotions off like a switch. Finally, the real woman was beginning to show through.

"What do you mean?"

Mona turned to her, tears in her eyes. "I thought... I thought when Mrs. Bellinger said—that Robin was withdrawing that it was because of me. That she'd started painting these... horrors... because I wasn't there for her. But these dates go back long before we became estranged. She started doing them while we were still friends. And I never saw it." She hung her head.

"She hid it from everyone," Charlotte said gently. "You couldn't have known."

Mona didn't look up. "But I should have."

Charlotte sighed, glancing back at the paintings. "Don't beat yourself up over this. She went to great lengths to conceal these. It was obvious she didn't want you to know. *No one* could have predicted this was what she had been hiding."

Mona nodded slowly, still staring at the images in front of her. "There's one for every month for the past three years," she said, her voice hollow.

Charlotte felt a chill run down her spine. "Three years of misery," she murmured, carefully pulling out different examples. The subjects in each painting seemed only to endure more torment as she went on. "Three years of pain... and they only got worse." This was the work of a woman fighting demons... and losing.

"What happened three years ago?" Charlotte asked.

"Nothing," Mona replied. "Nothing significant, anyway. But something must have. And she never told me."

They stood in silence for a moment, the entirety of Robin's suffering staring them in the face. As much as it unnerved her, Charlotte knew they'd have to go through each painting, one at a time. Maybe even get an expert in here to figure out if there was any pattern in the paintings, anything that might give them a clue about Robin's state of mind, or who she might have shared this secret with.

"There are some missing," Mona finally said.

Charlotte glanced up, nodding. "The two we have back at the station."

"No, look," Mona said. "Two others. We're missing four in total."

* * *

It was like Mona couldn't breathe—like a thousand-pound elephant was sitting on her chest and was pressing harder and harder.

As she watched the techs pull out each painting and place it in a protective plastic bag before adding a corresponding number to it, her vision began to swim. They'd been here for two hours already, directing the extra people Whittle had brought in on how to catalog and organize all the paintings, all the while taking photographs of each of them. But the longer it had gone on, the more despair and anguish Mona had seen in the paintings until it had just become too much, and she'd had to take a break.

She bent over, trying to catch her breath. Why was it she could look into the eyes of her dead friend's corpse and not be bothered, but the sight of all these paintings was giving her a mild panic attack? What sense did that make? Maybe it was because Mona had been with her when she was making these paintings and never knew about it. She had been so blind to her friend's pain in those moments. It was possible Robin had gone home and painted after their nights out, her pain pouring from the paintbrush onto the canvas, perhaps even her anger at Mona for not seeing what was right in front of her face. How could anyone forgive that?

Seeing Robin's body hanging up there, while terrible, wasn't as bad. Because that wasn't her anymore. She was already gone. But having been in her presence and betrayed her in such a way made Mona's heart ache like it never had before.

"Hey there," Detective Dawes said, and suddenly she was holding Mona up. "Here, sit down before you collapse."

"No, I'm okay," Mona protested, but allowed Dawes to help her sit on the ground anyway.

"Can I get some water over here?" Dawes called out. A moment later, Mona felt the cool liquid coating her throat.

"Just sit for a second," Dawes said, crouching in front of Mona. "You're okay. Breathe."

Mona took a few deep breaths, which was easier now that she was sitting. "I'll be okay."

"You're about to hyperventilate," Dawes replied. "Trust me, I've seen it enough. You just need to take a few minutes. Let the team handle the storage unit."

The Oak Creek Police Department had responded to their call in record time. Whittle had arrived with his associates, all of them shooting glances at Mona and Detective Dawes, no doubt for giving them the biggest workload they'd ever seen.

Even Sheriff Franklin was at the scene, coordinating with the help of Detective Dawes. But Mona found all she could do was stand there and watch as they packed up Robin's things, all headed for the evidence locker.

Three years. She'd been painting those back before she and Mona had their falling out. And she'd never mentioned them to Mona. Were these paintings what had gotten her killed? And could Mona have prevented it if she'd only known?

Without meaning to, tears began to fall from Mona's cheeks.

It was so surprising that she thought she had accidentally splashed some of the water from the cup on her face.

"Mona?" Detective Dawes asked, locking their gazes.

"Detective Dawes... can I tell you something?" she finally said.

"I think we can drop the formalities," Dawes replied. "Just call me Charlotte."

She was so supportive, so understanding. Why couldn't anyone else be like that around Mona? She knew she wasn't the easiest person to get along with, despite always trying to have a smile and a friendly demeanor. But that only seemed to drive more people away. And despite Mona's flaws, Detective Dawes hadn't given up on her. Not yet anyway.

Mona thought back to the paintings and finally pulled her gaze away from her new partner. "I think I know why she started painting these."

Detective Dawes took a seat next to her and they both watched the team pack the boxes. She didn't pressure Mona for more information, she just waited. Mona appreciated that, because she wasn't sure how she was going to say this. She'd forced it down for so long, it was difficult to put words to it.

"Um... you said you wanted to know what happened between me and Robin. I wasn't exactly honest with you before. We didn't just drift apart. About a year or so ago—" Her voice cracked and she had to take another sip of the water. "A year ago she told me..." Mona took a deep breath. She could do this. It was okay. Dawes was a friend. "She said she had something important to tell me about her father."

"Her father?" Dawes asked.

Mona nodded. "I remember she wouldn't make eye contact with me. She kept looking away... He abused her. During most of her childhood."

The other woman didn't say anything. Just looked straight ahead. "She confessed that I was the first person she'd ever told.

I'm not even sure *why* she told me. We'd been celebrating her store opening and we'd both been sharing some wine. She just... came out and said it."

"She must have trusted you a lot to be that vulnerable," Dawes said softly.

"That was the problem," Mona replied. "She trusted me."

Dawes narrowed her gaze. "You didn't—"

"No," she replied. "You're the first person I've ever told. I swore I would take it to my grave."

"Then what—"

Another tear fell from Mona's eye. "I didn't know how to handle it," she confessed. "I didn't know what to say. Sheriff Franklin is the closest thing I've ever had to a dad which wasn't the same thing at all. So... I just... I just pretended like it wasn't a big deal, that she could get over it."

Mona glanced over to find Detective Dawes—Charlotte— staring at her. "My entire life, my mother always told me things would work out just like they're supposed to. That there was a plan—so that's what I grew up believing. I'd never dealt with anything like that before and I'd only been on the force a short time then. And I just... I just—"

"You turned your emotions off. Pretended like nothing was wrong."

Mona nodded, more tears coming. "I think I crushed her spirit that night. She was looking to me for compassion, for understanding, and I just continued like everything would be fine. That it was all part of some predetermined plan. I... discounted everything she'd been through because I didn't know how to deal with it." She took a few more deep breaths. "After that, she stopped talking to me. I would go to her house and she wouldn't open the door. She blocked my number. I think... I think all she saw when she saw me was someone who didn't care enough to acknowledge that an awful thing had happened to her. Like our entire friendship had been a farce.

"But it wasn't like that at all. I just didn't know how to process it. I mean, how do you fix something like that? I don't know why it's so hard for me to face tough emotions, I've just always pushed them away. For a long time I thought it was a benefit. Until that night. And I guess... I guess I thought she knew that about me. That there was something wrong with me. What did she think I would say?"

"We all have our own ways of coping," Charlotte said. "Maybe your way wasn't the way your friend needed. She wasn't looking for you to fix anything. Just to listen. But that doesn't mean you're a bad person or there's something wrong with you."

"That's just the thing," Mona replied. "I think there *is* something wrong with me. Who does that to their best friend? I didn't fight to get back in her life because—deep down—I knew I deserved to be shunned."

"Listen," Charlotte said. "This is a hard job. And we see a lot of hard things. It's not a crime to insulate yourself from some of them. You'd go crazy if you didn't. Hell, if I could do what you do, I'd have a lot fewer nightmares, that's for sure. I'm sure if you could have sat down with Robin and told her what you've told me, she would have understood."

"I don't know. I thought we understood each other, but maybe I was just lying to myself. Maybe she just put up with me because there was no one else around. But now it's too late," Mona said, her voice barely above a whisper. She put the cup down and instead pulled her knees up to her chest, wrapping herself in the smallest ball she could.

Minutes passed without any words between them. Had she really just opened up to the woman who solved the Don Perlinio case? Charlotte was the first person she had felt truly comfortable with since... since Robin. It was a strange world sometimes. Had someone asked her a week ago if this was where she'd be, she wouldn't have believed it.

Finally, Charlotte spoke up. "I know how it feels to be an outsider. I pushed everyone around me away, never accepting they could just love me for who I was. I always needed to do *more*, to be *better*. And what did it get me in the end? A pat on the back and a cheap gold watch."

"Do you regret it?" Mona asked.

"Every day," she admitted. She rubbed her hands on her knees. "But the world isn't going to stop for me and my problems. I can commiserate when I'm dead. What we need to figure out is *why* Robin started painting this series. What drove her to it?"

"Her relationship with her father, I assume," Mona replied.

"Okay. But he's been dead for how long—a decade? Why did she suddenly start painting these three years ago? What happened?"

She thought of the grotesque images she'd seen in the other paintings. It was clear Robin had been suffering. And given the nature of each of the pictures, she hadn't been getting any better. "I wish I knew."

"Do you think she was suicidal?"

"I think she was more traumatized than I ever realized," Mona admitted.

"Whatever the reason, our killer has decided to take things a step further and use them as his calling card." Beside her, Charlotte took a deep breath. "With two more paintings missing, it means we're possibly looking at two more victims. He planned this from the start. It was never just about Robin. He's going on a spree."

"How do we find him?" Mona asked.

"I wish I knew," she replied. "No one seems to recognize the location of the second painting. Without that, we're dead in the water."

Mona turned to her partner; a thought came to her. "Remember how I said she always painted in series?"

"Yeah," Charlotte said. "You're thinking maybe she—"

Mona shot up. "Maybe she used the same location more than once." They both rushed over to where the team had begun stacking the paintings as they were pulling them from the unit. "Here, arrange them in order."

"What are you two doing?" Franklin said, walking over as Mona and Charlotte began spreading out the paintings on the gravel.

"We're missing June of '22, September of '22, March of '23 and December of '23," Charlotte said once they were all spread out.

Mona scanned the paintings, then pulled up the image of the one found at the barn. It looked to her like it would fit in the September '22 slot. She carefully examined the paintings in July, August, October and November of that year.

"There," she said, pointing to November. "That looks like the same location, just a different angle." In it, the same chaise lounge from the previous painting was in the center of the picture, but instead of a figure lying across it, the figure was now standing on it, holding what looked like their own eyes.

"I think you're right," Charlotte said. "The ceiling matches."

"Wait," Mona said, her heart in her throat. "I know where this is. We need to go. Now."

TWENTY

The bright light of the community center welcomed them from the road as they pulled into the parking lot. Charlotte and Mona had left the storage unit in a hurry with a contingent of officers on their tail, all of them arriving at the same time. Charlotte stepped out of the car, motioning for everyone to circle up behind one of the patrol vehicles. She directed two of the officers to take up positions across the street and keep their rifles trained on the building.

There was no telling what they would find in there. But Mona had been insistent the painting was from the building's top floor, as she'd recognized the shape of the windows in the next painting in the series. She'd told Charlotte it was a place both she and Robin had frequented in their teens as a good way to get away from everyone for a while. Apparently, it had been a refuge for both of them from the stresses of the other kids. From the constant bullying. On the way over Mona had described how they used to each bring a stack of books and read them together, letting their imaginations run wild with the stories. There had been a smile on her face as she told the story, clearly a happy memory.

But when they pulled up, the conversation died as Charlotte stared up at the windows along the top floor. There was no mistaking them—a dead match to the ones in the paintings.

"Okay," Charlotte said with Mona at her side. "We have no idea what we're walking into here. Whoever is doing this, they're smart. Keep a close eye for anything that looks out of place. Watch for trip wires. Assume your life is in your hands because it is."

"Isn't that a little extreme?" one of the officers, Roberts, asked. He and his partner had both been at the site by the river. "Do you really think they trapped the building?"

"I don't know what they've done," Charlotte admitted. "But given what we've seen so far, I wouldn't put it past them. Just watch your six and stay in pairs. Each team will take a floor. Alberhasky, Roberts, you're on ground. Nichols, Drew, second floor. Detective LaSalle and I will head to the top. Understood?"

"Yes, ma'am," they shouted in unison. Whatever qualms the department had once had about Charlotte's presence had dissolved once Robin's body had been found. Apparently, once this case exploded into more than just a dumped body, people stopped being so petty. They realized Charlotte was there to help and thankfully—for the most part—allowed her to do her job.

Charlotte turned to the community center, its wide windows reflecting the pale light of the streetlamps outside. The building was technically on the verge of closing for the night, but a few cars remained in the parking lot. They needed to get anyone still inside the building out—in the small chance this really was a trap.

They split up, each team approaching the building from different angles, headed for different entrances. Charlotte and Mona headed for the south entrance, crouched low as they ran across the open parking lot. Despite having rifles trained on the building, Charlotte wasn't taking any chances. Still, she couldn't ignore what had become a constant ache in her fingers. Ever since Robin's house with Adam, the sensation hadn't completely gone away. This was the longest it had lingered, and Charlotte had no choice but to ignore what that meant for her, long term.

As they reached the door, Charlotte glanced back at her partner. Mona gave her a supportive nod, but there was a new kind of tension in her—a vulnerability that hadn't been there before. Gone was the overly cheerful mask that had unnerved Charlotte. Now Mona looked more human, more real. And despite the gravity of their situation, the fact that Mona had opened up to her meant Charlotte was more comfortable with the woman watching her back.

"There should be a staircase right inside the door," Mona said quietly, her voice tinged with something akin to nostalgia. "It'll lead to the third floor. This is the door Robin and I used to use. We'd sneak up to the attic to hang out, away from everyone."

Where before Mona had been an impenetrable wall, now the cracks were starting to show. This case had hit her hard. The revelation of Robin's pain had shattered something in her.

"Take point," Charlotte said, motioning Mona forward. "I'll be right behind you."

"You sure?" Mona asked.

"Don't argue." The fact was, Charlotte wasn't sure she trusted herself to take a shot if the situation arose. Despite her state, Mona was still a solid detective. Charlotte trusted her aim over her own for the moment.

They approached the entrance with weapons drawn, the quiet hum of the nearby heating units adding to the tension in the air. Mona nodded to Charlotte and pulled the glass door open, sweeping the inside of the building before whispering a quiet "all clear." She crept forward with Charlotte on her tail, finding the stairs right where she said they'd be.

Down the hall, Charlotte caught sight of the other officers coming into the main foyer, heading in different directions. She held a silent hope they weren't about to find another body. But a part of her suspected they were already too late. Whoever had orchestrated this was clever, and he wouldn't lead them somewhere by accident.

On the second landing, Mona stopped, causing Charlotte to come up short behind her. "What is it?"

"Civilian... maybe," Mona whispered. Charlotte climbed two more flights of stairs and caught sight of a man in a chair not far away, scanning his smartphone. Headphones covered his ears. At least... that's what it looked like from here. But they couldn't take anything for granted. Charlotte nodded for Mona to approach while she brought up the rear.

A shout from one of the teams below caused the man to lean forward, removing his headphones when Mona was only about halfway there. Apparently, the teams downstairs had found someone. The man in the chair made a move to get up. "Stop right there," Mona ordered him, her weapon trained on him.

He turned, and his eyes went wide, his hands shooting up. "W-what's going on?"

"Sir, stay there," Charlotte said, coming around Mona, both of their weapons on the man. She approached slowly. "Identify yourself."

"Stanley. Stanley Cromlish," he said. "What—"

"Mr. Cromlish, I'm going to need your full cooperation," Charlotte said. "Get down on the ground, interlock your hands and place them on the back of your head. Do not make another movement—do you understand me?" The odds Cromlish was their killer were low, but Charlotte wasn't about to make any assumptions until they were sure. The fact was, they were dealing with someone so unhinged, he might very well wait for them to arrive in person, pretending to be someone else.

"I don't understand," Cromlish replied. "What did I do?"

"Get down on the ground, right now," Charlotte commanded.

The man seemed to realize if he didn't comply, he might never walk again. He nodded quickly, falling to his knees and interlocking his hands behind his head.

"All the way," Charlotte added. Cromlish went to the ground, face first. Charlotte heard a whimper. He might have accidentally broken his own nose.

She circled around him, pulling the pair of cuffs from her back pocket and holstering her weapon as Mona kept her weapon on the man. She cuffed him quickly, pulling his arms behind him. When she lifted him back up, sure enough, his nose was red with blood.

"Damn," she said. "Get someone up here to help him," she told Mona. The other woman holstered her weapon and called down over the railing for one of the other officers. A moment later Nichols and Drew appeared at the stairs.

"Take care of Mr. Cromlish's nose," Charlotte said. "And hold him until we've cleared the building."

"Roberts found another couple downstairs," Nichols said. "And the janitorial staff."

"Keep them all outside until you hear from us," she ordered. He and his partner took Cromlish by the arms and led him to the stairs, as the poor man kept his head back, blood covering his face.

"We need to get to the top," Charlotte said.

They made their way to the staircase that led to the top floor. Unlike the rest of the staircase, this part was older and not open to the public. As they climbed, Mona's voice broke the tense silence.

"I remember we used to think it would break under our feet

every time we came up here," she said quietly. "It's only occurring to me now that she probably suggested we come here so she didn't have to go home as often. It worked out for the both of us —both our moms often worked evening shift, which meant we could spend as much time here as we wanted. And trust me, we spent *a lot* of time here."

Charlotte grimaced. Ever since Mona had revealed the circumstances of Robin's abuse, it had been in the back of her mind. And it was clear that the abuse went far deeper than anyone could have ever expected, especially given the subject matter of Robin's paintings. She had been dealing with some strong demons, and if painting was her outlet, Charlotte wasn't sure it had helped. If only she had spoken to someone other than Mona. If Haley had ever been through anything like that...

The truth was, Charlotte didn't know much about her daughter's life anymore. She had been an overly independent child, which had only been exacerbated by Charlotte's behavior. And Charlotte couldn't say for sure something like that *hadn't* ever happened to her. If it had, it was unlikely she'd tell her estranged mother. But it made her wonder, how much had Mrs. Bellinger known about the abuse? Or Adam, for that matter?

They reached the attic door, an old wooden slab with a rusted handle. It looked untouched at first glance, but the dust around the knob had been disturbed. Someone had been here recently.

Charlotte's pulse quickened as she reached for the door. She motioned for Mona to draw her weapon again, as she did the same, poised to move.

With a swift motion, Mona pushed the door open. Charlotte's breath caught as the hinges groaned in protest. The air inside was musty, thick with the smell of dust and decay. But it wasn't the smell that stopped Charlotte in her tracks.

It was the scene before her.

The attic was large, filled with old furniture and forgotten storage. But at the center, draped over a dilapidated lounge chair, was a woman's body. Her limbs were splayed, her palms facing upward, each marked with a deep, deliberate X. Her lifeless eyes stared up at the ceiling, and her face was frozen in an expression of haunting stillness.

"Jesus..." Charlotte said, forgetting for a moment they hadn't secured the scene. Instinctively she ducked down, as if expecting someone to swing something at her from the shadows. She and Mona moved around the scene, but there was no one else there. The room was otherwise empty.

It had been as Charlotte had suspected. They were already too late. She holstered her weapon as she approached the body, the air tinged with the coppery tang of blood. Unlike the open nature of the barn, this room was much smaller, and thus the smell was much more pungent.

"Please tell me that's not who I think it is," Charlotte said. The woman was completely nude, her blue eyes open wide, as if the last thing she ever saw was an unspeakable horror. The glasses she'd been wearing when Charlotte had last seen her were nowhere to be found.

"Dr. Pekannen," Mona said, stepping forward, as if drawn to the scene.

"I don't understand," Charlotte said, her mind feeling like an impenetrable fog had settled over it. Where before she thought she was making some progress, this made no sense. "Why would he kill *her*? Did Pekannen know about the paintings?"

Mona didn't answer. She was staring at the body, but not in the same way she had "studied" Robin's body. Her eyes were beginning to water, and Charlotte recognized the telltale signs of someone on the verge of breaking down.

Before that could happen, Charlotte guided her away from Dr. Pekannen to the side of the room, turning her away from the body. It was a stark contrast to how Mona had responded to finding Robin's body. It was as if opening up about her relationship with Robin had broken something in Mona—something that allowed the grief inside.

"What's wrong with me?" Mona asked, pleading. "I don't understand."

"It's a completely normal reaction," Charlotte replied, once again thankful her new partner was showing more of her human side. It was perhaps a cruel thing to wish for, but that cold detachment of hers had unnerved Charlotte. Seeing Mona like this was reassuring in a strange way. "Give yourself a few minutes. I'm going to take a look around."

"No, I can help," she protested. Charlotte leveled her gaze with the woman, who was wiping away the tears. "I've got control of it."

"It's okay if you don't," Charlotte said, softer.

"I'm good," the other woman replied after a moment. "Let's get to work."

Charlotte nodded and began to search for anything that stood out about the scene. The X marks on the woman's wrists, for instance. The cuts weren't deep enough to be the cause of her death; instead, she thought they were purely aesthetic. To match the second painting. He had staged her precisely, mirroring the painting down to the smallest detail. If there was a message here beyond that he had an uncanny ability to mimic the paintings in real life, it was lost on Charlotte. Unless he was just taunting them—showing them what he could do—how much control he possessed.

For a few moments the women stood in silence. Charlotte's mind was going a hundred miles per hour, trying to figure out how Dr. Pekannen fit into this narrative. Was he choosing his victims at random? Or was there something connecting them?

"The only thing that makes sense," Mona said, "is Robin

must have confided something to her. Either professionally or just as friends."

"You think she knew about the paintings?"

"I don't know," Mona replied. "But before we... before everything, she had mentioned to me that she was thinking about therapy. She thought she needed help. I hope she did. I hope she found some peace."

Given how the paintings only seemed to get more disturbing as they went on, Charlotte wasn't sure that was the case. But if Robin was seeing Dr. Pekannen, then that might be the connecting thread between them. The question then became: How would the killer have found out about that? Doctor-patient confidentiality would have prevented him from uncovering any files. Unless... Robin had been the one to tell him. And maybe not directly. She thought back to the missing diary from her bedside table.

That was the disturbing thing about this killer. He seemed to know more than he should—more than anyone should. It was something that had begun to gnaw at Charlotte like an unrelenting mosquito. Nothing about this case was regular. And frankly, it was beginning to strain the limit of what she considered plausible.

"Okay, let's assume—for argument's sake—Robin was seeing Dr. Pekannen," Charlotte said, finally turning away from the scene. "How does killing her fit into our unsub's plan?"

Mona shrugged. "Maybe he's killing anyone who knows about the paintings?"

"Why would he do that?" Charlotte asked. "Why does he care?" She rubbed her temple, the acrid smell of the blood in the room only serving to piss her off. They were up to three bodies and still no answers. The only reason she could conceive their killer would want to eliminate anyone who knew about the paintings was because he wanted to cover up their origin. But they already knew Robin painted them. If that had been the goal, it had failed miserably. "It doesn't make sense."

"Or—maybe he thinks the paintings are about him," Mona suggested.

"What kind of egotistical—" Charlotte stopped short, staring at Mona. "You said Robin's father was dead. Are you sure?"

"Yeah, he died when she was a teenager," Mona said.

"How?"

"A car accident of some kind," she replied. "I'm not sure of all the details. But I remember going to the funeral."

"Was there a body?"

"Detective, I don't mean to sound... combative, but are you suggesting Robin's *father* killed her?"

"Was there a body in the casket?" Charlotte demanded.

"I don't know. It was closed. They said the accident was pretty bad."

"I'm not leaving anything to chance," Charlotte said, pulling out her phone. "Not anymore. I want to pull the reports on this man's 'death.' And if we have to go exhume a grave to make sure, we will."

She pulled out her phone to call the precinct to inform them of the discovery. As she did, Mona stepped closer to the body. Charlotte paused, watching her. Mona was inspecting the woman's neck. "Detective," she said. "Look at this."

A ring of bruises circled around the woman's neck, similar to that Whittle had showed them on the decomposed corpse. "A match to our Jane Doe?"

"It looks similar," Mona replied. "Maybe the same kind of rope."

Charlotte nodded. "I'll take care of Franklin. You call Whittle. Tell him he's got another long night ahead of him."

TWENTY-ONE

Mona checked her phone. It was closing in on 11 p.m. and she could feel the exhaustion in her bones. The day had been one thing after another. And they were still no closer to finding the person responsible for all this.

Ever since finding Robin's mood board, Mona had found it harder and harder to keep her head clear. Not only had she never faced a case with so many variables, but she had erroneously assumed she'd been the root cause for Robin's descent into madness. And while that wasn't the case, if she'd figured out what was going on before Robin started painting, maybe none of this would have happened. But more than that, it felt like something had cracked deep within Mona, breaking open a part of her she didn't know still existed. Where before she could do her job with impunity, now she found herself questioning everything, most of all herself. Maybe Franklin had been right: She might not be the person for this case, given how it was beginning to affect her. And the worst part was, there didn't seem to be anything she could do about it. An ache had developed deep within her chest, one that felt like it would never go away.

It was a sensation she hadn't experienced in a long time. And she was having trouble figuring out why. Normally, she would have gone to her mother with something like this, but given how things were going on that front, it wasn't much of an option anymore. This was something she'd need to figure out on her own.

After discovering the body of Dr. Olivia Pekannen, they had secured the scene and returned outside to interview the few civilians that had remained in the building near closing time. Detective Dawes had called to get the coroner's report on Robin's father, while Mona had gotten in contact with Whittle to let him know they had yet *another* scene he needed to process.

It turned out the man who had accidentally broken his own nose trying to comply with their orders was a teacher at the local high school and had a rock-solid alibi for the time of Robin's disappearance. He was also part of the coaching staff for the basketball team and had been at the game all Friday night, working with the team to beat the Killoway Knights and had come to the community center to review some online papers from his students.

The other two people that had been apprehended were the night janitor, who had just come on his shift and hadn't been there more than ten minutes when they arrived, and an elderly couple who had stayed late organizing an upcoming charity drive. None of whom fit the profile of the killer they were chasing down.

Detective Dawes had confessed to Mona that she believed if they didn't make progress soon, a case of this magnitude would draw the attention of the feds, and they would come in to take over. Which meant their already tight clock had just sped up. Regardless of her feelings, Mona *needed* to be the one to solve this case. If for no other reason than to let Robin's spirit rest in peace. She may have failed her friend in life, but she wouldn't now... not again.

What was really bothering her, though, was how the killer seemed to have some deep knowledge about Robin that no one else seemed to possess. She kept secrets from those closest to her, yet she was willing to open up to a random killer? It didn't make sense. Not unless he tortured her for the information, but how would he have even known about this darkness inside her?

As she and Detective Dawes returned to the attic with Whittle's team, it was clear that the constant deluge of work was beginning to take its toll on them as well. Whittle even mentioned calling in a few more favors just to get more bodies out here to process everything they had gathered so far, given the punishing workload. For a town that only had one or two murders per year, three bodies in as many days was extreme.

Even worse, the media had picked up the scent of the case, though they didn't know all the details, thankfully. All they knew was a body had been found by the river, and two more had been discovered in town. Franklin had still been at the storage unit when Detective Dawes spoke with him. He made it clear they needed to keep a lid on as much of the case as possible. The town was already on edge after learning about Robin. He complained he'd have to hold a press conference sooner or later, unless he wanted people beating down his door. A second murder of a local would only send everyone into a panic. No additional details, no talking to reporters. They also didn't need some crazy copycat seeing the story on the eleven o'clock news making their jobs harder.

As Mona climbed the stairs, returning to the top floor with Detective Dawes, she could feel the weight of her eyelids beginning to win out.

"Detectives? Over here," Whittle called out just as they reached the landing. Mona followed Charlotte as they made their way over to the man. "I'm beginning to get PTSD every time I see the two of you." He pulled back the cover on one of the old pieces of furniture a few feet from the chaise longue to reveal something underneath.

"Shit," Detective Dawes said. "He's leaving a goddamn trail of breadcrumbs."

Before them was yet another painting, presumably one of the missing ones from the storage unit. Mona squatted down to look at the painting that had been deliberately propped up underneath the sheet. The subject in this one was against a dark background, the body having been impaled by two sharp spears, angled into an X shape as they stuck out from the ground. It hung limp from the spears and Mona couldn't determine from the brush strokes whether the victim was male or female. It was similar to one of the images from Robin's mood board, taken from the internet. It was almost as if she was copying the grotesque images, looking for... something. Inspiration? The style of this one was messier—more frantic than the last. Like Robin had been unraveling as she painted it. That ache in her chest deepened.

"I think I already know the answer to this, but do you recognize the location?" the senior detective asked.

"No," Mona admitted. "But maybe we can do the same thing. Put it back in the sequence. See if it reveals anything." Detective Dawes turned the painting over, revealing another one of those strange symbols on the back.

"They have to mean *something*," she said.

She remained convinced it wasn't a signature of Robin's but looking again, somehow, it seemed vaguely familiar. She'd seen it somewhere before. Maybe researching an old case? "I'll send it over to Michaels—see if he can come up with anything."

Her partner nodded. "Bag it and tag it," she told Whittle. "We'll add it to the pile." She cursed as she turned, walking away.

It was obvious that this case was taking its toll on the older detective. It was taking its toll on all of them. Mona followed, trying to catch up with her. "There's nothing else we can do," she said, causing Charlotte to turn to her.

"I don't accept that," she replied. "There must be a way to get ahead of this guy. To figure out what his ultimate game is. Why only four paintings? Why not take them all and go on a town-wide killing spree? And why these specific four? He has an endgame in mind. And we need to figure out what that endgame is before anyone else gets hurt."

"How are we supposed to do that?" Mona asked. Charlotte finally stopped walking, but she didn't turn around. She just stood there for a moment. Mona had asked the impossible question.

"There *has* to be a pattern," Charlotte finally said. "There's always a pattern." She turned to face Mona, her eyes tired and sunken back into her head. "I just can't see it yet."

Mona nodded. Obviously, the bodies of Dr. Pekannen and Robin were of the same nature, recreations of subjects in paintings done by Robin. And the marks around Dr. Pekannen's neck could be a match to the Jane Doe's, but they wouldn't know for sure until Whittle did a full autopsy. Until then, there was still no direct evidence that it connected to the other deaths at all, except for coincidental timing. But it had led them to a much larger investigation. Mona couldn't believe they all weren't related in some way.

"We'll need to inform Dr. Pekannen's family," she finally said. "I think her daughter lives in Savannah."

Something about Mona's words had caused Detective Dawes to stop. "She had a daughter?"

Mona nodded. "I knew her, briefly, when we first moved here. She's a little older than me. Moved away when she went to college."

The older detective paused, leaning against the nearest wall. It was like the fight had gone out of her. "Are you okay?"

"Fine," she replied, still facing away from Mona. "I've been thinking a lot more about family since taking this case. It's not something that normally happens." Mona couldn't really add anything; she knew exactly how that felt. She couldn't help thinking about her own mother whenever she thought of Robin, as so much of their childhoods had been intertwined. Of how much time she had spent at Mrs. Bellinger's house or how much Robin had spent at hers. But one thing this case had reminded her of was that she still had the capacity for empathy. And now that she had felt it, she didn't want to lose that lifeline.

"You have a daughter, don't you?" Mona asked.

"Depends on who you ask," Detective Dawes replied. She turned around to find Mona's face drawn in confusion. "Ask my daughter, and you might get a different answer. But yes, I do."

"I guess you're not close."

A wistful look came over the older woman's face. "I'm not sure we ever were. She always complained—rightfully so—that I put my cases before her. I regret it, and at the same time, I'm not sure I know how to be any different."

"What about her father?" Mona asked.

"Happily remarried," she replied. "Which is just as well. Ronson and I... we never really fit. It was a whirlwind romance, one that burned out quickly. I don't resent him for leaving. And I don't resent Haley. I've just always been a better cop than wife and mother."

Before Mona could respond, her phone buzzed in her pocket, the sound cutting through the tension. She pulled it out, her stomach dropping when she saw the name on the screen.

Mona's heart thudded painfully in her chest as she answered. "Mrs. Bellinger?"

The voice on the other end was strained, filled with worry. "Mona, I... I'm so sorry. I wasn't sure what else to do. You told me to call if something... I'm just beside myself here and I can't..." She sounded like she was on the verge of hyperventilating.

"It's okay, Mrs. Bellinger," Mona said, struggling to keep her voice level. "Just slow down and tell me what's going on."

"I can't find Adam," she said. "I've tried calling and calling, but he won't answer. And he hasn't been home since yesterday."

Mona's heart thudded in her chest. Her eyes wide, she put the phone on speaker so Charlotte could hear and the moved into a quiet corner of the attic. "Okay," she said. "When was the last time you saw him?"

There was a pregnant pause on the other side of the line and Mona could imagine Mrs. Bellinger trying to maintain her composure. "Last night. He went out, said he'd be back later. I ended up going to bed. When I checked this morning, his room didn't look like he'd come home. I figured maybe he was out blowing off steam with his friends. But he's not answering his phone and I don't know where he could have gone. Mona, you don't think—I mean after what happened to Robin—"

"Mrs. Bellinger, this is Detective Dawes," Charlotte said. "I'm here with Mona. What time did he leave?"

"Maybe an hour after you came by? I'm not sure... I've just been so..." She trailed off.

"That's okay," Charlotte said. She gave Mona an encouraging nod for her to go ahead and reveal what they knew.

"We just saw Adam a few hours ago," Mona said. "We found him at Robin's house looking for anything that might help the investigation. But we informed him it was best if he went home, which was what he led us to believe he would do."

"Oh, God," the woman on the other end cried. "I can't lose him too, I just can't. Mona, you *have* to find him. Please. *Please*." The desperation in her voice was palpable.

Mona's throat tightened. She glanced over at Charlotte, who had stopped pacing, her attention fully on the conversation now. She felt that familiar pull, the mix of guilt and fear twisting inside her. "We'll track him down for you," she promised, her voice steady despite the knot in her chest. "What kind of car does he drive?"

Mrs. Bellinger quickly gave the details—the beat-up silver Pontiac they had seen when they'd arrived at the house had been his. Mona scribbled the license plate down on the back of her notepad. "I've got it. We'll get the information out to the station immediately."

"Mona, please. I just..."

"I know," Mona replied. "As soon as we hear something you'll be the first person I call."

When she hung up, she turned to Detective Dawes, who was shaking her head. "He's not missing. He's angry. I'm sure he'll go home when he cools off."

"She's scared," Mona protested. "Isn't it concerning he isn't answering her?"

"A teenage boy not taking a call from his mother? No."

Still, Mona felt a pinch deep in her gut. She'd feel better if they knew where Adam was, just in case. "We still don't know how the killer is choosing his targets. What if Adam is next on his list?"

"You think he knew about the paintings after all?"

Mona shrugged. "If so, he might be a potential target."

Dawes sighed. "To be on the safe side, get a BOLO out on his car," she said.

Mona immediately stepped out of the attic, making the necessary calls. Each word felt heavier, each second longer than the last as she informed dispatch and sent out the alert. When she returned to the attic, her partner was waiting, her expression unreadable.

"Not good," she said, her voice tight. "If this killer is targeting people connected to Robin... people who might know about the paintings..."

"We'll find him," Mona said, though she wasn't sure who

she was trying to reassure more—herself or her mentor. She didn't allow herself to consider what would happen if Adam did become the next victim. If she let those thoughts into her brain, they could cripple her. Especially after what she'd seen done to Robin and Dr. Pekannen. Adam was just a kid. Maybe he was a hundred-and-ninety-pound, six-foot-one kid, but a kid all the same.

"The more I think about this, the less I like it. He's angry and already not in a good headspace," Dawes added. "Someone could easily bait him into dropping his guard."

A surge of adrenaline flooded her veins, obliterating the former tiredness. "I need to go," Mona said, and turned for the exit.

"Go where?" the woman said behind her.

Mona headed for the staircase. "To find him. I promised his mother."

"Mona, we've been going full throttle all day," she said. "The BOLO is out there. In a town this small, patrol has a better chance of finding him than you do."

"But maybe not quickly enough," Mona replied. "I need to be out there. I wasn't there for Robin. I need to be there for him." She paused. "You go back and get a few hours' sleep. We can join back up later."

Detective Dawes sighed, looking off to the side before resolving something in herself. "No, I'm coming."

"You sure?"

"Yeah, just feeling my age," the woman replied. "Youth. Don't take it for granted." Mona noticed Charlotte flex her hand again. Though she wasn't even sure the woman knew she was doing it.

As they headed out to the car Mona could practically feel the situation pressing down on her. This case was spiraling, and now Adam was potentially caught in the middle of it.

And deep down, she couldn't shake the feeling that they were still just following the killer's plan, step by step.

TWENTY-TWO

The headlights of the car barely cut through the thick night, casting weak beams of light across the empty streets. The clock on the dash ticked over to 4.16 a.m., and Charlotte couldn't remember the last time she'd felt this exhausted. Her eyes were dry, her fingers ached for no discernible reason at all, and her mind was sluggish, weighed down by too many hours of dead-end searches and empty roads.

Beside her, Mona slumped in the driver's seat, her face pale under the dashboard lights. Neither of them had spoken in over an hour. They had been driving in silence, each of them too tired to muster up conversation, fueled only by the dregs of coffee and energy drinks they had guzzled over the past five and a half hours. Fast food wrappers littered the floor at Charlotte's feet, crumpled remains of greasy burgers that had done nothing to stop the gnawing fatigue.

"Okay, I'm calling it," Charlotte said. "We've been around every corner of this town and not a single sign of him. He's not here."

"I can't give up," Mona said. "I promised her. Let me drop you off, I'll—"

"Mona," Charlotte said, placing her hand on her partner's arm. "Face it. Either he's hiding, or someone is hiding him. And the chances of us just happening upon him are close to nil."

Mona didn't respond. Her eyes were fixed on the windshield, watching the darkened storefronts roll by as she turned down another empty street. The possibility of Adam's involvement hung between them, heavy and suffocating. They both knew the stakes. If Adam really was the killer's next victim, then they had just released him into the killer's waiting arms. He had been there, in the house with both of them and Charlotte had pushed him back out, more worried about contaminating a potential crime scene than the boy's safety. She hadn't even considered he might be a target. And if they found his lifeless body, Charlotte would never forgive herself. It would haunt her for the rest of her days, not to mention becoming her legacy. Instead of her last case being a botched drug deal, it would be a quadruple homicide where Charlotte had been an accessory.

Charlotte rubbed at her aching hand, the familiar pain flaring up again, worse than before. She flexed her fingers, trying to work through it, but it wasn't helping. She was too tired, too strung out to think clearly.

Her body was failing her, and it terrified her. Maybe she really was too old for this kind of work, too slow to keep up with a case like this. She could feel it creeping in—every missed connection, every hesitation. And now there was a boy missing, and the clock was ticking.

As they made their way back to the station and pulled into the square, a cluster of people stood close to the gazebo. At first glance Charlotte thought it might be some people from the vigil, still holding steadfast over the makeshift memorial that had been erected to Robin. However, as they grew closer, Charlotte realized that wasn't the case at all.

"What the hell?" she muttered.

Mona straightened in her seat, frowning as she took in the scene. "Is that... a mob?"

"Looks more like a horde."

As they pulled closer, the noise became clearer—raised voices, agitated tones. A group of about fifteen people—mostly men—had gathered in front of the stairs of the gazebo. And from the shouting, they were riled up about something. Charlotte glanced at the clock again. No good ever came from a group of agitated men gathering in the dark hours of the morning.

Mona parked the car on the square, and both women stepped out, leaving the engine running. The chill in the air seemed sharper now, and the tension hit them the moment they approached. Standing in the gazebo was Ken. The same friendly man who had served them coffee and chatted with them earlier was now pacing back and forth like a man possessed, gesturing wildly as he spoke to the crowd.

"They ain't doing a damn thing to stop this!" Ken's voice rang out, sharp with anger. "How much are we gonna take, huh? How many more people have to die?"

Charlotte's stomach twisted. This wasn't good. Word had spread, too quickly.

"What the hell's going on here?" she shouted, stepping up toward the edge of the crowd.

The mob turned to face them, and all eyes fell on Charlotte and Mona. The tension in the air thickened, and the friendly faces they'd seen around town earlier were gone, replaced by suspicion and frustration.

Ken's gaze landed on them, his eyes narrowing. "Look who it is! Waiting around until you find another of our community members murdered?"

Charlotte held up her hands, trying to keep her voice calm. "Ken, this isn't the way to handle this."

Ken barked a laugh. "Because your way has been so effective so far. We may seem like simple country folk to you, but we will not stand by as some psychopath picks us off, one by one. I offered you our help and you refused, and look what's happened. If you can't protect this town, we will!"

The crowd murmured in agreement, and Charlotte could feel the hostility rising. It wasn't just anger; it was desperation. These people were terrified. Both Robin and Olivia Pekannen had been beloved members of the community, and now they were gone.

"The police aren't doing anything," someone in the crowd shouted. "They're just sitting on their hands while people are dying!"

"That's not true," Mona said, stepping forward, but Charlotte pulled her back. "Don't they realize everyone is working overtime on this case?"

Charlotte could feel her pulse quicken, her exhaustion turning into frustration. "Listen to me. Vigilantism isn't going to solve anything," she said firmly, meeting Ken's gaze. "This is a police investigation, and we're doing everything in our power to find out who is behind these murders and bring them to justice."

Ken sneered, his face twisted with anger. "You're a stranger here. You don't know us. How can we count on you to protect us?"

The words stung more than Charlotte cared to admit. The truth was, she didn't know this town. She wasn't from Oak Creek, and it was becoming painfully obvious that these people didn't trust her. She may have earned the respect of those in the department, but the town was another matter. But before she could respond, Mona stepped forward, her voice cutting through the rising tension.

"She might not be from here," Mona said, her voice steady but firm. "But I am. This is my home. And I'm not going to let this town tear itself apart. Let us do our jobs. We *will* find the killer."

The crowd wavered, murmurs passing between them as they looked at Mona. There was a flicker of doubt, a crack in the mob's anger, but Ken wasn't done.

"You weren't born here," Ken said, crossing his arms. "And you haven't bled for this community. We take care of our own; we don't wait for outsiders to come in and fix our problems."

"We take care of our own!" someone echoed from the crowd, and more people joined in, nodding in agreement.

Charlotte stepped forward again, her patience wearing thin. "Anyone who takes the law into their own hands will be arrested," she said coldly. "You want to make this worse? Go ahead. But I promise you, if you start playing vigilante, you'll be behind bars before you know it."

The threat hung in the air, but Ken didn't seem fazed. His eyes glinted with something dark, something that chilled Charlotte to her core.

"And the boy?" Ken said, his voice low. "We just supposed to leave him out there to the wolves?"

Charlotte's stomach dropped.

She hadn't wanted the information about Adam's disappearance to get out for this very reason. There was only so much a town like Oak Creek could handle, and they'd obviously reached the limit. News of Adam's disappearance would only add fuel to the fire. And despite Sheriff Franklin's orders, someone must have leaked the BOLO. It didn't surprise her. Secrets tended not to stay secret very long in places like this. What would the town do when they learned of the condition of the bodies? If they were this stirred up over the murders, how bad would it be when they learned the truth?

Charlotte wasn't sure she wanted to stick around to find out.

"Mona," Charlotte said quietly, her voice urgent. "Call the

sheriff." Her eyes flitted to the station on the other side of the square. Despite the lights out front being on, the building was dark. There might be a few officers on call this late, but everyone not on patrol was probably trying to get a few hours of shuteye before beginning all over again.

"It's four in the morning," she replied.

"Do it," Charlotte replied, the energy of the mob coming off them in waves. She wasn't a hundred percent sure they were safe here.

Mona nodded, already pulling out her phone, but the strained look on her face told Charlotte there was no answer on the other side. "He's not picking up," Mona muttered, her voice tight with frustration.

"Try Ramsey," Charlotte said quickly.

Mona made the call while Charlotte kept her eyes on the crowd. There was no telling if there was a rat among them. Charlotte didn't know the people of this town well enough to know if there were a pair of accusing eyes that didn't belong. But she watched nonetheless. They continued talking amongst themselves; however, Ken's gaze hadn't left her own. He watched her intently, almost like he was studying her. She knew if she was the first one to break eye contact, it could cause an eruption. Her best bet was to project calm and order. Still. There was only so much the two of them could do.

"Ramsey, it's Mona," her partner said, her voice sharp. "We've got a situation at the square. Yeah, no, we need backup, immediately. Ken's riling up the town, talking about taking things into their own hands."

Ramsey's voice crackled through the line, but Charlotte couldn't make out his words. She was searching Ken's eyes, looking deeper, for what, she wasn't sure. But the man who had seemed so pleasant seemed to have no trouble switching over to mob boss.

"Just as backup. No one has become violent yet," Mona

replied to some question Charlotte didn't hear. "Okay, yeah. Thanks." She hung up before stepping forward.

"The police are on the way. I suggest if you don't want to spend the next six hours over at the station answering questions, you disperse and return to your homes."

"You can't arrest us for just standing here," one voice called out.

"Yeah!" another voice replied. "Do your jobs!"

Charlotte could see the situation spiraling out of control in her mind's eye. The town was angry, scared, and desperate for answers. And now, with Adam missing and the killer still out there, they were on the edge of doing something dangerous.

"You are now impeding an official investigation," Charlotte announced. "I don't know how you do it here, but in Chicago that's a Class B misdemeanor and it means a minimum of six months in prison. You're right, I'm not from here. And I'll have no qualms about arresting each and every one of you. So, you can either test me, or you can return home. It's your call."

Finally, the threat seemed to have worked as some of the air went out of the crowd. A few of the ones at the back began to head off in different directions, but Charlotte was confident this was far from over. Especially by the looks she was receiving from Ken. After most of the others had left, Ken and a few remaining men headed off in the direction of his café, where only a few of the interior lights were on. She didn't think they would back down so easily.

Just another variable they had to add to the list. But the crowd had dispersed and tensions had calmed... for now. Charlotte was satisfied that they wouldn't start roaming the town in pickup trucks with guns. At least... not yet.

"Think your algorithm could have predicted this?" she asked Mona as they headed back to the car.

"I don't know," Mona admitted. "I think I'm starting to understand what you meant by people being unpredictable."

Once they were back inside the car, the heat warming them back up, Charlotte motioned to Mona. "Better call Ramsey and get him to back off. But we'll need to keep an eye on Ken."

"Can't," Mona replied. "Backup was never coming."

Charlotte's eyebrow shot up. "Really?"

"Yeah, Ramsey said they were already stretched too thin with everything else."

"Wow," Charlotte said, impressed. "Make sure I never play cards with you. You've got one hell of a poker face."

"Thanks," Mona said, her smile returning for the first time since they'd found the stash of paintings. But there was something different about it this time. Somehow it seemed more... genuine.

But the moment was short-lived. This wasn't just about catching a killer anymore. This town was on the verge of falling apart.

And Charlotte had no idea how to stop it.

TWENTY-THREE

John stepped through the door of the small, cluttered home and locked it behind him with a quiet click. His heart was still racing from the scene at the café, the adrenaline coursing through his veins like a drug. It was exhilarating, watching the fear and anger ripple through the townsfolk, seeing the frustration etched into the detective's face as she realized how close things were to spiraling out of control.

He was really beginning to like small towns after all. The people here, while they wore smiling and welcoming faces on the outside, were really just scared, selfish creatures at heart. It had only taken a quick slip of a few details to some of the townsfolk to really get them going, though that Ken had whipped the crowd up all on his own... A welcome surprise.

"Beautiful," he whispered to himself, running a hand through his hair as he moved deeper into the house, stepping over the papers and goods that had been strewn all over the place. His mind buzzed with the electric thrill of it all. The town was cracking under the pressure. And Charlotte Dawes—this outsider—had unknowingly become his best weapon. "Did you see it?" he muttered. "They nearly pounced on her the second she arrived." He was practically giddy with excitement.

He crossed the living room, ignoring the mess, and headed toward the small office at the back of the house. It was quiet here, a sanctuary from the outside world. He liked the quiet. It gave him time to think.

Robin was already waiting for him in the room.

She sat in the corner, right where he'd left her, her pale face turned toward him, her expression unreadable. Her hair hung in dark, matted strands around her shoulders, and her skin had the sickly pallor of death. "You're not looking too good, sweetie," he said. Occasionally she would brighten—her form becoming less a pallor of death and instead regaining an ounce of the life it once had. But those moments were rare, just like they had been with Carol. What mattered was she was still here. Still with him.

"They're close," John said, dropping into the office chair in the middle of the room. He let out a long breath, leaning back and staring at the ceiling. "You should have seen it. Like a master class in strategy. A few whispers, a few choice words and everything just... *tips*." He made a motion with his hands as if he were knocking over a chess piece.

Robin didn't move or respond. She just sat there, watching.

John rubbed his face, feeling the manic energy beginning to slip from him, leaving behind a faint trace of frustration. "It's unfortunate," he muttered. "In a few days they'll have discovered all of it, and then... then we'll be done. It will be over." He leaned back, a chuckle beginning in the back of his throat. "And I just don't think I'm ready for that yet. I'm not ready to let it all go. This is too exhilarating. Too exciting."

Robin tilted her head slightly, her dead eyes watching him. *It all has to end eventually*, she whispered, though her lips never moved.

John laughed softly, shaking his head. "Yes, yes, I know that.

Of course it does. I just feel... Have I made this too easy for them? That Mona, she is quick. And she's following along exactly as she should. I suppose I just thought..." He leaned forward, staring at Robin, looking for an answer. "You know her, right? Tell me more about her. How can I push her a little further?"

The silence stretched between them, thick and heavy. John's mind raced, running over every detail of the game so far. He had laid out the clues, carefully crafted the scenes. And still, something wasn't right.

"Right. I need to go back to the basics," he muttered, more to himself than to Robin. "They need to understand... to really understand the gravity of what all this means. But there's a risk. It might push things *too far*. Or it could lead them in the wrong direction." He glanced at Robin, his eyes narrowing. "It's a gamble. But is it too much?"

Robin didn't answer, but John could feel her disapproval.

You're changing the game, she said softly, her voice like a faint echo in the room. *You're not playing fair.*

John's jaw clenched, irritation bubbling to the surface. "Fair? Fair went out the window when *Dawes* showed up. I gave them a path to follow, and they brought in that outsider. That wasn't part of the plan."

Robin's eyes flickered, her dead gaze holding him captive.

John stood up abruptly, pacing the length of the room. His mind was spinning, bouncing between frustration and excitement. He wanted them to play the game right. He wanted them to see the brilliance of it all. But maybe... maybe Robin was right. Then again, she couldn't see what he could see. She, like all of them, didn't understand. This was going to change it all.

"Listen, it's like a Dungeons and Dragons campaign," he said, his voice rising with renewed energy. "New obstacles arise, old ones fall away. The game... is unpredictable. You're on one path, and suddenly, the path disappears, having been wiped away by a magic spell. And you are forced to adapt. That's what makes it exciting. They think they know this game... I believe it's time to change their path. Because when they finally do reach the end, it will make things so much more satisfying." He turned to face Robin, his eyes gleaming. New ideas were popping into his head, new directions to follow. He needed a twist... and he knew just how he would do it.

His grin widened, the pieces falling into place in his mind. He reached into his inside jacket pocket, pulling out the diary that had directed him thus far. Inside it had been a road map to Robin's life, all of her hopes, all of her dreams... and demons. It had been the perfect tool—all he had needed to craft the perfect game around it. But now, it was time for a curveball. Push them to the breaking point. He needed to test them, really test them, to see if they were worthy of playing all the way to the end.

"They think they're clever?" he muttered to himself, flipping through the pages and pages full of handwritten memories. "Let's test that theory, shall we?" He retrieved his phone, opening the specific app he would need to make this plan work. It would be tight, but there was still time. All that was required was a little patience and the propensity for teenage angst. The latter was a given, which meant this was all but set in stone.

Robin's image flickered in the doorway, her form wavering like a candle about to go out. *What if they can't do it?*

"Then it was never meant to be," he whispered, his eyes gleaming with anticipation.

TWENTY-FOUR

Mona made her way across the parking lot to the police station as the morning sun rose over downtown Oak Creek, cutting sharp shadows across the square. She happened a glance to the empty gazebo. Some of the flowers from Robin's makeshift memorial had been trampled in the mob last night. The town seemed different this morning—harsher, in a way she'd never seen it before. It was as if these killings had transformed the town and its people into darker versions of themselves. Mona shuddered as she entered the station. She had slept, if only for a couple of hours, but it wasn't nearly enough to shake off the exhaustion that hung over her like a dead weight. Every muscle in her body ached, and her mind was still foggy from too many hours chasing down dead ends.

She still couldn't believe what they'd seen in the early hours this morning. Those had been people she'd known; that she'd sat and had coffee with, discussed their kids' hockey games with. And they had been ready to grab their pitchforks and start hunting the town like it had been overrun by Frankenstein's monster. Of course they were frustrated and scared. So was she, but that didn't mean she was about to go out and take matters into her own hands. There was no place for vigilante justice in modern society. She was just glad Detective Dawes had been there to help calm things down. Mona wasn't sure she could have handled it by herself.

After downing a mediocre cup of coffee from the machine, Mona poked her head into Sheriff Franklin's office only to find it was still empty. She hadn't seen him since they'd begun cataloging all the materials from Robin's storage unit yesterday. There must have been more there than they'd thought. And given how strapped they were for manpower; Sheriff Franklin was probably pulling double duty.

"Have you heard from the sheriff this morning?" she asked, finding Ramsey at his desk. Given how sunken in his eyes were, the man was as tired as she felt.

"No, I've been too busy putting out fires everywhere else," he replied. "I stopped by Ronnie's this morning and had a talk with Ken. He was under the impression they were on the verge of being arrested."

"If you'd seen them six hours ago, you would have agreed," Detective Dawes said, coming up beside Mona. After dispersing the crowd, they had both agreed they needed at least a few hours' sleep and showers before they could begin looking for Adam again. Her new partner was fresher faced than Mona expected. Maybe it was something that came with years late-night stakeouts and long shifts. Maybe you just got used to it.

"Don't go around threatening my townspeople," Ramsey said, turning his attention to her. "That's not how we do things."

"Tell your townspeople not to form mobs in the middle of the night and I won't have to," Dawes replied. "You ready to start again?" she asked Mona without waiting for a reply from Ramsey.

"Of course," Mona said. "Just let me grab another cup of coffee." The first one hadn't done a thing.

"I mean it," Ramsey said, apparently not liking that he'd

already been cut out of the conversation. "I'm in charge until Franklin gets back. I can send you back to Chicago anytime I want."

Going back empty-handed wasn't an option, especially not now. And it drove a pit into Charlotte's stomach to even entertain the idea. But she wasn't about to let Ramsey see her sweat.

"Be my guest," Charlotte replied. "In the meantime, we'll be out looking for the boy." She turned and headed for the doors. Mona shot a quick look at Ramsey—whose face had turned a slightly brighter shade of red—before she caught up with her.

"I really don't know how you stand working with that guy," Detective Dawes said, leading the way out to their cars.

"You don't have insufferable know-it-alls back in Chicago?" Mona asked, feeling more emboldened than usual.

"Oh, we do. They just know to stay out of my way," she replied. "Are you driving or am I?"

"Is everything okay?" Mona asked, feeling like the detective was more on edge than usual.

She blew out a short breath. "I heard back from the coroner in Kerns County on Robin's father; she sent over the report this morning. It was a meticulous and detailed account of a car wreck victim, down to the shearing effect the edge of the windscreen had separating the man's head from his neck."

Mona grimaced. It had happened before she'd become a cop and she'd never had an inclination to look into the details of his death. "Oh."

"I thought for sure I was onto something," Dawes added. "But I think we can definitely say Robin's father is *not* our killer."

"I had a thought," Mona said, hoping to change the subject as they reached her car. "Where would Adam most likely go when he's frustrated or scared?"

Her partner looked at her like she had two heads.

"His friends, right?"

"But his mother already checked with his friends, didn't she?"

"That's true," Mona said. "I spoke with her again this morning. She's already called all the parents of the friends she knows, but I'm thinking maybe there's someone else. Teenagers keep secrets, right? She might not know *all* his friends."

"So how are we supposed to find out?" Detective Dawes asked.

Mona took a deep breath. "We'll have to infiltrate." Her partner arched an eyebrow. "Sorry, I mean, we need to talk to the ones we know about, to find the ones we don't."

"The school?"

Mona nodded. "We're running out of options. None of the patrols have reported anything."

Charlotte sighed, like something was weighing her down. "Yeah. Let's give it a shot."

As they drove Mona couldn't help but feel something more was bothering the older detective. Something more than a coroner's report that disproved her theory. While she might look like she got more sleep than Mona had, she seemed distracted in a way Mona hadn't seen before. While she had often witnessed people experiencing distress or discomfort, her default mode was to ignore it and hope it went away. But she couldn't do that forever, and she didn't want to be that person anymore—the emotionally stunted detective who didn't care about anyone else around her. Working with Charlotte had helped her open up in ways she hadn't been able to before. It was strange, allowing her emotions to flow free during an investigation. It gave her a new perspective on things, allowed her to look at details in a different way, and as hard as it was, Mona liked it. If she wasn't careful, she could fall back into her old habits in no time. She needed to work to maintain what little of a breakthrough she'd made already.

"Hey," she said, testing the waters. "Is there something the matter? Something else, I mean?"

"Didn't sleep well," Charlotte replied.

"I figured you'd have slept about as hard as I did," Mona admitted. "I was so exhausted I don't even remember my head hitting the pillow." But the other woman didn't reply. Instead, she just looked out the window as they drove. "Do you want to talk about it?"

"It's nothing important," Charlotte said.

"Weren't you the one to tell me that you needed me to be honest with you about what was going on? So that I didn't freeze up at a critical moment?"

The older woman turned to her, a rueful smile on her face. "I did say that, didn't I? Guess I don't like taking my own advice." She took a deep breath. "This business with Adam... it's just bringing back some painful memories."

"Your family?" Mona asked.

She nodded. "Just thinking about Haley. She blames me— and rightly so—for not really being there for her. Says I was too focused on the job, and it only got worse as she became a teen. When I saw the anger and hurt in Adam's eyes, it was like I was seeing Haley the day she left the house for good."

"I'm so sorry," Mona said. "I had no idea."

"How could you?" she replied. "Those aren't the stories that make it into the news. They may talk about how I solved this case and that, but they never go into the deeper effects behind those cases. I ended up driving everyone away, and the shitty thing was I knew exactly what I was doing and didn't stop myself."

Mona winced at the words. It was difficult accepting someone else's pain, and not something she was used to doing. In a way, it physically hurt her. She wished there was some way she could make the detective feel better. "But look at all you've accomplished. All the lives you've saved. You're a legend. At least around here."

"That's sweet," Charlotte replied. "But it doesn't make up for the fact that my house is empty when I go home. This job... it can consume you if you let it. And soon enough, I won't even have this anymore." She made a small gesture.

"Wait—you're retiring?" Mona asked, alarm in her voice.

"It's more of a forced retirement, but yes. This will be my last case."

Mona's foot came off the gas pedal as they slowed to a stop sign. She turned to the woman. "But... *why?*"

"It's not worth rehashing," she said. "Let's just say your former partner was right, I haven't had the best track record lately. And I just finished up a case that may have cost the city a lot of time and wasted resources. And it ended without a conviction or any usable intel. As fuckups go, it was at the top of the pyramid."

"There has to be something you can do," Mona said. "Can't you appeal, or—"

"I appreciate your enthusiasm," Detective Dawes said. "I really do. But at some point, there's no use fighting anymore. I managed to snag this case by the skin of my teeth. But this is it. I just hope my final case won't turn out like my previous one."

"It won't," Mona replied, more determined than ever. "We're going to find out whoever is doing this. And no one else is going to die. As soon as we find Adam, we're going after this killer. Somehow we will track him down."

Detective Dawes motioned ahead of them. "That's the high school?"

Mona nodded. A large fence surrounded the property, and at the front gate a man in an oversized jacket sat on a chair, one leg crossed over the other. "That's Owen Tate, the security manager for the school. He'll let us in, and we can get to work."

As they were about to pull up, the radio crackled. "This is

Unit 114, calling in," the voice on the radio said. "Got a hit on that silver Pontiac, plate two-one-six-George-Ida-Sam. Location, six-one-eight-seven Olympic Boulevard. Standing by."

Mona grabbed the radio. "Unit 19, responding, that's the car. Stay there, we're headed your way." She threw the car in reverse and backed away from the school. "*Finally*. See? A little bit of luck after all."

"Where is that?" the other woman asked.

"An abandoned iron ore factory," Mona replied, though as she said it, her heart dropped. What would Adam be doing in a place like that?

Her partner must have read her expression. "Don't make any assumptions until we get there. We don't know what we're going to find. And whatever it is, we'll deal with it as soon as we arrive. How far away are we?"

"About fifteen minutes," Mona said. "It's a few miles outside of town." But her heart was hammering in her chest. It didn't make sense for Adam to be in a place like that, and the only other reason she could think he was there was because someone had *put* him there. She wasn't sure she'd be able to handle the heartbreak of Mrs. Bellinger's face if they had to tell her Adam was dead too.

Stop it, she told herself. It was like her partner said, no assumptions. They would deal with whatever they found when they arrived. Not before.

Still... it was hard not to let her imagination run loose.

TWENTY-FIVE

The abandoned iron ore factory loomed over them, a hulking skeleton of rusted beams and broken windows. It sat on the edge of town, surrounded by overgrown weeds and crumbling concrete, a place long forgotten by most of Oak Creek. Whereas it had once provided a booming and stable industry for the town, the vein must have dried up and necessitated the closing of the site. Given the condition of the building, Charlotte guessed that had been at least twenty years ago.

Adam's car sat off the side of the road, parked just outside the gates, which had been forced open.

Mona pulled up to the edge of the lot, where a lone patrol car sat, about fifty feet away from the other vehicle. The officer inside stepped out as they approached, his face tense.

"No movement around the car since I arrived," he said, glancing toward the factory. "And no sign of the boy. I wanted to wait for your call before heading in. Place like this, you never know what you'll find."

Charlotte watched her partner's face, a range of emotions running across her face all at once. While she was grateful for the changes she was seeing, she hated it was taking an event such as this to bring them out. The pain on Mona's face was unmistakable, and Charlotte really hoped they wouldn't find the boy's body inside the factory. But the pragmatic part of her knew it was already too late. This killer had been three steps ahead of them this entire time. Why should this be any different?

She scanned Adam's car, sitting there like a beacon in the otherwise deserted lot. The windows were fogged with dew, and the tires were caked in dust, but it was definitely the one they'd seen that first night visiting the Bellinger home. Based on the moisture on the car, it had been here at least a few hours, if not longer. They hadn't ventured this far outside of town last night during their search. But if they had, could they have intercepted him in time?

The inside of the car was a mess. Empty soda cans and fast-food wrappers littered the floor, and there was a faint smell of marijuana as they approached. But it wasn't the clutter that caught Charlotte's attention. It was the edge of a perfect rectangle she caught sight of right behind the driver's seat.

"Shit," Charlotte said, and fumbled to pull out a pair of nitrile gloves from her pocket.

"What?" Mona asked, coming up beside her, and gasping upon seeing the object. "Is that..."

"Goddammit," Charlotte muttered, finally getting the gloves on and trying the door, but it was locked. And none of the windows were down. "Do you have a slim jim?" she asked the officer.

He nodded and ran back to his patrol vehicle, retrieving a long, slender piece of metal with indentations on the end. He handed it to Charlotte who slipped it between the glass and the rubber of the window. She moved it around a bit before finally feeling it catch and pulled up. The button on the inside of the car popped up, and she opened the door.

Inside the smell of weed was stronger, but she didn't catch

the tang of blood. As far as she could tell, the painting was just sitting in front of the backseat, propped on its side. Reaching in, she pulled it out carefully, examining the subject. This one was of a woman on an iron X structure, being drawn and quartered. Another figure stood off to the side, operating the machine. Of the four they'd found, this one was the messiest, the faces of the subjects completely obliterated by the chaotic lines and frantic nature with which it was painted.

"I don't understand," Mona said. "What's it doing in his backseat?"

"I don't know," Charlotte said. Even though she knew there wouldn't be any fingerprints on it, they needed to bag it anyway. "I need an evidence bag." The officer trotted back to his car again, coming back with a bag that Charlotte placed the painting inside. "Get that back to evidence. We need Whittle to take a look, immediately."

"What about that?" the officer asked, pointing to the abandoned factory.

"We'll take care of it," Charlotte said, giving the car a quick examination. As far as she could tell, there wasn't anything else of note inside. The glove box only had a few registration papers and other than the cans and food wrappers, the car was empty. She snapped off her gloves.

As the officer headed off, Mona dropped her voice. "Should we wait for backup on this one? What if—what if it's like with Dr. Pekannen?"

"I don't think that's the case," Charlotte said, more confident now. The painting in the back of Adam's car was an anomaly. And the gears in her head were churning. "Plus, if he's hiding in there, it's better if it's just the two of us, right?"

"Yeah," Mona replied with some hesitation.

"If it makes you feel better, you stay out here by the car, I'll go in."

"No," she said, more resolved. "You need someone watching your back."

The iron ore plant was a massive complex of rusted metal and decaying concrete, with long-forgotten machinery scattered like the bones of some long-dead beast. The air was thick with the scent of rust and damp, and the factory itself was silent, save for the occasional creak of metal in the wind. Broken windows lined the walls of the main building, and jagged shards of glass glittered in the dirt like tiny traps waiting to be sprung.

Charlotte felt a chill crawl up her spine as they stepped inside, the shadows swallowing them whole. The place was a labyrinth of corridors and staircases, with broken equipment piled high in every corner. It was the perfect place to hide. Or to stage something horrific. As the glass crunched under their feet, all she could think about was turning a corner and finding yet another scene, this time with Adam's body skewered on two pikes sticking out of the ground. But something about this felt wrong. In the other scenes with Robin and Dr. Pekannen, they had found the bodies first, then the paintings later as clues to the next scene. This time they'd found the painting first. And it hadn't just been luck. Anyone meticulous enough to lead them through this mental labyrinth wouldn't just casually leave the last painting out for anyone to find. He would want it discovered after his most recent horror. So why the change in tactics?

"Anything?" Charlotte asked as her flashlight cut through the darkness of the areas not exposed to the outside. The factory's roof had long since decayed, leaving most of the remaining equipment to rust in the elements.

"No," Mona replied from behind her. "Something feels off."

"I agree," Charlotte said, but she couldn't put her finger on it. This didn't fit the pattern the killer had established after the first body was found. Then again, he had already changed up his tactics once, why not a second time? Whoever he was, he obviously wanted to keep them on their toes.

It's like he's playing a game, Charlotte thought as they continued to search the factory. *But he's not making it impossible for us. He* wants *us to find him, eventually.* A normal criminal would use every means to cover up his crime, but not this one. He seemed hell bent on leaving information for them to find. Not just information... puzzles.

"How good are you at brainteasers?" Charlotte asked as she continued deeper into the factory.

"I'm okay, I guess, why?" Mona asked.

"Because he's toying with us," she replied. "Leaving these cryptic messages for us to find. Hints, clues, but never enough information to track him down." She stopped, clicking off her flashlight.

"What are you doing?" Mona asked.

"Adam's not here," Charlotte replied.

"Are you sure?"

"I think it's a distraction," she said. "Look at it, a painting in the back of his car, right out there in the open? *Before* we find the next victim?"

"You're saying it's on purpose? But why?"

Charlotte went back over the details of the case so far. Could they have missed something even bigger here? Could it have been sitting under their noses this entire time and she just didn't see it?

"Who do we know who is really angry and isn't willing to hide it?" she asked. "And who is also very smart?"

Mona furrowed her brow. "Adam?"

Charlotte nodded. "What if we've been thinking he's been a victim this entire time, when he's been the one pulling the strings?"

"No," Mona said sharply. "That's not possible. Robin was his *sister*."

"I once had this case," Charlotte said, heading back to the

car as the idea formed up in her mind. "Guy killed his mother because she forgot to feed his dog when he was out of town for one day. Wrapped her up, buried her in the walls of his house. And no one would have ever found her if not for the black mold that started growing because he didn't know how to properly wrap a body. And the whole time she'd been missing he had been canvassing the neighborhood, putting up 'missing' posters, speaking with the local media... the whole bit."

"But... Adam's not like that," Mona protested. "He's not a killer."

Charlotte turned to her. "People are unpredictable. You never really know what is going on behind someone's eyes. And here's what I'm seeing. Robin's brother has a lot of anger. He's not afraid to break the law—as we saw when he was going through her house. By your own admission he also is very, very clever. Clever enough to set up false leads and make us jump through hoops." Now that she thought about it, his presence at Robin's house could have been to *intentionally* destroy evidence —anything that might have connected him to the crime.

"But what about Dr. Pekannen?" Mona asked. "Why would he—" Before she could finish the thought, her phone buzzed loudly, causing her to turn and answer. Charlotte knew Mona would be resistant to this idea, but it was an avenue they needed to consider. Adam had the means and the opportunity. He was a strong kid, and there was no doubt he could have strangled the woman left by the river. At the moment, it was just an idea. But the painting in the back of his car had given Charlotte pause. Adam may not have anticipated they'd be looking for him. He might not have found his third victim yet, and so he hadn't been able to plant the next painting.

"Yeah," Charlotte heard Mona say, but her voice was far away. When she turned to look at her, her face had gone completely white. "We'll be right there."

"What?" Charlotte asked. "What is it?"

"That was Ramsey," Mona said. "We need to get back to the high school."

TWENTY-SIX

As they pulled up to the school, six Oak Creek police vehicles were already on the site, along with an ambulance and two fire trucks. They had just been here less than thirty minutes ago and the site had been quiet. But as the security man waved them through the open gate, Charlotte reflected on just how fast things could change in half an hour.

Groups of school kids were gathered outside, all being shepherded by their teachers, while a line of cars had already begun queuing up near the side of the school where the buses operated from. Some kids had broken off from the groups and were running for their parents' cars. Some of those parents stood outside their vehicles, staring as Mona and Charlotte pulled in. And it didn't escape Charlotte's notice they were some of the same men she'd seen gathering at the gazebo, their eyes already accusing.

Mona pulled up beside one of the patrol cars, and Charlotte noticed it was the same one that they'd just seen at the iron ore factory. The painting, still in its evidence bag, leaned against the passenger-side seat.

Charlotte followed her partner wordlessly through the main

doors into the school, passing the two officers standing at the front, preventing any of the staff or children from returning inside. When Mona had received the call, the entire school was in the process of being evacuated. As far as Charlotte could tell, the school was empty of everyone except police and emergency personnel.

At the end of the hall stood Ramsey, an ashen look on his face, like he hadn't seen the sun in a month. As soon as he saw them, he began walking forward.

"How many people saw the body?" Charlotte asked as they reached the Detective.

"A couple of kids, and their teachers," he said. "They're in the cafeteria. We got everyone else out, routed them away from the gymnasium."

"What about witnesses? Security cameras?"

"Cameras, yes. Witnesses, no. I have Michaels in the security office now, compiling the footage. They think it may have happened overnight. First period gym was just beginning. That's when they found him."

Charlotte's heart was hammering in her chest, and she willed it to settle down. Beside her, Mona hadn't said a word since she'd informed her of what had happened. And now, looking at her partner, that impenetrable gaze had returned. Charlotte couldn't read her at all.

"Let's get this over with," Charlotte said. Her mood had darkened considerably, and she wasn't relishing the thought of inspecting yet another gruesome crime scene.

Ramsey led them down an adjacent hall, following the signs to the gymnasium. They accessed it through one of two pairs of double doors, leading into the large space which housed a full basketball court. Along the sides, fold-up bleachers sat unused, but the real story was at the far end of the room. The school's logo had been emblazoned on the painted concrete wall; a giant elephant looking menacing as it dribbled a basketball. In front of the logo hung the body, impaled by two of the school's flag-poles, in an X pattern. Each flagpole had been suspended from the basketball goal using heavy metal cord and the body swayed ever so slightly as they approached. Below it was a large pool of blood as it drained from the body to the floor.

Whittle stood off to the side near two paramedics from one of the ambulances. And despite his familiarity with the grue-some and unpleasant nature of his job, he looked as though he may lose his breakfast.

"Sheriff Franklin," Charlotte said, looking up at the body. He'd been completely stripped, the expression on his face twisted in agony. His eyes were still open, staring into nothing-ness and his limbs hung limp, like some sort of botched crucifix-ion. The way in which he'd been staged exactly matched that of the painting, with one small difference. In it, the spears, or flag-poles, in this case, had been driven into the ground. Here they were suspended. Charlotte assumed that was because driving them into the polished wood floor of the gymnasium would have taken some serious equipment. Equipment that may have attracted too much attention.

"I don't understand. He was just with us at the storage unit," Mona finally said softly. "How..." The word hung heavy in the air, like a lead balloon.

However it had happened, it only further cemented in Charlotte's mind that Adam may not be the victim they had assumed him to be.

"He never went home," Ramsey said, coming up beside them. Gone was the bravado and arrogance. Ramsey's features were drawn tight, enough that Charlotte could tell he was on the edge of cracking. No one had seen this coming. "I checked with his neighbors first thing this morning, when you said you hadn't seen him. No one remembered seeing his car at home last night."

"Do we know when anyone last saw him?" Charlotte asked.

"Alberhasky said he saw him leave the storage unit around eight last night, after they'd finished wrapping things up. After that, no clue."

"We need to find his car," Charlotte replied. "And we need to figure out how our killer is targeting and grabbing his victims."

"What does it matter now?" Ramsey asked. "That's all the paintings. We've already looked. There's not another one here."

"No," Charlotte replied, explaining what they'd found at the iron ore factory. While she did, out of the corner of her eye, Mona approached the body of the sheriff, looking up at it. Charlotte broke away from Ramsey and pulled Mona back in time to keep her from stepping in the dead man's blood.

"Mona, come on," Charlotte said. "You don't need to see this."

"I'm fine, Detective," she replied, her voice hard. "The poles, they must have been driven through him with some force. Look, they go through the rib cage. That would have taken a strong person."

"I know, come on," Charlotte replied. The longer Mona stayed here, the worse it would get. Charlotte had seen how she had looked up to the sheriff, how she'd seen him as something of a mentor. No doubt he'd been the one to promote her. And for someone like Mona, who hadn't grown up with a strong father figure, seeing him like this would only cause her to shut down further. Charlotte wasn't sure she could live with that.

"Can you handle this?" she asked Ramsey as she led Mona away from the scene.

The man gave her a forced laugh, though she could see the panic in his eyes. "Honestly, we're in over our heads. And whatever expertise you were supposed to lend us hasn't gotten us any closer to our killer. I've already put in a call to the FBI."

"Listen to me," Charlotte said, pointing at him. "You give this to the feds and you can kiss finding your killer goodbye.

There is a reason for all this, he has set it up for *us*. We just need to figure out what it is."

"Damn, you're arrogant," Ramsey replied. "You think this is all about *you*?"

"I know this has all been very deliberate," Charlotte replied. "He's obviously been watching us. He's trying to lead us somewhere. I just don't know where that is yet."

"And I'm not sitting around waiting to find out," the man replied. "In case you haven't noticed, we're out of our league here. This is bigger than we—or you—can handle. You think people were riled up last night? What do you think's going to happen when the town finds out their sheriff has been hung up like a Christmas ornament?"

"Fine," Charlotte said, leading Mona away. "Do whatever you have to." She grumbled as they headed back outside. Part of her was using her anger at Ramsey to distract her from the fact they'd just found another victim. A victim that happened to be a close, personal friend of her boss. But another part of her was furious at the man for being such a contrarian. First he didn't want outside help, and now he claimed was the only thing that could save them?

And what was worse, Mona seemed to have gone into some kind of trance, not saying a word and barely blinking as they headed back out to her car.

"I need the keys," Charlotte said, holding out her hand. Mona produced them from her pocket without really looking at the woman. As she started the car's engine, Charlotte caught sight of the first of the news vans pulling up and a reporter piling out, trying to get a better look at the school beyond the fence. "Shit, here we go. This town is going to start tearing itself apart soon." She turned to Mona. "Is there anywhere else you think Adam might have gone?"

"He didn't do it," she said again, softly.

"Okay, fine, he didn't do it," Charlotte replied. "We still

need to find him. Because if he's not behind this, then that painting in the back of his car could indicate he's the next victim."

It was like a current snapped in Mona and she sat up a little straighter, finally looking at Charlotte. "Yes. Right." She glanced around, looking at the groups of kids standing outside. "I—uh, I'm not sure. Maybe we go back to the factory?"

The factory had been a dead end, but his car *had* been there. Could it have been nothing more than a decoy? A way to throw them off?

"We'll run back by," Charlotte said. "But then we need to find a way to throw a net over this town. We're already sitting on a powder keg."

"Yes," Mona said, somewhat absently. "I think you're right."

Charlotte glanced at her colleague as they pulled back away from the parking lot, noticing the hint of a forced smile on her lips.

TWENTY-SEVEN

The atmosphere in the abandoned office was stale, encumbered with one too many cigarettes smoked over the years which hung around Charlotte, tainting the air. A pair of old chairs sat stacked in the corner. She could hear muffled conversations outside, a constant hum of activity. Everyone was on edge. With the discovery of Sheriff Franklin's body, more media trucks had descended on the town, meaning it wouldn't be long before the gruesome details of the case were made public.

Ramsey had already spoken to the FBI multiple times, and Whittle was working tirelessly through the autopsies, trying to pinpoint commonalities between the victims so far. For her part, Charlotte was exhausted—not just from lack of sleep, but from the unrelenting feeling of failure that had settled deep in her bones. It wasn't just her body that was tired; it was her spirit. The reality of finding body after body with no clue where to turn next was suffocating.

She glanced at her phone, the screen still glowing with her boss's name. This was not a call she wanted to make, but she couldn't put it off any longer. Her finger hovered over the call button, drawing out the moment. Better to just get it over with. She took a deep breath, steeled herself, and pressed call. The line connected almost immediately, and his voice filled the silence.

"Dawes," he said, his tone apprehensive. "Tell me you've got someone in custody."

She hesitated, trying to find the right words. She had rehearsed this conversation in her head half a dozen times, but now that it was real, everything felt wrong. Having just come from spending four hours at the scene, she could still see the chaos in her mind. The blood-stained gymnasium, the look of shock on the Oak Creek officers as they set about securing the area and the hollow stare in Mona's eyes as she tried to process what had happened. It was a look she wouldn't soon forget. And while she'd tried to distract herself by arguing with Ramsey or helping Mona process what she'd seen, it had all been a smoke-screen—a way to push off dealing with the fact the sheriff was dead.

But she could only do that for so long.

She'd known Jeremy Whiteside a long time. He was a hard man to crack, not prone to wearing his heart on his sleeve. But he was a good boss, and he'd trusted Charlotte with this job. Now it felt like everything had fallen apart, and she was power-less to stop it. She had come down here to do a job, and she'd failed, resulting in the death of her boss's colleague and friend. There was no easy way to do this.

"I'm sorry to have to tell you this. Franklin is dead," she said, her voice steady, even though her hands were trembling. "We're still gathering details. It looks like..." She paused, swallowing hard, trying to block out the image of the blood dripping down Franklin's arms and legs into small pools beneath his body.

Her practiced words died in her throat.

There was silence on the other end—for long enough she

thought he might have hung up. When he finally spoke again, his voice was thick, weighed down by the loss. "How," he said, and she could hear something breaking beneath his usual steely tone.

"The killer... targeted him. We still don't know why. He's our fourth victim."

"*No*. How did he get the jump on a veteran police officer?"

After returning to the station, Charlotte had reviewed what little footage had been recovered from the school. Most of it had been erased, except for a small section that showed a dark form dragging the body of Sheriff Franklin in through the doors around 2 a.m. The only explanation was the killer had left that section on purpose. For what reason, she wasn't sure. But it turned out while she and Mona had been out searching for Adam, the killer had been setting up their next surprise. She thought they had been so clever—that they were going to get ahead of him for once. And all he'd done was throw it back in their faces again.

Franklin's car had been found at a gas station between the storage unit and his home. Apparently, that was where he'd been abducted, but there hadn't been any evidence left behind there either. All they knew was it would have taken someone with a lot of strength and power, and the dark form on the video had looked suspiciously like a young, healthy male—though there was no way to be sure of that.

"We're still working on that," she said, and relayed what few details they had so far. "He was tired—we've all been pulling double shifts. We had no reason to think he was a target."

"I knew him almost twenty-five years," Whiteside finally said. "Stubborn, hard-headed as hell about his command style. We didn't agree on everything, but he was a good cop. He didn't deserve to go out like this." She knew he was waiting for her to reply, to prove that she had things under control, that she was still capable of doing this job. But if she was honest with herself, she wasn't sure she'd been the right person for this. And after asking for it, she had a hard time admitting she'd been wrong.

"Where are you in the investigation?" he added, as if to drive the point home. But there was something else behind his words. A fury he hadn't fully let loose.

"Ramsey has taken command," she replied, blowing out a long breath. "And called in the FBI."

"You don't think that was the right move?"

She grimaced. "I think this killer is following a specific script—playing a game. If the FBI comes in here, they're going to blast right through this, scorched-earth style and we'll lose him. He'll just move on. But if we keep playing—"

"More people will die," Whiteside said.

"I don't think so," she replied. "He only took four paintings after we found the Jane Doe. I think that means there's only one more victim. And I think that's part of his endgame. Trust me, if you want to find this guy, we have to be smart about it."

"We don't have the luxury of waiting for this psychopath to lead you to whatever impossible choice he's set up," he replied. "I agree with Ramsey. Bring in the feds. This needs to end, right now."

"But, sir," Charlotte said. "We're so close."

"Dawes, I don't think either of us expected anything like this when you asked for this assignment. And the fact is, it's bigger than any one person can handle. Hand it over to the FBI. Close up shop and get yourself back home."

Charlotte closed her eyes for a moment, taking a deep breath. This was it. The end of the line for her. She had failed to apprehend Victor Karkoff, and now she had failed to catch a serial killer who was terrorizing this small town. There would be no more chances, no more opportunities. Just days filled with mindless activity designed to pass the time. No making a difference. And she would leave the job embarrassed and ashamed. Something she'd carry with her until she reached the grave. There had to be a way to turn this around, for everyone's sake, including her own.

"I have a suspect," she said, her desperation getting the better of her.

"Who?" her boss asked, his voice cold.

"Adam Bellinger, the sister of the second victim," Charlotte replied, grimacing as she did.

"Evidence?" Whiteside asked.

"We found the last painting in his car," she replied. "They're still checking it for prints. And we have a BOLO out for him right now."

"Be straight with me, Dawes. Does he look good for it?"

Charlotte stiffened, knowing full well all they had on Bellinger was circumstantial. But at the same time, it *could* fit. He could be their suspect... but it wasn't rock solid. Still, when she thought about her empty townhome, and sitting all alone in a dark room with her failures, she couldn't imagine a worse fate. "Yes."

"Then bring him in. Immediately," Whiteside replied. "I don't care what it takes."

She didn't respond, at war with herself about how to proceed.

"Is there a problem, Dawes?" Her boss's voice hardened, turning cold, that quiet anger of his reaching a boil.

"If the FBI interferes, the kid will run," she said. "He's already on a hair trigger. The woman I've been working with—Detective LaSalle—she's a friend of the family. I believe she's the only one who can bring him in—safely."

"Then do what you have to do. I'll coordinate with the FBI, see if I can't slow them up a little. But you're on borrowed time. You need to find this kid, yesterday. Understand?"

"Yes, sir," she replied, feeling an unease in her stomach. "I'll take care of it."

"Good hunting, Detective."

The line went dead, and Charlotte let out a frustrated breath. She stared at the phone for a moment longer, as if maybe she could will Whiteside to call back and tell her not to bother—that it would be too flimsy. But he had no way of knowing that. She'd given him the name of a suspect that she wasn't sure was the culprit in an effort to save her own skin. And now she had to deliver.

She just wasn't sure if she was ready to inform Mona. The woman had already been through enough. Despite her protestations, they needed to bring Adam in, either for his own safety or to formally charge him. Something Charlotte wasn't sure the other woman would be able to handle. She was already teetering with the loss of Sheriff Franklin. This might push her even further over the edge.

But as she went over the specifics of the case in her mind, Charlotte couldn't see another way forward. At least not an immediate one. Whoever was playing this game was being very careful, very deliberate. Did Adam have the capacity for that kind of deception and ruthlessness? He was only seventeen. She hadn't seen it in him, but then how did he get one of the paintings in his possession?

As much as she hated to admit it, it really didn't matter. Until they could find Adam and question him, the evidence pointed to him as their prime suspect.

She pushed open the door to the small office, stepping out into the hallway. The noise of the station hit her like a wave, the voices of officers and ringing phones filling the space. She spotted Ramsey across the room, his face set in a grim expression. She made her way over to him, her steps purposeful, even though every muscle in her body ached from exhaustion.

"We need to find Adam Bellinger," she said as soon as she reached him. "We can't afford to wait any longer."

"Please, fancy city cop. Tell me how to do my job some more," he replied, his eyes dark. "We already have every available patrol out looking for him." He sat back, rubbing his forehead. "Doesn't matter anyway. It's about to be the FBI's problem, not mine."

"I'm glad to see you're taking the burden of command so seriously," she replied.

"Look," he replied, leveling his gaze at her. "I already have enough on my plate trying to keep this place from completely falling apart. We are stretched to the breaking point here, Dawes. In case you haven't noticed, we don't have the resources of a department like yours. Right now, all I'm concerned with is keeping things from getting any worse until reinforcements arrive. Maybe instead of standing here accusing me, you should actually be doing something useful. Otherwise, I don't know why you're still in my town."

Charlotte sneered, leaving the man to continue playing sheriff. Obviously, everyone was on edge, more than they had been with the other bodies. When they'd found the painting in the community center, there had been no indication who the next victim could have been. The fact that it ended up being Sheriff Franklin gnawed at Charlotte—it just seemed so random. The Jane Doe, Robin Bellinger, Olivia Pekannen and now Sheriff Franklin. What did they have to do with each other? This was a close-knit community, and in towns like this everyone was connected in some way. Unlike Chicago where random killings were just that: random. What was she missing that connected these people? What was the common denominator?

She sighed, drawing yet another blank. She couldn't do this alone. Mona knew this place—these people. The only problem was, Charlotte wasn't sure she could handle the emotional load.

But there were bigger concerns at the moment, and Charlotte couldn't let her personal feelings get in the way of the case, not when so much was riding on its outcome. She couldn't let this case get away from her like she had back in Chicago. She needed to close.

Which meant roping Mona back in, no matter the consequences.

TWENTY-EIGHT

Mona sat at her computer, absently tapping away, not really paying attention to what she was doing. Instead, her mind was spinning, trying to resolve everything she'd seen over the last twenty-four hours. It was like she was stuck in a bad dream, one that had crossed over into reality and that she couldn't escape from. First Robin, then Sheriff Franklin? And now Adam was missing too, and... everything was just falling apart.

Was this what it meant to be a police detective? Growing up she'd always thought it was a glamorous job, chasing down criminals and putting the guilty behind bars. But that had been on TV and in movies, and it turned out life was a lot more gruesome... and personal. She had separated her emotions from her job for a reason, but when Detective Dawes had come into the fray Mona had begun to question that approach. She saw how the woman operated, how she used her emotions to help her navigate the specifics of a case and how they helped her find her answers.

But that hadn't been the case for Mona. All she'd found when she'd opened herself up was pain and heartache. Finding Sheriff Franklin's body had almost crippled her—a loss of that magnitude would have taken her down for good if she hadn't thrown her walls back up at the last minute. Maybe keeping herself open to her cases wasn't the best idea after all. It required too much emotional currency—too much risk. Better to keep herself shut off from the world, separate, as she'd trained herself to do from a young age. Maybe that meant alienating people, but it also meant protection. That way she could never get hurt—not like she had been in the past two days.

But there was something else bubbling under the surface. Something that had been growing in the back of her mind ever since they found Dr. Pekannen. At first, she'd dismissed it as nothing but a coincidence, only for Detective Dawes's words to come back to her: *Too many coincidences make me nervous.*

The fact was, something *did* connect Robin, Dr. Pekannen and Sheriff Franklin. She just wasn't sure she was ready to face the truth of it.

But before she could consider the matter further, her partner rounded the bank of desks and took a seat next to her. She wore a grim expression, like she had more bad news to share. Mona only barely glanced at her and instead pretended to be more involved with working on her most recent string of reports than she really had been.

"Mona," the woman said. "I need to inform you that I've identified Adam as our primary suspect. And as soon as we locate him, I'll be arresting him until we can get all of this figured out. Just as a precaution."

For a second she thought about pretending she hadn't heard. But that didn't work with Detective Dawes. The woman was relentless, no matter the situation. Still, she didn't respond.

"I know that's not what you want to hear. But given how little we have to go on, and the fact that the painting was found in the back of his car, I hope you can see my line of reasoning."

"It doesn't mean he's guilty," she finally said.

"No, but it doesn't mean he's innocent either. That's why we need to find him. So we can clear all of this up."

Mona felt the detective's eyes on her—the intensity of her stare was almost unbearable. It was all she could do to force her feelings to the back of her mind and close herself off just so she wouldn't have to feel it any longer. "Then I hope you find him."

"I wanted to talk to you about that," Charlotte said, pressing even further. It was like an iron weight was on Mona's chest, and Detective Dawes was pushing it harder and harder into her rib cage. "You know him better than anyone else here. Before we were looking at a possible victim. Let's change tactics. If he were the perpetrator of all this, where might he go?"

"Why is that any different?" Mona asked. "Plus, I thought you said the killer wanted us to find him."

"Remember how I said we needed to get ahead of him?" she asked. "Maybe we did that when we found Adam's car. He may not have anticipated we would consider he might be a victim himself. And that one mistake might have given us the edge. It let us get ahead of him, to find the painting before he could take the last victim. He may be regrouping, planning his next move."

"If he's as smart as you say, he wouldn't hide anywhere I would know," Mona said.

"Aren't you the one who told me that people were predictable on some level? That with enough information, you could figure out their next moves, before they made them? Who has more information about Adam than you?"

Mona hated how Detective Dawes was throwing her own words back at her, just to prove a precarious point. She glanced back to the computer. "I don't have enough data to—"

"I'm not talking about in there," she said. "I'm talking about in here." She pointed to Mona's forehead. "You know Adam. You were best friends with his sister for a long time. You may know more than even you realize."

Mona's thoughts flashed back to her times with Robin.

Their friendship had seemed so rock solid it was strange to think all it took was one misstep for it all to fall apart. But during those good years, they had spent a lot of time together. Occasionally, Adam had tagged along. And there was one place she hadn't really considered looking, not until now. She wasn't even sure the place still existed. "It doesn't matter what you say, he didn't do it," she protested, though it was barely above a whisper.

"Then help me find him and clear his name," she replied. "For his sake, at least." Mona hesitated. For the first time since she'd met the woman, she felt like Detective Dawes was drawing her into a trap. "Look. The FBI are on their way. We don't have a lot of time. Would you rather them find him? Or us?"

Mona closed her eyes, sighing. She turned back to her computer and typed in an address, pulling up the building on her maps. It turned out the building did still exist.

Detective Dawes leaned over her shoulder. "A laundromat?"

"It's been closed for years," she said. "Robin and I worked there in high school. Sometimes Adam would tag along. It's a place he'd be familiar with, that no one might think to look." She turned to stare at Dawes. "It's the only place I can think of."

"Why didn't we look here before?" the other woman asked.

If Mona was a hundred percent honest with herself, she would have to say it was because she didn't want anyone else finding him before she did. She had considered the laundromat when she'd first planned to head out looking—*before* Detective Dawes decided to join her. But she trusted Detective Dawes... didn't she? So why did she hide this place from her?

"I forgot about it until now," Mona lied. "Just one of those things, I guess."

The older woman nodded. "Okay. Let's give it a try."

Mona grabbed on to her arm. "But just to clear his name."

Dawes winced, and in that moment, Mona saw the truth. Dawes was more interested in getting a collar than solving the case. "We'll do everything we can for him."

Mona's hand fell away as Dawes stood and made her way for the stairs. She looked back at Mona, as if to say that she could stay here if she wanted, that she'd take care of it and Mona wouldn't have to be involved.

But Mona had already let down her friend. She needed to do everything she could for Adam, no matter the circumstances.

She grabbed her jacket and followed the senior detective, her face completely absent of all emotion.

The air outside was crisp, a sharp contrast to the stifling tension that filled the car as they drove. Detective Dawes's eyes stayed on the road, her jaw clenched, her hands gripping the wheel tightly. Mona sat in the passenger seat, her arms crossed, her gaze fixed out the window. Neither of them spoke, the silence between them heavy and unbroken.

Mona's mind raced, her thoughts spinning in a thousand different directions. What if he really was part of this? How would they approach him? What could he be thinking? Despite her protestations of Adam's innocence, she didn't have a good explanation as to why his car had been at the factory or why he'd had one of Robin's missing paintings in his possession. But he had to know by now that the police were looking for him. The BOLO had gone out on all the local short-waves. And given his propensity for tinkering with anything mechanical, it was unlikely he was unaware of what was happening.

"We'll go in slow," Detective Dawes finally said, breaking the silence. "If he's in there, we don't want to spook him. We'll reserve the use of force as a last resort, agreed?"

Mona nodded, though her heart was pounding. "Agreed." The entire time she couldn't help but think this was a mistake.

She never should have revealed this option. If Adam really was here and they managed to arrest him, it would all be her fault. Her only solace was he would be safe in custody.

They pulled up to the location, a two-story building set off an old, abandoned strip mall about two miles from the iron ore factory. As soon as they pulled up, a flood of memories of the place in its heyday invaded Mona's mind. Memories of her and Robin working the late shifts, bringing in dirty laundry by the slat full and dumping it into the industrial washers. It had been an easy, mindless job, one where they could goof off together during their shifts, a reminder of better times before everything went to hell.

Back then, the laundry facility ran twenty-four seven, which had been ideal for a couple of students trying to make a little spending money on the side.

But now it sat abandoned, dark and foreboding. Most of the equipment had been removed, and there was a chain-link fence up around the building that had been cut open using a pair of bolt cutters. Detective Dawes killed the engine, and they stepped out of the car, the crunch of gravel beneath their feet the only sound in the otherwise silent lot.

"You take the lead. I'll go around back and cover the exits," her partner said, her voice low.

Mona nodded, her heart in her throat as they approached the building. She could feel the tension in the air, the pressure of what they were about to do squeezing her, like a child clutching a balloon until it popped. She took a deep breath, steeling herself as she pushed open the door and stepped inside.

The facility was dark, the only light coming from the holes in the corrugated metal roof and through the few windows that had been broken. The others were caked in years of dirt and grime. Her footsteps echoed through the cavernous space. She didn't hear anything as she walked, but she made sure to keep her steps even and deliberate. She didn't want to startle him.

"Adam?" Mona called out, her voice bouncing back to her. "It's Mona. Are you in here?"

There was a rustle of movement, and Mona's eyes snapped to the far corner where the building's offices used to be. A dark form stepped out from the shadows. His face was set in a grimace, and he held the bolt cutters in one hand. "What are you doing here?" Adam asked, though it wasn't accusatory. It was more like confusion.

"We need to talk," Mona said. She looked around the space. "I know you must be scared."

"Scared of what?" he asked.

Mona furrowed her brow in confusion. "Didn't you come here to hide?"

"No," he replied. "I'm looking for old records about Robin's time here. I thought maybe whoever took her might have had something to do with this place."

"Why would you think that?" she asked.

"Because nothing else makes sense. Robin didn't have anything worth killing her over. So, I figured someone must have had a grudge against her. Since I couldn't find anything at her house, I thought this might be the next best place to look. Maybe she had a boss or another co-worker who worked with you guys who had... I dunno... a crush on her or something." He dropped the bolt cutters. "I know it's stupid. But I didn't know where else to turn. I'm running out of ideas."

How could anyone think this boy—this child—was a cold-blooded killer? Even Mona, who had on more than one occasion been accused of being emotionally stunted, could see what was right in front of her face.

"How long have you been here?" she asked.

"Most of the night," he replied. "But there's not much here. Is that why you're here?"

Mona shook her head, giving him a small frown. "I wish it were."

"Did you and that other lady find anything at her—" The crunch of glass caused him to snap his head to the side, where Detective Dawes stood, her hand hovering near her holster. His eyes flashed.

"No!" Mona yelled, but it was too late. He turned, bolting further into the facility. "Adam!"

"Dammit," Detective Dawes said, drawing her weapon. Mona grabbed the woman's hand, causing her to look up in surprise.

"You can't shoot him."

"Detective, remove your hand from my weapon," Dawes said, as serious as Mona had ever heard her. Mona lifted her hand away. "We will bring him in, alive."

"Promise me," Mona replied.

"I promise," Dawes said. "Now, take the right, he's probably looking for another way out." She ran off after the boy. Mona flinched, then headed to the right side of the building, looking for any emergency exits Adam might want to use. But before she could spot anything, she heard footsteps above her. Looking up, Mona saw Adam's silhouette climbing the metal stairs to the landing above.

"Adam. Please, we just want to talk!"

"Bullshit," the boy replied. "I saw the look in her eyes. You came here for me, *didn't you?*" His voice dropped off as he ran further away.

Mona found the nearest staircase and raced up to catch him. More light from the broken windows reached the second landing, making it easier to see in the darkness. But it was empty. She glanced up again. He wouldn't go to the roof. Not unless...

She raced up the next staircase, bursting out into the sunlight. Adam stood at the far end of the roof along the edge, looking down. And less than fifteen feet from him on the other side stood Detective Dawes.

"Adam," Mona yelled. "Just come with us. I promise everything will be okay."

"Can't you just tell the truth for once," he yelled back. "You always *lie*. You lied about coming to help my sister, and now you're lying about helping me. I don't even know what you want with me." He took a step back toward the edge.

"Okay, okay," Mona said, holding her hand out to try and stop him. They were at least thirty feet above the ground. And as she reached the edge of the building, she could see the remains of a fire escape lying in a mess of twisted metal on the ground. There was no other way off this roof. "We found a painting in the back of your car. It matched other paintings we've found at crime scenes. We just want to know where it came from."

One look from Detective Dawes told Mona she hadn't wanted her to release that information—not yet. But Mona didn't care, Adam's life was on the line here. To her, he was the same little kid who would try to tag along with her and Robin, always wanting to join in. In a way, he was like a little brother she never had. But he wasn't a killer.

"I don't know what you're talking about," he cried out. "I don't even own any paintings—she never gave them to me." All his focus was on Mona, and Dawes had used his distraction to inch closer to him without him realizing it.

But just as Mona was about to respond, he turned his head and saw Dawes bearing down on him. Mona watched in her mind's eye as Adam's foot slipped from the edge and he went tumbling off the roof, impaling himself on the metal below.

Mona blinked and Adam still stood before them, inches from the edge. She dashed forward, using his distracted attention to grab him and roll them to the side before he could go any further. As they hit the ground, the breath came out of Mona and Adam cried out. But before she could help him up, Dawes was on him, a knee in his back as she pulled his arms behind him into cuffs.

"Adam Bellinger, you are under arrest for first-degree murder. You have the right to remain silent. Anything you say can and will be used against you in a court of law."

As she continued to Mirandize him, Dawes got Adam to his feet before offering Mona a hand. But Mona only glared at the woman as she got up on her own, a fiery anger erupting from somewhere deep within her. An anger she didn't even know she possessed.

Adam said nothing as they led him back down, and on the few times when his eyes locked on Mona's, she found she couldn't meet them. Her heart ached. She had wanted to protect him, to help him, but now, as she watched Dawes load him into the back of the car, she knew she had failed.

The drive back to the station was silent, the tension in the car almost unbearable. Mona sat in the back with Adam, her eyes on her lap, her thoughts racing. She'd wanted to assure him that everything would be okay, but she hadn't really believed that. And she knew, deep down, that he hadn't believed her either.

As Dawes drove, Mona watched the woman in the rearview mirror. She never took her eyes off the road, and it was a good thing she didn't, because if she'd looked back, she wouldn't have seen Mona. She would have seen someone completely unrecognizable.

TWENTY-NINE

"Well, that's going to be the nail in the coffin," Ramsey said, slapping down an evidence bag on Charlotte's makeshift desk. She looked up at the man.

"What's this?"

"Found it stuffed underneath the floormats of the kid's car. Want to guess what it is?"

Charlotte picked up the clear plastic baggie but recognized the contents immediately. It was a black journal, the kind you could buy at any office supply store. "Robin Bellinger's diary."

Ramsey nodded. "Complete with information about how to find the paintings in some of the entries." He handed Charlotte a file. "That's not all."

She took the file carefully, then opened it before turning her full attention to it. As she read, her eyes narrowed. "Is this right?"

"Just confirmed it myself," Ramsey replied. "Spoke with the mother *and* the therapist's assistant this morning. That gives Adam Bellinger motives in each of the killings."

Charlotte knew going after Adam had been a stretch, but she'd had a job to do. And thankfully, they'd managed to bring him in without incident, thanks to Mona. But it had caused a rift between the two women, and ever since bringing Adam in and putting him through processing yesterday, Charlotte hadn't seen the younger detective. She figured she'd just need some time to blow off steam, and in the meantime, they could clear all this up with a simple interview. She had wanted to get this over with so they could cut him loose and focus on other suspects.

But this... this changed everything.

"Have you spoken to LaSalle?"

"Tin Man? No, and I don't really care to," Ramsey replied, taking the folder and evidence bag back. "But I do plan on speaking with the DA. Maybe we can get him to cut a deal before any of this gets any worse. I'm also going to speak to the media before we interview the kid. See if I can't calm things down out there." He straightened his askew tie.

Charlotte stood. "Okay, but that's still not enough for a conviction. It's still all just—"

Ramsey turned to her, that grimace back on his face. "Jesus, will you just take the win? You were the one who fingered him, and now that it turns out you were actually right, you want to renege? How the hell does anything get done in your department?"

"I'm not convinced he's our suspect," Charlotte replied. "Maybe the evidence does fit, but that doesn't mean it's right." She couldn't help thinking back to how the killer had led them along like a dog on a leash. What if this was nothing more than another distraction? Another angle in his game?

"Out here in the real world we don't always have DNA evidence or a solid alibi. Trust me, this is as good as we're going to get. I've already informed the feds. By the way, they want to have a word with you when they arrive later this afternoon." He sauntered off with a little extra pep in his step.

"Shit," Charlotte said, gathering up her things. She needed

to find Mona. "Alberhasky," she said, sticking her head into the bullpen. "Where's LaSalle?"

"Haven't seen her," he replied. Charlotte pulled out her phone and dialed Mona's number, but it went straight to voicemail.

Great, she's ghosting me. She fired off a series of texts anyway as she headed to the desk sergeant. "Where is the Bellinger boy?"

"They just brought him to interview one," the man replied.

"Anyone in there with him?"

He pulled out a schedule. "Ramsey and Tasker are scheduled to interview him. Could be another hour or so, though."

"Thanks," Charlotte said, and headed for the interview room. Because she had been the arresting officer, she had some prerogative here. But she hadn't fought to be the one to interview Bellinger because she didn't think he'd talk to her, given their history so far. She had hoped Mona would be able to get something out of him, but seeing how things went down, his trust in her was probably all but obliterated.

But now, thanks to Ramsey, that had changed. Charlotte didn't have a choice. She needed to get to the bottom of this, right *now*.

She knocked once on the door before opening it. Inside, Adam sat with a cuff around one arm that was attached to the table. A camera in the corner of the room sat idle, its little red light on, watching.

Upon seeing Charlotte, Adam just turned to the side, obviously uninterested in anything she had to say. That was fine, because she was pretty sure if the boy *was* really innocent, he'd be talking up a storm in less than two minutes flat.

"Have you spoken to Mona since yesterday?" Charlotte asked, taking the seat across from him. No surprise, he didn't seem interested in responding. She'd hoped she might have been able to glean something from his body language, but he wasn't giving anything away.

"Okay, I'm not supposed to be in here, so I'm going to make this quick. And you're going to want to listen, because your head is on the chopping block here—get me, kid?"

He glanced her way before rolling his eyes.

"I know what your father did to your sister. I also suspect you knew about it. What I didn't know until five minutes ago was that Dr. Pekannen was your therapist."

Adam sat up straighter. "That's supposed to be private."

Charlotte held up her hand. "Your records are still sealed. Mona told me about what happened to Robin. All I know of your relationship with Dr. Pekannen is you were on her patient list. But that's part of the problem."

"Wouldn't surprise me if you broke in there and stole them," he muttered.

"Furthermore, I have *also* just learned that your mother dated Sheriff Franklin for a short time. Last year? Is that right?"

"Yeah, and he ghosted her after one date. So much for cops being the good guys," he said with all the attitude a seventeen-year-old could muster. At least now she partially understood his mistrust of cops. But his attitude told Charlotte he didn't know the full impact of what was happening around him. If he was really a mastermind killer, the fact they had figured out he was in some way connected to three of their four victims should have produced *something*. A reaction—something more than just bluster. Charlotte was getting a sinking feeling that she had made a grave mistake.

"You took your sister's diary from her house that night, didn't you?" He turned to the side, looking anywhere but at her. "I don't need you to admit it, they found it in your car. But I don't care about that right now. I'm here to warn you."

"Pssh," he said. "You're just trying to trick me."

"Look around this place—haven't you noticed things aren't exactly calm? Why do you think that is?"

He furrowed his brow.

"Both Dr. Pekannen and Sheriff Franklin are dead. Which means you have a personal connection with three of the four victims." Charlotte leaned forward as the realization dawned on the boy. "That gives you motive. And you had evidence in your possession identifying the location of your sister's paintings. At this point, they don't need more evidence. They are going to crucify you in the court of public opinion. I need to know. *Did you do this?*"

"I don't... how..." The boy began stuttering, sweat forming on his brow as he fidgeted in his seat. "Dr. Pekannen is really dead?"

"Yes," she replied, though she could tell he hadn't known. Either that, or he was the greatest liar in the history of all criminals. "I'm willing to guess you don't have an alibi for the last two days, do you?"

"I already told you; I've been out looking for the person who killed Robin. I tried to get some of my friends to go with me, but they all bailed. You *saw* me. I was at her house, looking for... something that might help." He dropped his gaze.

"That's right, we saw you," Charlotte said, lowering her voice. "And you removed something from the scene. Which, in this state, is considered evidence tampering. But that is the least of your worries. Listen to me, you need to get a lawyer. When the other officers come in here, do not answer any of their questions, do not say anything other than the word 'lawyer,' understand?"

"But... but I didn't do anything," Adam replied, all his bravado gone in an instant. Charlotte could finally see the scared kid underneath.

"That doesn't matter," she replied. "Don't let them pretend

like they're your friend. They're not. Don't talk to anyone other than the lawyer, not even your mother. *Do you understand me?*"

"I..." He winced. "Why are you trying to help me? You're the one who arrested me."

"Because someone is jerking me around here and I don't think you're devious enough to be a criminal mastermind. You're smart—smarter than a lot of kids your age. That doesn't mean you're a killer. Tell me the name of the Jane Doe down by the river."

"What?" he asked, wide-eyed.

"Yeah, thought so," Charlotte replied, silently cursing. There hadn't even been a flinch of recognition on his face. She never should have named him to Whiteside. That had been a last-ditch effort to save her own skin and now she was sorely regretting it. "I've been in this job a long time, kid. And I know a killer when I look them in the eye. That's not you. Mona was right. I should have listened to her."

The door behind her burst open to reveal Ramsey and another detective behind him, presumably Tasker.

"Dawes! What the hell are you doing in here with my suspect?" Ramsey shouted.

"Technically, he's my suspect," she said, standing and facing him. "I'm just gathering some additional information."

"You're interfering with an investigation, that's what you're doing," he said. "Did you reveal confidential information to a *murder suspect*? I'm going to have your ass for this."

"What else is new," Charlotte replied, walking past him. "Considering I'm the one who found him and brought him in—despite the fact you wanted to wait for the FBI to show up." She noticed Tasker give him a disapproving look. "I have some reports to review. Apparently, I have a meeting to prepare for."

Ramsey grumbled something under his breath that Charlotte didn't catch, but she was sure it wasn't worth hearing anyway. As she headed out, she could only hope that Adam listened to her advice. There was probably a fifty-fifty chance, given their history. Adam as a suspect had been a dubious means to an end at best, but now that he was Ramsey's number one target, she felt a deep need to defend the boy. She should have just swallowed her pride and gone back to Chicago. Now an innocent child might be convicted for murder. What was worse, the real killer was still out there somewhere and Charlotte didn't have the first idea of where to find him.

* * *

Mona sat, idly typing away at her home computer. She couldn't stand to be in that police building one minute longer, not when she'd been forced to watch as they fingerprinted and photographed Adam, his information going into the record as he was formally charged with murder.

Why hadn't Detective Dawes listened to her? It was like the woman had been on a relentless mission to take Adam down, no matter the cost. And now he would be charged as an adult, for at least one murder, maybe more. Murders she was positive he didn't commit.

Ever since moving to Oak Creek, Mona had had difficulty making friends. It had been a pattern that repeated itself over and over through her life, but Robin had been the exception. Somehow, she had been the one person that saw Mona's eccentricities as benefits rather than detriments. And in a way, Mona had been accepted as part of the Bellinger family. As her own mother's mental health waned, she found comfort and security with Robin's family. Mrs. Bellinger was like a second mother to her. And Adam had been like a brother.

As Mona stared at her computer screen, staring past the algorithms she'd built and tested as they ran scenarios over and over, she made a decision. The only way to get Adam out of this was to find the real culprit. And since there hadn't been any leads thus far, she only had one option left.

Mona opened her remote access to the department and downloaded every file available to her regarding this case, starting with the body that showed up by the river. Once she had it all in her home system, she began uploading it to her algorithm, providing it every piece of information they'd discovered so far. Places, times, medical reports, witness statements—everything. She couldn't leave anything out. She even uploaded the photographs from the crime scene.

She had sworn to herself she would never do this—never use her predictions for a real case. The software was too new, too untested to produce anything reliable. She'd been using cold case data for training purposes only. Running scenarios, marking results. Determining reliability based on the real outcomes of certain cases. And with every new data set, she'd adjusted. But a program like this was probably a decade away from anything resembling practical trials. And by using it in this way, she was violating her duty as an officer.

Was this a risk? Absolutely. And no police station on earth would sanction something like this, which is why she had to do this alone. But she had built this system from the ground up, believing that given enough data, it could accurately predict crime before it happened. They still had one more potential victim out there. And it was up to Mona to stop the killer before he struck a final time.

She was the only one who could.

As she pressed enter, watching the little wheel on her screen spin, she tried not to anticipate the results. Maybe she wouldn't get anything back at all; it might not have enough data to make a determination. Or worse, what if it decided to point the finger at Adam after all? It was just a computer, and it could make mistakes. So how much faith could she really put into the result?

Finally, the wheel stopped spinning, and the algorithm began to generate a report. Mona's breath caught in her throat, her heart pounding as anticipation and fear twisted together. Mona watched as the words appeared on her screen.

"Just as I figured," she said, looking at the report which read: *inconclusive*. So it had been a failure after all. Detective Dawes and everyone had been right. What prompted her to think she could predict crime anyway? But as she was about to turn away from the screen, she saw an additional report at the bottom stating *more information required*. Below it were images of four symbols—symbols Mona had only barely glimpsed during the case. Each of them had been on the back of a painting, along with a specific number. In the moment she had thought maybe they were nothing more than doodles, or a way for Robin to catalog her paintings, but as she looked at all four of them together in a row, something tickled the back of her brain.

Frowning, Mona headed upstairs, rooting around some of her yearbooks from school stored in an old plastic tote. Now that she had seen the symbols lined up in that manner, they felt familiar somehow. Maybe it was something Robin had showed her before and she'd forgotten. But Mona had recalled whenever Robin would sign her yearbook, she'd always add extra "art" around the signature.

Finally, she managed to find all her high school yearbooks, pulling them out one by one and flipping to the back signature pages. Sure enough, there were the doodles she had remembered, but they didn't match the symbols in any way. Mona pored over each book, looking for a clue, but there was nothing.

Defeated, she slumped back, staring at the tote full of things from her younger days. Why did those symbols look so familiar? Beside the yearbooks sat a small stack of journals Mona had kept as a child. Back when she'd been young, she'd been obsessed with the idea of cataloging every event of her life. She had planned to record her entire experience as a human.

However, as she'd grown older, she'd realized just how impossible that became. If she were to try and write down all of her thoughts every day of her life, she wouldn't have enough hours in the day to sleep, not to mention anything else.

Mona picked up one of the journals, flipping through it and was surprised at just how full it was. She hadn't wasted any space, the words filling from one edge to the other. She took a few minutes to read, lost in the memories of being twelve again and all the silly worries she'd had at the time, like whether her haircut looked stupid or if she was wearing the right kind of shirt so the other kids wouldn't laugh at her.

Smiling, Mona picked up a few more journals, absently flipping through them, until she came to one that made her stop cold. Dropping the others, she flipped back through one of her oldest journals, which had to have been from elementary school, when she had just learned to write.

"I don't understand," she said aloud as she inspected the journal further. There on the page were the exact same symbols that had been present on the backs of the paintings. But how was that possible? As she investigated further, she noticed the symbols formed a language all their own, as she'd written a key for the symbols in the back. Each one corresponded to a different letter of the alphabet. And the more she read, the more the memories of the symbols came back to her.

It was something she'd completely forgotten she'd done. But now that she read back through, she found she was able to read the symbols easily without the codex.

Journal in hand, Mona ran back down to the computer, looking at the symbols that it had highlighted on the screen. And like a switch had been flipped in her brain, whereas before they had seemed like gibberish, she was now able to read them quite clearly.

Find me on Clearfield.

A cold shudder ran down her back. Clearfield Road had

been the road she and her mother had moved to as soon as they'd arrived in Oak Creek. The house—1039—was an older home, far away from anyone else. They'd lived there for almost fifteen years before Mona had needed to move her mom into healthcare and find a place of her own.

Her mind raced as she tried to rationalize what she'd discovered. A secret code that *she'd* created, written on the back of the paintings of each murder, all of it pointing to her old home? Did this mean all of this was about *her*?

Had everything been connected to her from the start?

No, that was absurd. She had no idea who the woman by the river had been. But as she began to ponder the fact, the pieces started to fall into place. The cold truth she hadn't wanted to face before was that *she*, not Adam, had a connection to each of the victims "predicted" by the paintings. Her connection to Robin was obvious. And she'd gone to see Dr. Pekannen when they'd first moved to town. She couldn't really remember why; she just remembered her mother insisting and Mona protesting each session. It hadn't lasted long. The one thing Mona *had* remembered was Dr. Pekannen telling her if she didn't want to be there, there was nothing she could do for her. That had been enough to get Mona out of it for good.

And Sheriff Franklin had been her boss. Not just her boss, but her support, her mentor in many ways. Someone she could look up to, who inspired her. Now that she thought about it, Mona didn't like where all this was leading. Was someone trying to get *her* attention, specifically? And if so, for what purpose?

She steeled herself. She couldn't tell Ramsey about this discovery; he'd have her committed. Probably fired for taking the case files and loading them into a non-licensed program. And she couldn't tell Detective Dawes—the woman had turned against Mona, going off to follow her own erroneous theories. But going to the location by herself would be considered reckless—unless it was the final location of the last victim. And if that was the case, Mona couldn't sit around, wasting time, worrying about procedure. Obviously, *someone* wanted her to find it, and maybe that was the last piece of the puzzle. Maybe all she had to do was go to the location to get the answers she finally needed.

Grabbing her service weapon and her badge, she pulled on a heavy overcoat and headed for the door. If she ran into trouble, she'd radio from the house. But there was no time to waste, the clock was ticking.

THIRTY

As Charlotte drove through the streets of Oak Creek, a growing sense of unease had formed in her chest. After her "interrogation" with Adam, she'd been even more desperate to get in contact with Mona, only for her calls to continue to go to voicemail and her texts left unread and unanswered. She wasn't even sure the woman had her phone on.

That, and the fact no one had seen her since bringing Adam in, was beginning to worry Charlotte.

She'd seen the look on Mona's face when they'd apprehended Adam, knowing full well the woman placed the responsibility for what happened to him squarely on Charlotte's shoulders. She had hoped they would be able to question Adam, clear him and then release him without much fuss—but given what Ramsey had "found," that was now impossible, unless they could find another suspect that fit the evidence. The boy was in there due to a series of unfortunate coincidences, and even though there was no hard evidence connecting him to the murders, Charlotte could easily see how the town might swoop down to prey upon the boy.

And the real killer would use the opportunity to get away, scot-free.

The boy had been set up as a patsy, and Charlotte had fallen right into the trap. The only way out was to track down Mona, put their heads together and find a way to track down this killer before it was too late. Because the fact was, she didn't trust anyone else in this town to do it. Ramsey was tightening his grip in Sheriff Franklin's absence, and Ken's "mob" would be more than happy to crucify Adam just because he happened to fit the narrative.

Turning down a quiet street, Charlotte pulled up to Mona's house. At least—it was the only house listed in her personnel file, which she'd coaxed out of Michaels. The sun had set only a few minutes before, but it was as if night had settled quicker than normal, pressing down on her with a mix of urgency she could hardly ignore.

The house was dark, but Charlotte stepped out of her car and walked up to the door anyway, knocking firmly. She waited, but there was no answer. She knocked again, her gaze scanning the front of the house. The curtains were drawn tightly, and there was no sign of movement inside. She turned the doorknob, but it was locked. Everything about the place seemed cold, abandoned.

She peered into one of the windows beside the door, but the darkness within gave her nothing. No sign of where Mona might have gone, no hint of what she might be doing. Just emptiness. Charlotte sighed, stepping back from the door, her frustration mounting.

Part of the problem was she didn't know the woman well enough to predict where else she might have gone. Instead of taking the time to get to know her, like a normal person would, Charlotte had focused all her attention on the case and left any questions about her new partner in the dark. Part of that was because she hadn't wanted to answer those questions herself—

hadn't wanted to expose too much of her personal life. But in keeping that private, she'd kept the woman at arm's length, and now it was biting her on the ass.

Charlotte pulled her phone out and called the only other person she thought might help her in a situation like this.

"Hello?" the meek voice answered almost immediately.

"Michaels? It's Detective Dawes again?"

He hesitated on the other end of the line. "How are you, Detective?"

"Not great," she replied. "Listen, I need another favor. Can you pull Detective LaSalle's next of kin for me? Her home was a no-go."

"That's not really information that should be available," he said. "I'm not sure I'm allowed—"

"I know," Charlotte interrupted. "But this is something of an emergency. She's not answering her phone or her texts, and no one has seen her since this morning. I'm worried and I need to find her."

There was a pause on the other end.

"Look, I know Ramsey has probably told the entire department not to cooperate with me. That's fine. But Mona is one of your own. And I may not know her very well, but I know this isn't like her."

The man sighed on the other end. "Yeah... okay." She could hear him typing in the background. "Next of kin is listed as Katherine LaSalle. Resides at Golden Ridge Retirement Village. Do you need the address?"

"No, I think I saw it coming into town," Charlotte said. It had been on the road as she'd come from the site where the body was found by the river. "Thanks, Michaels. That's three I owe you." She hung up and hooked a U-turn in the middle of the road.

Visiting someone's family—especially without notice—was

personal and intrusive. But given the circumstances, Charlotte was willing to take the chance.

Because she couldn't keep from thinking about that final painting.

The nursing home was quiet, the sterile smell of disinfectant lingering in the air. Charlotte walked down the hallway, the soft murmur of voices and the occasional clatter of a meal tray echoing around her. She reached the door to Kathy LaSalle's room and paused, taking a deep breath before knocking lightly.

"Come in," a frail voice called from inside.

Charlotte pushed the door open, stepping into the room. A woman sat in a chair by the window, her thin frame wrapped in a blanket, her eyes distant as she gazed out at the garden beyond. She turned her head as Charlotte entered, her face lighting up with a smile. Charlotte had to work to hide her surprise; the woman couldn't be older than sixty. She'd been expecting someone much older. But this woman was probably only ten years Charlotte's senior.

"Mona!" the woman said, her voice filled with warmth. "Oh, sweetheart, how are you?"

Charlotte's heart sank. It wasn't as if her diagnosis was written on the door somewhere, but Charlotte recognized the signs immediately. Dementia. "No, Mrs. LaSalle, I'm not Mona," she said gently, stepping closer. "I'm a friend of hers. My name is Charlotte."

Kathy blinked, her smile faltering for a moment before returning, as if she hadn't quite heard what Charlotte had said. "It's so good to see you. It's been ages; you're so busy lately with that new job of yours. I know you're working hard, but you need to take care of yourself too."

Charlotte nodded, deciding not to correct her again. "Mrs. LaSalle, I was hoping you could help me. I'm trying to find

Mona. She's not at home and not at work. Do you know where else she might have gone? Does she have any favorite places she likes to blow off steam?"

The woman blinked a few times, the smile falling from her face. "Oh, I'm sorry," she said. "Do we know each other? I must have had one of my episodes."

Stepping further into the room, Charlotte gave the woman a warm smile. "That's all right. My name is Charlotte Dawes. I'm a friend of Mona's."

"It's nice to meet you, Charlotte." Mrs. LaSalle took a deep breath. "How is my daughter these days?"

Her tone indicated that perhaps Mona didn't spend a lot of time here with her mother. "She's good. Busy. We've been working on a case together."

"A case?" she asked. "Did she... did she get a promotion?"

Charlotte hesitated. She wasn't sure she wanted to get in the middle of what could end up being a hornet's nest. "She's been a detective for a few months, I believe."

"Oh," Mrs. LaSalle said, her face falling. "She might have already told me. Sometimes I can't remember things very well."

"I wanted to ask," Charlotte said, more urgency in her voice before the conversation drifted even further. "Do you know anywhere she might want to go to get some time away? To be alone?"

The woman frowned. "You don't know my daughter very well, do you? She hates to be alone."

"She does?"

"Always has, ever since she was a little girl." The woman's eyes turned glassy as she looked out the window again. "Never liked being by yourself, did you, babygirl?"

"Why didn't she like being by herself?"

Mrs. LaSalle turned back to Charlotte, that faraway look back in her eyes. "I did everything I could for us, didn't I? I moved us here, got you settled in a new place. We even tried therapy, but it just wouldn't take."

Therapy? "Mrs. LaSalle—" Charlotte could see her approach wasn't working. She was making progress, but the woman's memory was too fractured to rely on it. She decided on a different tactic. "Mom. You took me to therapy?"

"Yes, don't you remember? When you were still little. Dr. Olivia? She was so nice to you, but you were having a tough time. She said you needed other outlets, projects. That's when you got into working with computers. You used to spend *hours* on them." She chuckled. "Remember when I tried cutting it off, but you figured out how to make it work again? You were always so smart—so good with puzzles." She sighed, looking longingly out the window. "Just like your father."

Wait. Mona said she didn't remember her father. "My... father?"

"Oh yes, he was always fixing things too. Always coming up with these elaborate puzzles for the two of you. I could never keep it straight."

Charlotte's stomach dropped. "Mrs. LaSalle, is Mona's father still alive?"

The woman frowned, as if her entire face had been pulled down by some invisible force. "How do you know about Mona's father?"

The whiplash was going to give her headaches for a week. "I... She told me about him. A little."

"She did?" Mrs. LaSalle asked. "She never talks about him. I didn't even realize she remembered him. She wasn't supposed to remember..." She shifted forward in her seat, an anxious energy about her that hadn't been there before. "I did everything I could to help her forget. Moving towns, starting over. The hypnotism sessions with Dr. Pekannen... getting rid of everything from our old lives... but I guess it didn't take. Somehow... the memory of him must have been too strong."

"Mrs. LaSalle, I need to know. Is Mona's father still alive?"

"I don't know," the woman admitted. "I left him over twenty years ago and haven't looked back." She reached up with a frail hand and pulled back the collar of her shirt to reveal four old scars that swiped across her clavicle. "I never wanted Mona to be on the receiving end of this."

"What's Mona's father's name?" Charlotte asked, her voice insistent.

"I don't know what he's calling himself if he's still around. But to us he was John. John McCormick," the woman said, though her words were tainted by a darkness. "He tricked me... didn't show me his true face until it was too late. He tricked all of us."

"What happened?" Charlotte asked.

The woman's eyes narrowed, and a sharpness came over them that Charlotte would have said was impossible only five minutes earlier. "He pretended. He *always* pretended. Pretended to be a good husband, a good father. It wasn't until later when I saw who he *really* was. *What* he really was. By then it was too late. I was cut off—isolated. We had a daughter—both of us were in danger. And he had us cornered."

"Mom," Charlotte insisted. "What happened with Dad?"

"I didn't have a choice," she said. "I had to get you to safety. I knew it was only a matter of time before he came after you too. He would spend hours and hours with you playing those intricate games. He always teased he was training you, but I knew that it was no tease. He *meant* it. Deep down, he was looking for a protégé. I knew if I didn't get you out of there, he'd turn you into another version of himself.

"It was late one evening. He'd been up all day working on his most recent project. There was *always* a project. And never enough food. He'd been tired. I slipped a sleeping pill into his dinner and he was out. I didn't bother taking anything but the car. I grabbed you, your stuffed animals, and we left. Drove for two days before we stopped. I made sure to always take the back roads, never the Interstate. By the time I was done we were six states away. After a month without him finding us, I settled us here. It seemed small enough to disappear into. He'd never been a fan of small towns."

"You did what you had to do," Charlotte said, trying to reassure the woman, hoping any other relevant details might emerge. "I don't blame you."

"I was so afraid you would," she said, her eyes beginning to water. "You kept asking about him, about when we'd be going back for him. I thought... I thought the therapist could help you get over it, if she could help you disassociate. I had to tell her who your father was. What he'd done before she'd help us. She taught you how to keep things tucked away. To keep them separate."

"It's okay, Mom," Charlotte said, putting a supportive hand on hers. "You did the right thing."

"Did I?" She began wailing. "Sometimes I look in your eyes and all I can see is him. All I see is that fake smile he used to give me, pretending like it was all going to be okay. If you end up like him, I'll never forgive myself." She was straight out shouting now. "Never forgive! Never forgive!"

The thundering of feet preceded a couple of nurses rushing into the room, concern etched on their faces. Charlotte stepped back. Mrs. LaSalle was in a full-blown fit, rocking back and forth in her chair as she screamed at the top of her lungs.

"What is going on in here?" a woman in a long white coat asked as she walked in.

Charlotte produced her badge. "I'm sorry. I was speaking with Mrs. LaSalle about a current case. I thought she might have information that could help us."

The woman stepped between Charlotte and Mrs. LaSalle, almost like a shield as the other two attended to her, helping her calm down. "If you had checked with me before barging in here,

I could have saved you a lot of time. Mrs. LaSalle is suffering from advanced dementia from brain damage sustained when she was in her thirties. She has difficulty caring for herself, let alone remembering what day it is."

"I understand she has a daughter," Charlotte says. "Does she visit often?"

"A few times a week usually, though I haven't seen her in a while," the woman replied. "Not that it matters. Mrs. LaSalle never remembers."

"I see," Charlotte replied. "Well, thank you for your time. I'm sorry for disturbing your patient." She turned and headed back out to the parking lot.

Despite what the doctor had told her, she had seen the truth in Mrs. LaSalle's eyes. The woman had been lucid, if only for those few moments. It turned out Adam wasn't the only one with a connection to the victims. Mona was as connected to them as anyone, which perhaps explained that look Dr. Pekannen had given her that first night at Ronnie's café. She had been the woman's patient as a child. Sheriff Franklin had been her boss, and of course, Robin had been her best friend. The only wild card was the Jane Doe—but Charlotte had a sneaking suspicion that person wasn't connected to *anyone*. She had been put there to throw them off at the beginning. Could Mona's father be the one behind all of this? If he had a propensity for complex puzzles and games, then it would make perfect sense. Not that there was much Charlotte could do about it. Even if what she'd learned about Mona's father was true, Charlotte was no closer to tracking him down.

As Charlotte got in her car she kept going over what Mrs. LaSalle had said. How long had her relationship with Dr. Pekannen endured? And why hadn't Mona mentioned any of it when they found the therapist's body? Had she really repressed the memories and didn't recall her time with the therapist? Or had she been intentionally hiding that information?

One thing was for sure, Mona could be the key to all of this. In fact, she could be the man's final victim. The only problem now was tracking her down. If the killer really was Mona's father, and all of this had been to draw Mona in, that meant the clues were there, in the case somewhere. He would have wanted her to figure it out. But given how careful and meticulous he'd been, Charlotte was willing to bet the puzzle had been for Mona and Mona alone. Without her, Charlotte probably wouldn't be able to crack the code.

But that didn't mean she couldn't try.

THIRTY-ONE

Mona looked up at the house, a flood of memories coming back to her—memories long forgotten. Of playing on the porch with a plastic horse, of running around the backyard and almost breaking her ankle in that gopher hole. Of Mom calling her and Robin from the back door to come in and get ready for dinner every night before she had to go to work.

It had been Mona's life—but there had been something else, something before all that. Something that sat on the edge of her mind, like a smell she couldn't quite place. She didn't remember much of her time before Oak Creek, and Mom had always been scant on the finer details. Whether that was on purpose or not, Mona couldn't say. But whatever was there, teetering in the darkness, it was strong. And Mona was sure if she walked through the door of that house, it would tip over, and she would finally have her answers.

Then again, it all might be nothing more than an elaborate ambush. Detective Dawes had warned them that they should treat every location from here on out as a trap, and Mona was inclined to agree. Especially since this particular message seemed like it had been for her and her alone. Part of her knew she should turn her phone back on and call someone to let them know where she was. But something stayed her hand. Almost like an imperceptible sense that the second she called for help, everything she was searching for would disappear into the wind. She didn't know *why* she felt that way, but the feeling itself was strong. Everything about this felt very structured… like there were rules that needed to be followed. Rules, that if violated, would upend everything she'd worked so hard to find. Then Robin's life would have been taken for nothing.

She took a tentative step forward, pushing down the fear and anxiety in her chest and plastering a smile across her face. If she was walking into the lion's den, she wasn't about to do it looking scared.

The house stood abandoned, looking like no one had lived in it since they moved out. The grass was brown and unkept, and weeds had poked out between the sidewalk and died. Debris of all kinds littered the property, and the house itself was in need of a good wash. Its once white color had faded to a sickly ivory and a few of the windows on the front were missing, either from weather or unruly teens looking for some entertainment late at night.

It was the kind of house someone could hunker down in and no one would bat an eye.

Drawing her weapon, Mona stepped up to the front door. Unsurprisingly, it was unlocked, and she turned the knob like she had hundreds of times before, the door swinging in on creaking hinges.

Inside the house was dark, its old wood floors reaching out into the shadows. The staircase in front of her led up to the second floor, where her one-time bedroom sat just to the left. Her mother's room would be to the right, and a bathroom would be at the end of the hall, between them.

With daylight waning quickly, Mona had to pull out her phone and turn on her flashlight to get a good look at the place. No furniture remained in the house; it was just an empty husk of a place, no longer a home to anyone.

She walked carefully, noting the creaking of the floor under her feet as she explored each room. Where she might have expected to find more symbols, or perhaps something even more shocking, there was nothing. Perhaps she'd misinterpreted the symbols, and maybe there had never been anything here at all. She had to consider all of this was part of her imagination trying to make sense of a case that had no answers.

But as she rounded the living room into the dining room that connected to the kitchen, she heard something. Mona stopped, listening carefully. It seemed to be coming from below her. The house had a basement, but she'd rarely ever gone down there as a kid. It was always dark and damp down there, and the only reason to venture down had been when Mom asked her to retrieve the laundry.

Even into her teens, she'd spent as little time down there as possible.

Her heart ready to thud out of her chest, she stepped into the empty kitchen, to the door which led down into the basement. Her hand trembling as she reached out, Mona opened the door, revealing a warm glow coming from below.

"Hello?" Mona said, feeling foolish that she wasn't being more assertive. "This is the Oak Creek Police. Come out with your hands up!" The words emerged with little authority, and she regretted giving herself away so soon. Her weapon was pointed down the stairs, and thanks to the glow coming from somewhere beyond them, she could see the concrete floor below. She also noticed what looked like tracks or marks on the stairs, fresh ones that dug into the old wood. It looked like someone had pulled something heavy down to the space below.

"Show yourself!" Mona called again, keeping her weapon trained on the bottom of the stairs, but there was no answer. Cursing, she accepted the fact whoever they were, they wouldn't come to her. She would have to go to them. There was no way around it. "I am armed and am coming down the stairs. Do not make any sudden movements if you don't want to get shot."

Her voice sounded pitiful yelling into the darkness; she wasn't commanding like Detective Dawes. But she was going to get to the bottom of this.

Because there were walls on both sides of the stairs leading all the way down, Mona couldn't check the corners until she was at the bottom. As she reached it, the stairs opened into a large multi-purpose room they had used for storage. The old wood-paneled walls were still there, though they'd grown moldy over time. And the room reeked of mildew and decay. She had never liked this basement, and it felt like it had begun to shrivel and wither as if it were itself a corpse.

When she turned the corner, coming fully into the room, a man stood in the center besides stacks of old boxes, his grizzled whiskers twisted into a smile.

"You did it," he said, almost as a whisper. "I knew you would."

"Don't. Move." Mona trained her weapon on the man, but he seemed completely unfazed.

"God, I can't believe you're real," he said, his voice gravelly, almost like he'd been yelling. "Can you believe she's here? I have to admit, I thought maybe it wouldn't happen. That I'd made things too challenging for you. But no... here you are. You're gorgeous, babygirl."

It was as if she had been kicked in the head by a steel-toed boot. A surge of energy shot through Mona's brain as those words registered with something deep and dark and long forgotten. It was as if she'd reached into a dark sewer hole, grabbed hold of something, and pulled out a memory. "... Daddy?"

He nodded, his smile growing bigger. "That's right, honey. I found you. I finally found you, after so long." He raised his hands almost as if he were about to cover his mouth, causing Mona to retrain her weapon on him, it having dipped as she'd made the realization. "I know this is a shock. But just look at what you've done."

Mona barely heard the man. It was taking all her effort to maintain her composure as the memories came flooding back to her. Night after night of sitting on the floor with the man in front of her, working on puzzles of all kinds. Sometimes they were simple picture puzzles, other times they were games with intricate parts. But he'd been there with her, helping her figure them out, letting her take the lead, showing her shortcuts. And all of it had been in a house she could barely remember. A place before here. A place lost to her past.

"You—you're behind this?" Mona asked, her voice quivering. "Why... What—"

"My little Ramona," he chided. "You made it this far, don't disappoint me now. You can figure it out; I know you can."

Ramona. No one called her that. Not even her mother. It had been so long since she'd heard the name uttered she'd almost forgotten it. "You're under arrest," Mona said. "Put your hands on your head and turn around."

The man *tsk*ed. "Now, now. I need you to drop those barriers, honey. It's okay. You're safe here with us," he implored.

Us? Mona glanced around the room. He was the only person here besides her.

"What do you want from me?" Mona demanded, her anger getting the better of her. It was almost as though she couldn't help it. The barriers she'd willingly dropped before—that had gone back up when Detective Dawes began her pursuit of

Adam—were just... *gone*. How could that be possible? "I don't understand."

"Oh, what have they done to you?" he asked, chidingly. "There was a time when you would have figured all of this out by now."

"Where have you been?" she asked as it was the first thing that had come to her mind.

He scrutinized her. "Maybe the better question is: Why don't you remember?"

As the realization that she'd forgotten him settled upon her, she began questioning everything. Her life here in Oak Creek. Her entire childhood, missing a crucial piece. As she thought she began to recall sessions with Dr. Pekannen, sessions she and her mother attended together. Sessions designed to make her forget.

Forget him?

"Why?" she asked. "Why would they want me to forget? Unless..." She narrowed her eyes.

"There you go," he said, grinning.

"Robin, Dr. Pekannen, Sheriff Franklin..." Mona said as it dawned on her. "You wanted my attention... but... why? Why did four people have to die?" Now that her protection was gone it was as if her heart was a raw nerve exposed to the whole world. She wanted to crumple under the weight of it all —that *she* had been the impetus behind all these murders. Had it not been for her, her friends, her *family* would still be alive right now. The only thing keeping her on two feet was her ability to keep her job front and center in her mind. Even if he was her father, she wasn't going to let that stop her from doing her job.

The man nodded a few times before lowering his head and walking to Mona's left. She kept the weapon trained on him the entire time. It was only now that she realized he'd been standing in front of a large wooden cross that looked eerily similar to the one from Robin's final painting. Straps had been affixed to each end of the cross, but there was no one on it.

"She doesn't remember," the man muttered, stroking his whiskers. Finally, he took a seat in a large wingback chair that sat on the other side of the room. He crossed one leg while staring at her. "It took me a long time to find you, longer than even I could have imagined," he said. "After your mother left with you that night, I searched for months, driving all over the southeast. But your mother hated the cold. I never thought she'd settle this far north," he said ruefully. "I guess I should have figured she'd do anything to get away from me. If she'd just left without you, I probably wouldn't have cared. But she took you with her, and that cut my heart out."

"She took me with her?" Mona asked.

"You don't remember Charleston, do you?" he said. "Where you were born."

"I was born in San Diego," Mona replied. "It says so on my birth certificate. We moved here for her job when I was five." But even as she said the words, she could feel their hollowness.

The man *tsk*ed again. "Damn. She was wilier than I gave her credit for. But it doesn't matter now," he replied. "The fact is, I'm here and you're here. And we can pick up right where we left off. You've proven that you still have the basic skills for survival I imparted on you all those years ago."

"Skills?" Her cheeks were wet from the stream of tears she hadn't realized had begun falling. It was as if her mind was being torn in two, one side trying to process the reality that she'd been taken from her father at such a young age and the other side grappling with the horrible things he'd done. How could she be related to someone so terrible?

"Deduction, problem-solving, analysis—everything you would need to succeed in this world," he said. "I knew you were different from the moment I held you in my hands. I knew that you were like me, and the two of us together would be unstoppable." He grimaced, turning to his right, as if he were speaking to someone else. "Unfortunately, her mother had other plans."

"Hey," Mona said, waving the gun, wanting to keep his attention. Whatever was distracting him was something she couldn't see. "What plans?"

"Your mother knew what I was from the moment we met. Whether she wanted to admit it to herself or not is another matter. But as the years went on, I could feel her turning against me." He chuckled. "You know, if she hadn't left, I probably would have taken care of the problem myself."

"You mean you would have killed her," Mona said.

"I would have... *relieved* her of her burdens," he replied. "In fact, I saw that place you stuck her in. But killing a bird locked in a cage is no sport at all. A far worse fate awaits her and I'm happy to let her stew in her mindlessness."

Mona sucked in a breath. She'd heard enough. This was all nothing but a spate of lies. It had to be. She needed to do what she came here to do. He hadn't yet found his fourth victim, and she would make sure he never would. "Stand up," she said. "I'm taking you in."

Her father looked at her straight in the eye, leaning forward so his elbows were on his knees. "You know how you survive this world, Ramona? You either get smarter or richer than everyone else. Now, I've never been great with money. Your mom could tell you that much. But one thing I have always been is clever. You don't know this, but in school I tested in the ninetieth percentile. I was destined for great things. But the money was never there. And I learned very quickly that in order to get what I wanted, I would have to outsmart everyone."

"You mean manipulate," Mona said, though her grip on the pistol loosened.

"Let's agree on *persuade*. But the other thing I've always been fascinated with is puzzles. It was something I noticed in you too, from a young age. A trait we share. I knew if I could help you master these skills, you could go even further than I could."

"I'm nothing like you," Mona replied.

"Oh, darling, but you are. I was alone as a youngster as well. Often by myself, criticized for my extreme ideas, shunned because I didn't fit in with everyone else. Your friend, Robin, she cut you off, didn't she? Because she thought you didn't understand what she was going through."

"She cut me off because I made a mistake," Mona said.

"And this program you've created, I understand in a few years you expect to be able to predict crime. That's all well and good, Ramona, but no tool will ever be able to replace you. Your skill, your intelligence."

Mona found she was at a loss for words. "I... but that's..."

"Did you use that program to help you find me?" he asked. "I considered the possibility, but of course it wasn't a requirement. I gave you everything you needed to do it on your own."

"The symbols," Mona said.

He smiled. "Our secret language. See, even by the time you were barely writing your name you were already coming up with your own codex. How many preschoolers can say that?"

"But I didn't come up with it," she said. "You did."

He sat back, pressing his lips together. "Well. I may have helped a little. Do you remember how we used to write secret messages to each other? And your mother had no clue what they said?"

More memories were beginning to surface. Memories of messages written to her, giving Mona instructions. She winced. She couldn't quite remember them, but they had been... horrible. Gruesome.

"You... you wanted me to hurt things. Hurt animals," Mona said.

"Now, now," he replied. "If you're going to make it in this

world, you have to harden yourself to the realities. Nature is cruel. In order to succeed, you have to match that cruelty."

"That's not true. Not everyone is cruel."

"My dear, sheltered Ramona," he replied. "We'll have to start your training over. At least a refresher course. Don't you see what I've done for you? I have removed every obstacle from your path. Every person who has betrayed you is now gone. You are free to do as you wish, to *level up*."

She furrowed her features, trying to reconcile his words. "But... they didn't betray me."

"Of course they did," he said. "Robin turned her back on you when all you did was try to comfort her." He looked to his right, tsking again before addressing Mona a second time. "Dr. Pekannen made you forget who you really were, taking away your very being. And Sheriff Franklin postponed your promotion twice, only granting you the role of detective after he was forced to when Detective Souther retired. He never truly believed in you. He wasn't the father you needed."

Mona felt more tears form in the corners of her eyes but she blinked them away, holding up the weapon again. "That's not true. He was proud of me."

"No, he never was, babygirl. He pitied you. Felt *sorry* for you. Because you had such a hard time fitting in. You should have been promoted years ago. But you don't have to worry about him anymore." Her father stood, walking closer to her. Her hand tightened on the grip, but she couldn't pull the trigger. No matter how hard she tried, she couldn't make herself do it.

He stopped with the barrel of her gun inches from his chest. If she pulled the trigger, it would pierce his heart in an instant.

"There's only one other person who's betrayed you, and to complete your training, you'll need to finish what I started."

"What?" Mona asked, tears in her eyes. She couldn't even think straight. Watching as her father wrapped his hand around the gun and removed it from his grip, she felt all the fight go out of her.

"You will bring her here, and together, we'll take one last roll of the dice. And then... then we can do whatever we like. Then you'll be truly free."

"W-who?" Mona asked, her voice shaking.

"The person who betrayed you when you needed her the most. Detective Charlotte Dawes."

THIRTY-TWO

"You're not listening to me," Charlotte said. "Your detective is in danger, and you need to find her."

Ramsey sat with his arms crossed, while the two FBI agents who had arrived, Jansen and Billups, stood off to the side, listening to Charlotte's pleas.

"So, you think because a mental patient who just happens to be LaSalle's mother told you her father is a stalker that he's specifically targeted her and now has her in his grasp," Ramsey said. Charlotte didn't miss the wink he shot at one of the FBI agents.

"Okay, fuck you, Ramsey," Charlotte said, turning to Special Agent Billups, who seemed like the more amenable of the two. "The Bellinger kid was set up. *Nothing* ties him to the case except circumstantial evidence. You're looking at the wrong suspect."

"I guess you missed Whittle's report while you were out talking with crazy town," Ramsey replied, regaining control of the conversation. "Kid's prints came back on the painting. We've got him dead to rights."

Shit. Charlotte grimaced. If Mona's father really was the

master game player that Mrs. LaSalle insinuated, there's no reason why he couldn't have found a way to plant those fingerprints, especially if he was able to get into the kid's car. "Did he check to see if they were transfers? Because that's easy enough to do with some tape and a lighter. You can't just—"

"I think I've heard enough," Ramsey replied. "As far as this office is concerned, we have our killer, oddly enough, thanks to you. So I will offer you a round of congratulations before telling you to get the hell out of my office. I think you know the way back to Chicago."

"You can't just hang Mona out to dry!"

"Detective LaSalle will return to this office when she's good and ready. She's been through a lot and deserves some time off." Ramsey's gaze was hard, almost impenetrable.

"Is this because she called you out, back on the site?" Charlotte asked. "Is your ego really that fragile? I don't know why you have such a problem with her but—"

"Careful, Detective," Ramsey said. "My personal feelings about LaSalle have nothing to do with this."

"*Bullshit*," she replied. "I saw how you treated her when I arrived. Like little more than a stray dog. Do you treat all new detectives like that, or just women? If Franklin were here—"

"He's not," Ramsey replied. "And I think it's time for you to go."

Charlotte turned to the agents again, feeling everything slipping through her fingers. "You have to see there is more going on here. One seventeen-year-old kid? A quadruple murder?"

"I'm sorry, Detective," Billups said. "But we have to follow the evidence. And everything we have so far points to Bellinger."

"God*damm* it," Charlotte yelled. "Can't you see what's happening? He's manipulating the situation to make it look like he's a ghost. And you're falling right into his trap!"

"Okay, that's enough," Ramsey said, pressing a button on

his intercom. "Alberhasky, get in here. And bring Roberts with you. I need you to escort Detective Dawes from the building."

She couldn't believe this was happening. Was he really threatening to throw her out? She looked to the agents for assistance, but it seemed they weren't willing to rock the boat. They had a suspect who fit the crimes. From their perspective, all they could see was a washed-up old detective on the verge of retirement, probably with a few screws loose and talking conspiracy theories.

"I know the way," Charlotte grumbled, and threw the door open to reveal Alberhasky standing there with Roberts. *"Move!"* The two men jumped out of the way as she barreled down the hallway, headed for the exit.

Fucking Ramsey. Self-important *asshole*. He had a suspect, so what did he care if it was the wrong one? As long as it fit his narrative and gave him the credit he needed to temporarily take over as sheriff, he'd do it. He was going to have hell to pay when they found Mona's body drawn and quartered sometime in the next twenty-four hours. But by the time Charlotte could say "I told you so," it would be too late for Mona. It didn't help matters that no one seemed to want to stand up to him. It had been just as she'd suspected; the FBI would only be interested in closing this thing up and confirming they had their suspect in custody.

She tried to think. Was there anyone else who could help her? Anyone who would believe her story? Then again, if she looked at it from their perspective, she could understand the skepticism. Mrs. LaSalle was a dementia patient with a shaky record at best. Maybe Charlotte wouldn't have believed her herself, if not for the steely-eyed look the woman gave her when talking about her ex-husband.

If Mona's father was as smart as she suspected, he wouldn't be traceable. In fact, finding anything about him after high school was probably a stretch. To Charlotte, he didn't seem like the type to make himself visible. But maybe there was another way to trace him. If he really had been operating in Oak Creek this entire time, he had to have left some imprint somewhere.

As Charlotte headed out to the parking lot, she had to press through a group of reporters that had gathered near the door. They shouted a bevy of questions at her, but she ignored all of them, not wanting to fan the flames. If she came out and said Adam Bellinger wasn't the suspect, Ramsey would probably have her arrested. And then she wouldn't be able to do anything for Mona.

Once she was through the reporters, Charlotte caught glances from other members of the town that had gathered. Ken the café owner among them, glowering at her as she passed. Had Adam not been brought in as a suspect, they would still be out roaming the streets. The town had their culprit; their blood-lust had been satisfied.

Charlotte got back into her car, flexing her hand as she did. The throbbing ache was back and worse than ever, despite the fact she had barely even used it. It was like her body was taunting her, telling her she was all used up and there was nothing left for her. How could she track down McCormick in time? It seemed impossible.

As she considered what Whiteside would say if she tried explaining her hunch to him, her phone vibrated in her pocket. She pulled it out and upon seeing the name on the screen immediately hit accept. "Mona? Where are you?"

"Detective Dawes?" the woman asked, her voice sounding like it had when they'd first met—overly happy and energetic. Like she didn't have a care in the world.

"Are you okay? What's going on?" Charlotte asked.

"Do you have time to meet?" she asked.

"Of course," Charlotte said. "Where? I can come to you right now."

"The address is 1039 Clearfield," Mona replied. "And I need you to come alone. I—I've found something."

The hackles on the back of Charlotte's neck rose. "What did you find?"

"I'll show you when you get here. Just... hurry." Mona ended the call before Charlotte could press her further.

Something was wrong. Very wrong. She was back to her default mode again—pretending everything was fine. And maybe that would have fooled Ramsey or one of the others, but Charlotte had seen the progress Mona had made over the past few days. She had seen the pain the woman had endured by allowing herself to come to terms with the reality of Robin's situation. So what could have happened to make her do such a heel turn?

Had she made the same determination Charlotte had—that her father was the one behind all this—and just shut down? Or was there something more going on here?

Whatever the reason, she needed to get to Mona as soon as possible. Charlotte considered going back inside the station and getting some backup. But odds were anything she did Ramsey would just counter. If he was willing to throw her out, she wouldn't put anything beyond him. Plus, he would argue that Charlotte was getting exactly what she wanted.

Still, she didn't feel right. In the absence of backup, she needed some assurances.

Charlotte turned over the engine and backed out of the parking lot, leaving tire tracks in her wake.

THIRTY-THREE

Upon arriving at the address Mona provided, Charlotte had to steel herself. The house was miles from the nearest neighbor, and far enough from any main roads that help would take a while to arrive, should she need it. There was no good reason Mona would be in a place like this, not unless she was in dire trouble.

Charlotte double-checked her weapon before stowing it. She didn't like walking into situations blind, that wasn't her MO. But she couldn't help but think about the operation at Victor's club, about how they had planned that op down to the last detail and things had *still* gone to shit. Sometimes there was just no getting around it and she would just have to trust that whatever was in that house, she could handle it.

She stepped out of the car, checking the roof of the house for anyone who might be up there watching, but she didn't see anyone. It didn't help matters it was near pitch-black out, the moon providing barely enough light for her to see. But once she was inside that house it would be hard to see anything at all. Charlotte took a deep breath in through her nose, the air chilling her. Mona's car sat off to the side of the house, dark and empty. Charlotte pressed her hand against the hood to find it cold. Whatever she was doing here, she'd been here a while.

This was stupid and reckless. But what choice did she have? It was either go in and try to help Mona or risk the woman's life by trying to bring reinforcements—if she could even convince anyone to come.

As Charlotte approached the house, she noted it was in a heavy state of disrepair. It didn't look like anyone had lived here for a long time. But footsteps in the dirt on the porch conveyed someone had been here recently, which at least told her she was in the right place. She drew her weapon, keeping it pointed at the ground as she approached the front door. It was unlocked, and she opened it carefully. She clicked on the flashlight she'd taken from her car and swept it inside the home, searching all the blind corners.

"Mona?" she called out. This was looking worse and worse by the second. If by some miracle everything had been on the up-and-up, Mona would have met her as she pulled up to the house. The fact she was nowhere to be found had Charlotte at full alert.

There was no answer as the word echoed through the house. Before her was a staircase leading up, but she didn't see anyone up there. Her first job was to clear this floor, then she could worry about the others.

Making her way through the house, she carefully checked each corner, finding the home desolate and empty.

"Detective Dawes," Mona called from somewhere deeper in the house. She didn't sound like she was in distress, but she didn't sound like herself either. Instead, she sounded like she'd been hollowed out somehow. Different than she had on the phone.

Coming into the kitchen, Charlotte found the door to the basement already open. Light seeped up from below, suggesting the power in the house was still connected. "Mona?"

"Down here," she replied, again in that strange tone.

Charlotte took the stairs one at a time, very carefully. Whatever was going on, whatever she was walking into, wouldn't be good. She had to be on her guard no matter what.

Reaching the bottom stair, she checked around the corner then pulled back, cursing under her breath. Mona was in the room, standing beside a man sporting a greying beard and a workman's jacket, wearing a wide smile. Charlotte had to assume the man was McCormick, seeing as Mona didn't seem to be under any duress. What worried her, though, was McCormick had Mona's gun.

"Detective," he called out. "Thanks for coming. Now, I abhor using these things, but seeing as it's the only kind of language you cops really understand, I'll make an exception. Drop your weapon and come out."

"Mona, are you okay?" Charlotte called.

"*Now* you're concerned? Where was that concern when poor Ramona was trying to tell you innocent, little Adam wasn't the culprit? *If you'd only listened.*" His voice was sarcastic, playful, almost joyful even. *Ramona?* Charlotte hadn't realized her name was shortened.

"I'd do as he says, Detective," Mona added.

She checked the blind corner again. McCormick didn't have the weapon trained on Mona, but if he really was behind all this, Charlotte had no trouble believing he would use his own daughter as a shield if she tried to get her sights on him.

"What do you want, McCormick?" she called, trying to think of a way around this. She couldn't just shoot the man, not in time anyway. He could potentially harm or kill Mona in the second it took Charlotte to aim. Not to mention the ache in her hand had graduated to a tremble, just like it had back in Victor's club.

Not now, she thought. *For the love of God, not now.*

"Well, well, seems your reputation is well earned. You surprise me, Detective Dawes."

"Why, because I figured out who you were?"

"Did you, though?" he asked. "What do you really know about me? And how long did you keep that information from your new partner here?"

"I spoke to your ex-wife," Charlotte replied. "Why don't you put down the gun and we'll discuss it."

"I don't think so." This time his voice was full of vitriol, like the act of speaking with Mrs. LaSalle had set him off in some small way.

"You might as well give up; I have backup on the way as we speak."

"For a detective, I'd think you'd be a better liar," he said. "The fact is, no one is coming. Don't you think I'm monitoring the police channels?" His voice was exasperated, like he'd had enough of this. "Mona, take care of this, please."

Charlotte frowned as she watched Mona's shadow grow larger on the concrete floor next to the stairs. Before she could think of another option, Mona appeared in front of her, a smile on her face and her weapon back in her hand, pointed at Charlotte. "Detective, please."

Charlotte frowned, though she wouldn't raise her gun to aim it at Mona. "Why are you doing this? Just arrest him!"

"The last time I listened to you, an innocent boy was arrested."

"Mona, he killed Robin. He killed Sheriff Franklin."

"I know," she replied, any hint of her former emotion completely absent. All that remained was that damn smile. "I need you to do as he says. It's what's best for everyone." She held out her hand for Charlotte's weapon.

Charlotte considered not giving it to her. Would she really pull the trigger? In the few days they'd worked together, she had seen glimpses of something else inside her.

Was this what she'd seen? The daughter of a monster, just waiting for the right opportunity to come out? Was there some deeper part of Mona that could do what her father had done?

"You're better than this," Charlotte said, sighing as she handed over her weapon. "Don't just bury everything. *You have a choice.*"

"I do," she replied. "It's just easier this way."

So that was it then. She had made her decision. And it was going to get them both killed.

"You're right, Detective," McCormick said as Mona motioned for Charlotte to round the wall and face the man. Underneath his overcoat she could see he had a patch on his workman's zip-up with a name embroidered across a patch that said *Don*. And for some reason he looked slightly familiar. But his eyes were full of life and fire. She could see the glee he was taking in this whole scenario, playing out just like he'd hoped. "Most of us are bound by the expectation of choice. I have broken free, and soon Mona will as well."

She needed to stall him. Find a way out of this. A way to turn Mona back. "How'd you do it?" Charlotte asked. "How'd you plan it all so perfectly?"

"As I believe Mona has already told you, given enough data, you can predict just about anything. I may not use as sophisticated measures as she does, but the principles are the same."

"What the hell does that mean?"

"It means time and patience are a man's best friends. I've been looking for Ramona ever since her mother stole her from me. And I found her, three years ago."

Charlotte furrowed her brow. "Three years?"

"Ah, but that's where the patience came in. Because I knew her mother had either poisoned Ramona against me, or found a way to make her forget me completely. I decided to learn as much as I could... by befriending her best friend." He glanced to his side, smiling. Charlotte shot a glance at Mona, but the action didn't seem to faze her.

"You seduced Robin," Charlotte sneered.

"It was mutual, I assure you," he replied. "Though I did ask Robin to keep our relationship secret in the beginning—it was easier to learn about Ramona that way. She didn't know my true identity until later, of course. But when she found out..."

"She turned on you," Charlotte said.

His eyes darkened. "Regrettably. I fled, assuming it was all over. That she would expose me to Ramona. But... she didn't. What I failed to consider was the guilt she would feel for sleeping with her best friend's father." He grinned a wicked smile. "That was all it took."

Charlotte looked to Mona for some sort of reaction, but her face was completely blank. Had she really lost herself? "Mona," she said softly.

"It's no use, Detective," McCormick said. "Ramona has remembered who she is now. She is my daughter, and she is immune to silly emotions."

"Wait, three years. That was when—*you're* the reason Robin started painting those horrors, aren't you? You were the catalyst we've been looking for."

He smiled. "Apparently, poor Robin had more demons than I had realized. I knew about her dealings with her own father, of course. But the paintings... those were a surprise. When I came across the image of one online and realized who had painted it, I knew it was time to return. To create the ultimate puzzle."

"Why did you come back?" Charlotte demanded. "Why couldn't you have just left her alone?"

"She is my daughter," he said. "And I needed see if she was worthy. I wanted—needed to know if she was my true heir after all. So I set some things in motion, starting with the first domino down by the river. After that, all I needed to do was sit back and observe."

"Wait," Charlotte said. "I've seen you before. You were at the gazebo that night, weren't you? With the mob? And you were at the vigil as well."

"My dear Detective Dawes, I have been *everywhere* this past week. Eating dinner next to you, following you to Robin's home, tailing you as you chased Adam across the city. I've been right in front of your face, and you never even noticed me." He glanced over to his daughter. "If you please."

"Detective Dawes," Mona said, motioning to a large structure that had been set up in the basement. It was essentially two large pieces of wood that had been bolted together into an "X," with straps at each end. Charlotte's stomach dropped. Mona was never in danger of being the fifth victim. That honor belonged to her.

"Now she sees," McCormick whispered. "Glorious."

"Then all of this, all this death was for *her*, to draw her in?" Charlotte asked.

"Do you have children, Detective?" he asked as Mona escorted Charlotte to the wooden cross and indicated she press herself up against it. She handed one of the guns back to McCormick who kept it aimed at Charlotte as Mona got to work on the straps.

There had to be some way out of this, something she could do. It was two against one. And if she was going to die anyway, why not die trying to take them out? But as she looked at the barrel of the gun and thought back to what had happened in Victor's club, she knew she'd never get two steps before finding a bullet in her stomach. Maybe twenty years ago she would have had a chance. But now her best bet was to keep McCormick talking, maybe she could find a way to hang him with his own words. "What, you don't know all about my family life?"

"Well," he said, chuckling. "You were something of an anomaly when I first learned you'd joined my daughter here in

Oak Creek. I... miscalculated, I guess you could say. You were never supposed to be here. But it turned out to be for the better. Look at what we were able to accomplish because of you. You made this game far more exciting, Detective." He laughed again, like someone had told a funny joke, causing Charlotte to narrow her gaze. "Yes, that's right, she *did* find one of the clues out of order. But that's to be expected."

"Who—who are you talking to?" Charlotte asked as Mona strapped one of Charlotte's arms to the X.

"I'm talking to *you*," he replied. "As a parent, you're willing to do anything for your kids. Even take the most extreme measures, if necessary."

"I would never kill an innocent person for my daughter," Charlotte spat. "Much less four."

"Then you're just not motivated enough," McCormick replied, vitriol in his voice. "It doesn't matter anyway. It isn't like you're special, or that you have anything worth saving. Not like my Ramona. She is a *prodigy*. A one-in-a-million kind of mind. One that can compartmentalize away anything that gets in her way, including her emotions. Do you know who taught her to do that?"

"Got it," Charlotte said. "So the key to being a good parent is to first train your child to be some kind of, what... unfeeling robot? And step two is kill a bunch of people. I'll make sure to write that down." The man grimaced, clearly not liking being made fun of. "Come on, McCormick, spell it out for me. I guess I'm just too stupid to understand." Maybe if she could catch him in his own logic, Mona might break out of whatever mindset he had her in.

"I needed to remind Ramona of who she really was," he said. "And make sure she still had the skills necessary to survive."

Survive? "And if she hadn't? What if we hadn't followed your little trail of breadcrumbs?" Charlotte asked.

The man didn't reply, but the look on his face told Charlotte all she needed to know. She turned to Mona. "Don't you see? He would have killed both of us in the end anyway. He's going to turn on you. One day you'll do something to disappoint him and that'll be it."

"There's no use trying, Detective," McCormick said with a smile. "Ramona already knows what's best is for her to finish excising her last demon—namely you. Then she will truly be free."

God, he really is insane, Charlotte thought. Her arms secured, Mona put Charlotte's weapon in the back of her pants and worked to secure Charlotte's legs. "Something doesn't make sense, and it hasn't since this whole thing began," Charlotte said. "The woman by the river. Who was she?"

At that, Mona stopped momentarily before continuing to secure the straps.

"What woman?" McCormick asked. "No one. She's no one."

"She was. You put her there. Who was she to you?"

"Shut *up*," he said, though he did it in a way that looked like he wasn't talking to Charlotte *or* Mona. "Listen, this has been great fun. But we're on a schedule here. I'd like to be at least a few states away before they find your body."

"They'll never stop looking for you," Charlotte replied. "Or her."

"Oh, I think they will," he said. "A well-timed car wreck with two burned bodies fixes that problem very easily. A carefully calculated plan will be required, but given enough time and preparation, I have no doubt we can pull it off."

"Sometimes you just can't control everything," Charlotte said, though she was looking at Mona as she said it. "Trust me, I know. This entire time I've been trying to put off the inevitable, to somehow keep myself from losing the one thing I put above everything else in my life. And you know what? I've finally realized I can't. I just have to accept what's coming. It's time to stop fighting."

"Very apropos," McCormick said. "It's refreshing to see someone accept their fate. Usually, it's a bunch of unnecessary screaming and yelling. Bravo, Detective. I salute you." He made an imaginary tip of his hat.

Mona stepped back, having fully secured Charlotte. McCormick smiled, then produced a long, sharp knife, handing it to his daughter. "Time's up, Detective. Your turn in this is over."

THIRTY-FOUR

Charlotte's eyes widened as she stared at the knife in Mona's hand. She still wore that pleasant smile as she approached, wielding the knife like a butcher, ready to start carving. Behind her, McCormick took a seat in the only chair in the room, crossing one leg and smiling himself. It was creepy how much he looked like his daughter in that moment. "This is it, Ramona. Remember how she turned on you. How they all turned on you, disregarded you. Didn't believe in you. Don't disappoint me."

"Of course not, Daddy," Mona said, her voice chipper and remorseless. She turned to Charlotte. "Don't worry, Detective. I know how to make this quick. You won't feel much."

"Mona," Charlotte said, but the woman put one finger to her lips. Charlotte's entire body tensed, the ache in her hand throbbing. But as it began to tremble, Charlotte realized the restraints around her arm weren't as tight as they appeared.

Mona was only inches from her, the knife between them. And one second the smile was there, then it was gone, like it had never existed. Charlotte saw the woman she'd seen after they'd found the paintings. The real woman, beneath the mask. "*Char-*

lotte, I need you to scream," she whispered. "Make it sound good."

Charlotte's eyes widened. Mona had never called her by her first name before.

Then it clicked.

Charlotte let out a bloodcurdling scream as Mona made slashing motions across her stomach. Even though her eyes were squinting in pretend pain, she could see McCormick vying for a better view.

"Move, girl, I can't see a thing," he yelled.

"Louder," Mona whispered, and Charlotte complied, realizing the straps around both her arms and legs weren't tight at all. In fact, they were completely loose. She'd been so preoccupied with the fact she was going to be rendered helpless, she hadn't even thought to check.

"Son of a bitch," McCormick said, standing and striding over to them, impatience etched across his face. In that instant, Mona turned and drove the knife deep into the man's shoulder, causing him to cry out.

Charlotte yanked against the restraints, her arms and legs coming loose in just enough time to pull Mona to the side as McCormick raised the gun with his good arm and fired. The sound was like a cannon going off, and had Charlotte not moved her, he would have taken Mona's head off.

"No, goddammit! You're breaking the rules!" he yelled, though the ringing in Charlotte's ears muffled his words a bit. He moved to fire again but stopped suddenly, cocking his head at something to his right, giving Charlotte an opening.

It was like a ballet; her body moved into a familiar position all on its own—the stance from years of practice and training—and she squared herself up, one arm raised to defend and another poised to strike. As McCormick stood there, almost like he was staring into blank space, Charlotte's hand made a fist, any sensation of pain draining away before she stepped into the punch and landed a hit straight across the man's jaw.

There was an audible *crack* and he flailed back, but she wasn't done. Without even thinking, Charlotte spun halfway around, her leg shooting out and striking the hand with the weapon, which now hung limp. The gun went flying off into the darkness as McCormick reeled back in pain. Charlotte grabbed the man's shoulders, driving her knee deep into his stomach, knocking the wind out of him before landing a final blow across his jaw that sent him sprawling to the floor.

"Wow," Mona said, coming up beside her. "I didn't know you still trained."

"I don't," Charlotte replied, wincing. "I think I just pulled something." As the adrenaline began to subside, a sharp pain came from somewhere in her groin. She looked at Mona carefully. "Are you okay?"

"Sorry for the deception," she admitted. "It was the only way I could get him to drop his guard. He had to believe I was in it with him."

"I guess that's one of the benefits of looking like you're able to turn off your emotions. You had me completely fooled," Charlotte said as they approached the prone body of John McCormick. "We need to get that knife out of him and get him medical attention."

"Or... we could just leave him," Mona said.

"He'll bleed to death." The knife had cut directly into his right shoulder and may have severed one of his primary arteries. Even now, as they spoke, a pool of blood was beginning to form under him.

"I don't think that would be so bad," she replied. "Considering all he's done."

"Mona, that's not justice. That's revenge," Charlotte said. "I can't imagine what you might be feeling—or even what he's put you through. But this isn't the way."

Mona turned to her, and Charlotte saw tears in the woman's eyes. "But *I'm* the reason they're all dead. He did this all to lure me in, to try and make me like him. If it weren't for me, they'd all still be alive. What if... what if he kills someone else? Or manages to find a way out? He's too dangerous—"

"And what about Adam?" Charlotte asked. "Without your father, he could still go down for all this. Your dad was smart, he didn't leave anything behind. We need him alive."

Mona drew in a deep breath before finally nodding. "Okay." She rushed over to him, attempting to apply pressure around the wound while Charlotte pulled out her phone to call it in. As she relayed the information to local 911, she could hear McCormick muttering something.

"—yes, 1039 Clearfield," she said. "Tell EMS we're in the basement, accessible through the kitchen. And make it quick, he's bleeding fast." She got off the phone and joined Mona, putting pressure on the wound to stave off as much of the bleeding as possible. But she also put her knee on the man's outstretched arm just in case. "What's he saying?"

"Why do you always have to be such a *bitch*," Mona replied, imitating her father's voice.

"Is he talking to you?"

She shook her head. "I don't think so. I think he believes there is someone else here with us." She glanced around the room, but they were alone. "He's been talking like there's another person here ever since I arrived."

Charlotte had noticed that too. But there was no question about it, they were alone. "Maybe he's not as sane as he thinks." Though she couldn't shake the feeling had it not been for whatever distracted McCormick in those brief seconds, both she and Mona would probably be dead by now.

Whatever—or whoever—it had been, Charlotte silently thanked them, regardless, even if it had been nothing more than the last remaining piece of McCormick's own conscience.

THIRTY-FIVE

"Hey," Charlotte said, pulling out a nearby chair and taking a seat. She'd just finished three hours of debrief with the FBI and had the immense pleasure of watching Ramsey sit beside her and squirm as she went over every aspect of the case and how he had attempted to impede the investigation at turn after turn. The FBI had taken over the investigation, not that there was much left for them to do now that McCormick was in hospital custody under twenty-four-hour guard. But still, they had grilled both Charlotte and Mona about every detail, going over the case inch by inch. Charlotte had to give them props for taking as much interest as they did, but given they'd nearly announced Adam as the suspect to be charged, and the amount of egg on their faces had they done that, she was pretty sure it was all in the good name of self-preservation.

"Hey," Mona said, though she didn't take her eyes off the screen.

"I don't think your friend Ramsey will be around much longer," Charlotte said, trying to get the woman's attention. "The FBI didn't go very easy on him, and your mayor is... well, let's just say he's upset. He might have wrangled the position until the next election cycle, but now there is talk of having an interim election to find a new sheriff."

"That's good," she replied, though Charlotte could tell she wasn't really listening. Instead, she was watching a video of McCormick, squirming in his hospital bed.

"Mona," Charlotte said, leaning forward. "Did you hear what I said?"

Finally, she turned to Charlotte, blinking a few times. "Oh, sorry. Ramsey is out? That's good news."

"It's not official yet," Charlotte replied. "But I'd be surprised if it doesn't happen."

"That will make things a lot smoother around here," Mona replied.

Charlotte motioned to the screen. "What are you doing?"

"Me? Nothing. Just... going over case information."

"You want to know more about him, don't you?" Charlotte asked.

"Not really, no," she admitted. "I learned everything I needed to know down in that basement. I saw him for what he was immediately. And I remembered... finally." Her face fell slightly at the memory. "Learning about him and Robin... I just can't believe it. Why didn't she ever tell me?"

Charlotte pursed her lips. "Maybe she didn't want you to suffer. And I think McCormick was right. Her guilt was probably eating her up inside. Maybe that was the real reason she pushed you away that night."

Mona blinked, though she was beginning to tear up. "How do you keep all these conflicting feelings inside at once without going crazy?"

"Time," Charlotte answered. "Patience... with yourself. Learning how not to close yourself off but to still keep a respectful distance, is one of the balancing acts of this job. But from what I've seen, you're already making great strides.

Choose your battles. Some you'll win and some you won't. But each one will give you experience for the next."

Mona sighed. "I just never want to cut myself off like that again. I've seen what can happen when you live like that all the time. As he stood there, talking, I began to remember what he used to be like. He would always pretend like there was nothing wrong. Even when he was attacking my mother. It was like it didn't even affect him at all. I never want to be like that."

Charlotte put a hand on Mona's. "I don't think that's very likely."

Mona wiped her eyes, smiling. "I don't know. You looked pretty scared down there. I mean... it was good, it made it seem more real, for him. But I guess you thought I had really jumped off the deep end." She paused. "Were you really ready to die down there?"

Charlotte frowned. "I don't know if anyone is ever really ready to die. But truly, I was more concerned for you than myself. I knew you had the capability to beat him, I just thought I needed to remind you of it. Turns out, you didn't need me at all."

"That's not true," Mona replied. "When I was down there, with him, he kept saying how by winning his game, he'd molded me into this perfect copy of himself. That the two of us would be inseparable. And I knew I definitely didn't want that. I decided to finally listen to what Sheriff Franklin was trying to tell me all along. And part of that was thanks to you."

"What was?"

"That I'd rather fight back than just take it on the chin." She smiled, though this time it was genuine, reaching her eyes.

"I'm not sure you want that, kid," Charlotte said, laughing and rubbing her inner thigh. "It comes with consequences."

"How *is* your groin?" Mona asked.

"Sore, but thankfully I only pulled a few muscles. That's what not keeping up with my training gets me," Charlotte replied. "I should be walking normally in about a week if I keep up with my PT."

Mona nodded, then turned back to her computer. "Here, I want you to listen to this. I've been monitoring him when he thinks he's alone." She scrubbed back a specific video showing McCormick in the hospital bed, a large bandage covering his shoulder and part of his chest, while both arms had been hand-cuffed to the bed.

"—I *know* that," he said, frustration in his voice. "I don't need you reminding me. Well, maybe next time I will. We can't, no, listen, we can't just... God, you are so *fucking* annoying. *I know how it works!*"

"Who is he talking to?" Charlotte asked. "There's no one else in there."

"I think he's talking to Robin," Mona said. "I think he believes she's still there, with him. *Tethered* to him, somehow." She opened a drawer and withdrew a file, handing it to Charlotte. "Look."

Charlotte opened the file. "Carol Demeter. Age thirty-one, born in Phoenix, Arizona." It was a missing persons report. "Is this...?"

Mona nodded. "Our Jane Doe. The FBI helped me track her down. Whittle confirmed via dental records that it's her. She disappeared four months ago from Arizona, last seen with a man matching my dad's description."

"I don't understand," Charlotte said. "How did you figure this out?"

Mona motioned to the screen. "He kept saying: *Carol would never talk back to me like that.* It was enough to start a search. I think... in some way... he still sees the people he kills. Some of them, at least. He talks to them. I think they maybe... kind of live in him. If I'd gone with him, I may have ended up like that eventually. Tethered to him forever."

"Are you saying he's being *haunted* by the people he kills?" Charlotte asked.

"No, nothing like that. I think some rebellious part of him may manifest them in some way, so he's not alone all the time. So he has someone to talk to. Even if it's really just another version of himself." She dropped her head. "It was something I used to do too. I would talk to Robin, when I got really lonely."

"I don't think you have to worry about that anymore," Charlotte replied. "As far as I can tell, everyone in the department is really impressed with your work. Some are even suggesting you make a run for sheriff yourself."

"Me?" Mona asked. "But I don't have that kind of experience."

Charlotte shrugged. "Sometimes it's more about how you relate to people than how much experience you have." She checked the time on the computer. "Something to think about. C'mon, we're going to be late."

"Late?" Mona asked.

"Trust me," Charlotte replied. "You don't want to miss this."

Twenty minutes later they stood outside the main lockup of Oak Creek jail. There was a *thunk* and a loud buzzer before the door to the cells opened, revealing Adam with a guard behind him.

"Mona?" he asked as the door closed behind him. "Where's my mom?"

"She's at home," Mona said. "We're just here to make sure you get there safely. There's..." She glanced at Charlotte. "... something of a crowd outside."

"A crowd?" he asked.

"This case has become national news," Charlotte said. "And it's my fault you're a part of that. Adam, I can't tell you how sorry I am."

The boy gave her a wary look, and she wasn't surprised to see it. She'd violated his trust and there was probably no getting it back, but there was one last thing she could do for him. "But Mona never gave up on you. She was determined to prove your innocence. So much that she had to take down her own father in order to do it."

Adam glanced at Mona. "Yeah? That true?"

Mona nodded solemnly. "I just wish I could have figured it out before you got dragged into all this."

Adam glared at her a moment before his façade finally broke. "Well, I guess I can't blame you. At least now we have something in common. Dads suck, amirite?"

Mona, who Charlotte was sure was waiting for the hammer to come down, couldn't help but give a start, then a chuckle. "Yeah, they really do." And just like before, her joy was genuine. It was striking to see the difference from the way she had been when Charlotte had first arrived. "C'mon. Your mom is waiting for you. We're going to get you through this. And don't worry about the media. Just... just don't say anything to them. Eventually they'll go away."

"Actually," Charlotte said, stepping forward, "you two go out the back. I'll head out the front and distract them."

"You sure?" Mona asked, her arm partially around Adam's shoulder.

"Yeah," Charlotte replied. "Let me take one for the team." She wiggled her eyebrows at them then limped outside where the throng of reporters was eagerly awaiting a statement.

THIRTY-SIX

As Charlotte finished throwing what few clothes she had back into her suitcase, there was a knock at the motel-room door. She paused, then headed for the door, checking the peephole before opening it. Mona stood there with a small basket of flowers in her hands.

"What's this?" Charlotte asked.

"A going-away present," Mona replied. "I figured your place could use some color when you got back."

Charlotte couldn't help but smile as she took the flowers. "Thanks. You really didn't need to do this."

"It gave me an excuse to come by one more time," Mona replied. "Are you sure you won't consider staying? We have plenty of B & Bs here in town."

Charlotte shot her a glare. "I think we both know my stance on B & Bs. No, I need to get back. There's a lot that needs to be taken care of."

It had been nearly a week since Adam had been released and John McCormick had been formally charged with the murders of four people, though the FBI was looking into the possibility of other murders. Thanks to Mona's surveillance of the man, they had managed to learn details about each of the deaths that had been previously unknown as he continued talking to "no one" in his room. Details like how he'd managed to plant Adam's fingerprints on Robin's painting and how he'd had her paint the symbols on the back of the four paintings before he killed her. He had meticulously planned the whole thing upon arriving back in Oak Creek, and yet it had been his belief that he could control everyone that had caused his downfall.

There had been five funerals, after they had discovered the body of Detective Perkins in his own home. Apparently, McCormick had killed him and faked the messages requesting personal time to Franklin in order to move Mona up through the ranks and get her on the case. With the death of both him and Franklin, the town was reeling and in need of some serious repose. Fortunately, the community had come together, determined not to let one person destroy everything they held dear, despite almost tearing itself apart.

Mona and some of the local business owners had petitioned the town to refurbish and rebuild the gazebo in the town's square in Robin's name, something that had won approval with the town council seven to zero and was to be seen as a new start for Oak Creek. And the mayor had appointed Detective Tasker as the interim sheriff until an election could be held; Tasker—to his credit—had offered Charlotte a position with the department. He'd seen how Ramsey's antagonistic attitude had begun to tear the department apart and decided he'd rather follow in Franklin's footsteps instead.

And while it had been a tempting offer, Charlotte had already decided she was done trying to fight the inevitable. She had been struggling so hard against the idea of retirement, she hadn't appreciated what an opportunity it was. An opportunity to reconnect with the people she had pushed out of her life, and to finally start putting people ahead of her career. Spending these last two weeks with Mona had made her realize just how much she missed Haley. There was a possibility her daughter might not want anything to do with her, but she wouldn't find out if she was still trying to convince Whiteside she deserved a spot on the roster. She'd already called him and informed her she'd be taking that retirement, effective immediately.

"At least you managed to go out with a bang," Mona replied. "I'm pretty sure they'll be talking about this one for decades."

Charlotte smiled, throwing the last of her shirts into the suitcase. "They will. And it's one hell of a case to start with. They'll be expecting big things from you."

"I'm not sure I care," Mona replied. "Plus, I have a lot of stuff to work out first. Dr. Pekannen's assistant was able to help me find a new therapist in Cagney, the next town over. I have a feeling I'm going to be doing a lot of commuting."

"That's good," Charlotte replied. "It'll give you plenty of time to reflect."

"You know," Mona said, "if you're ever back this way, there will always be an open booth for you at Ronnie's."

"You sure about that?" Charlotte joked, closing up her suitcase. "I don't think Ken would be too happy with me showing back up."

Mona was enjoying accolades from the whole town and Charlotte had quietly stepped back to allow her to take the limelight. At the same time, even though the killer had been caught, she could feel the animosity of the town. Despite everything, there needed to be someone to blame. And Charlotte was more than happy to step up to the plate.

"I had a talk with him," Mona replied. "And impressed upon him if he ever did anything like that again, he'd find himself on the wrong side of a jail cell."

Charlotte stared at the woman a moment, stunned. The woman who only a few weeks ago was hesitant about interviewing a witness was now making a name for herself in Oak

Creek. A name to be respected. Finally, she couldn't help but laugh. "I'm guessing he didn't take to well to that."

She shrugged. "People are complicated, maybe too complicated to predict. But when they step out of line, I'll make sure I'm there to take care of it."

Charlotte gathered up her suitcase and flowers in one hand, extending the other for Mona. "Detective LaSalle, it's been a pleasure."

"The pleasure has been all mine, Detective Dawes," she replied. "Charlotte." Then, without warning, she pulled Charlotte into a hug. "Thank you. For everything."

"Thank you," Charlotte whispered back.

Mona pulled back. "For what?"

"For reminding me that sometimes you need to pull on your restraints a little. They might not be as tight as they look." She shot Mona a wink before heading back out to her car. "Let me know if you ever get that algorithm working. I'd love to see it in action."

Mona nodded. "Keep in touch."

"You too," Charlotte said as she got into her car.

As she backed out, giving Mona one last wave goodbye, Charlotte noticed her hand didn't hurt in the slightest.

A LETTER FROM THE AUTHOR

Thank you for reading *The Darkest Game*!

I hope Charlotte and Mona's story kept you captivated and turning the pages late into the night. If you'd like to stay updated on my latest releases and enjoy exclusive bonus content, be sure to sign up for my newsletter!

www.stormpublishing.co/alex-sigmore

If you enjoyed this book, I'd truly appreciate it if you could take a moment to leave a review or recommend it to a friend. Even a short review makes a world of difference in helping new readers discover my books. Your support means everything!

Though I've been writing for nearly a decade, Charlotte and Mona's story has been rattling around in my head for even longer. I've always wanted to explore the intersection of the art world and something as dark as murder, and thanks to Storm Publishing, I finally had the creative freedom to bring that vision to life. This book allowed me to tell a story about loss, loneliness, and connection in a way I never have before, and I hope you enjoyed reading it as much as I enjoyed writing it.

Thank you for joining me on this journey and for trusting me with your most valuable resource—your time. It's an honor to write stories for you, and I can't wait to share many more. Stay in touch!

KEEP IN TOUCH WITH THE AUTHOR

www.alexsigmore.com

ACKNOWLEDGEMENTS

Writing may be a solitary process, but bringing a book to life is anything but.

To my editor, Kate—thank you for taking a chance on me and giving me the opportunity to tell this story. To everyone at Storm Publishing—Oliver, Alexandra, Jon, and the entire team who helped bring this book to life—thank you for your support and dedication through this process.

I wouldn't be where I am today without the incredible writers who have been with me from the beginning, pushing me to be better and reminding me that I'm not alone in the struggle of getting the story just right. Jess, Andrea, Jessie, Jen, MJ, Remy, Drew, and Doug—your friendship and guidance mean everything.

Most of all, thank you to you, the reader. Your time and attention are the greatest gifts a writer can receive, and I'm honored that you've chosen to spend them on my stories. To those who have been with me from the start, your support means more than I can say. None of this would be possible without you.

And finally, to my wife—my North Star. Your unwavering belief in me gives me the confidence to keep going, even when the words don't come easy. I love you to the moon and back.